BY ITS COVER

Donna Leon was named by *The Times* as one of the 50 Greatest Crime Writers. She is an award-winning crime novelist, celebrated for the bestselling Brunetti series. Donna has lived in Venice for thirty years and previously lived in Switzerland, Saudi Arabia, Iran and China, where she worked as a teacher. Donna's books have been translated into 35 languages and have been published around the world.

Her previous novels featuring Commissario Brunetti have all been highly acclaimed; including *Friends in High Places*, which won the CWA Macallan Silver Dagger for Fiction, *Fatal Remedies*, *A Sea of Troubles*, *Doctored Evidence* and *Beastly Things*.

Praise for Donna Leon and *By Its Cover*

'Donna Leon is a truly fine novelist, period, and should be acclaimed as such'
Times Literary Supplement

'Donna Leon's books are a joy'
Guardian

'Leon's command of the baroque Italian thriller is second to none'

Donna Leon

BY ITS COVER

arrow books

Published by Arrow Books 2015

1 3 5 7 9 10 8 6 4 2

Copyright © Donna Leon and Diogenes Verlag AG, Zurich 2014

First published in Great Britain in 2014 by William Heinemann

Arrow Books
The Random House Group Limited
20 Vauxhall Bridge Road, London, SW1V 2SA

www.randomhouse.co.uk

Addresses for companies within The Random House Group Limited can
be found at: www.randomhouse.co.uk/offices.htm

The Random House Group Limited Reg. No. 954009

A CIP catalogue record for this book
is available from the British Library

ISBN 9780099591283
ISBN 9780099591290 (Export edition)

Map © ML Design

Typeset by SX Composing DTP, Rayleigh, Essex
Printed and bound in Great Britain by CPI Group (UK) Ltd, Croydon, CR0 4YY

MIX
Paper from
responsible sources
FSC
www.fsc.org   FSC® C018179

Penguin Random House is committed to a sustainable future
for our business, our readers and our planet. This book is
made from Forest Stewardship Council® certified paper.

For Judith Flanders

Mean as he was, he is my brother now.

Saul, Handel

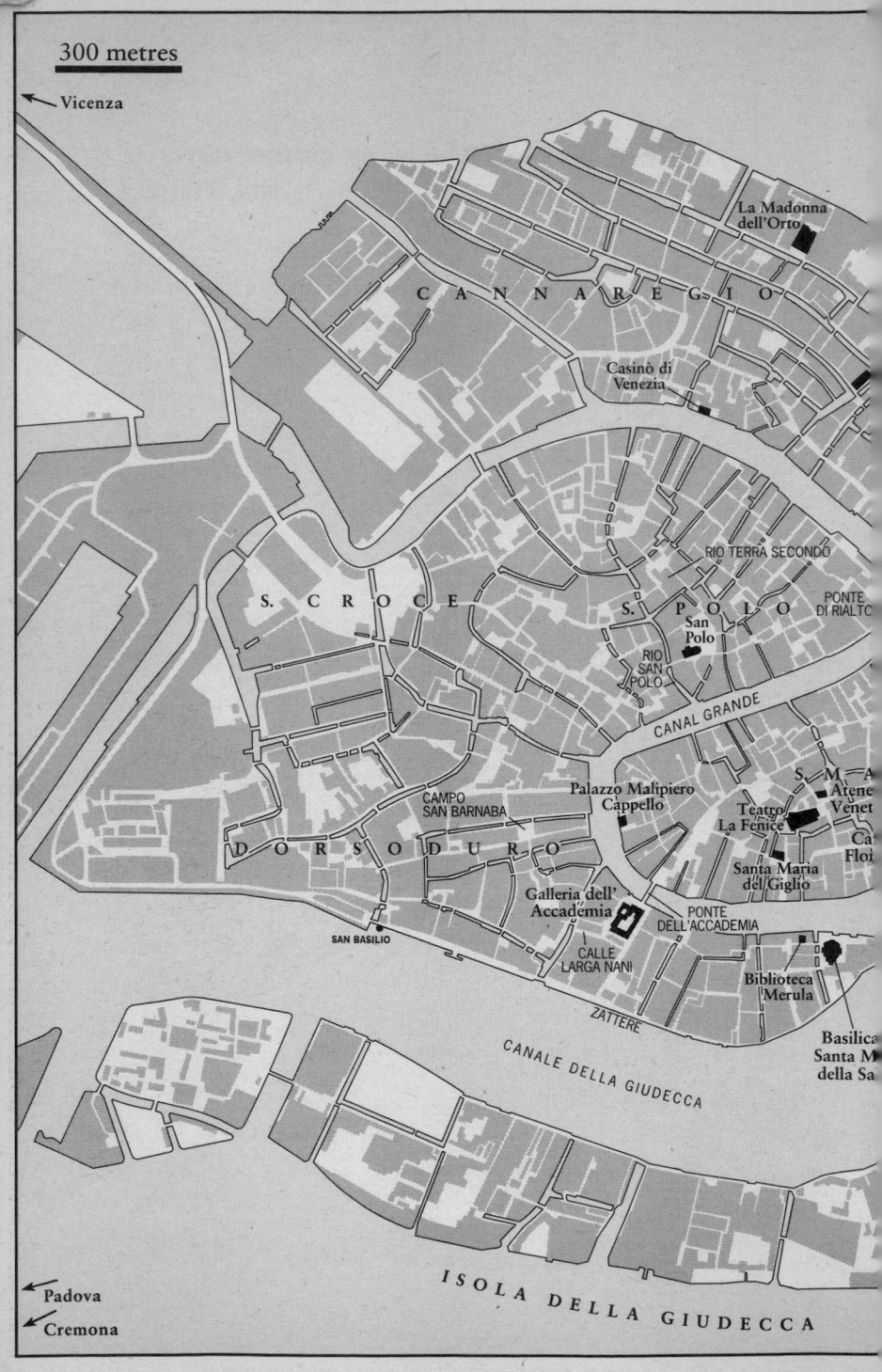

1

It had been a tedious Monday, much of it spent with the written witness statements about a fight between two taxi drivers that had sent one of them to the hospital with concussion and a broken right arm. The statements had been made by the American couple who had asked the concierge of their hotel to call a water taxi to take them to the airport; the concierge, who said he had called one of the taxi drivers the hotel always used; the porter, who said he had done nothing more than his job, which was to put the Americans' luggage into the taxi that had pulled up to the dock; and the two taxi drivers, one of whom had been questioned in the hospital. From what Brunetti could make of the various stories, the driver from the usual company was nearby when he received the call from the concierge, but when he arrived at the hotel, another taxi was docked at the landing. He pulled up, called out the name of the Americans, which the concierge had given him, and said he was to take them to the airport. The other driver said the porter had waved to him as he was passing, so it was his fare. The porter denied this and insisted he was simply helping with the luggage. The driver into whose taxi the porter had put the luggage had somehow found himself on the deck of the other taxi. The Americans were enraged that they had missed their flight.

Brunetti knew, but could not prove, what had happened: the porter had waved to a passing taxi so that he, instead of the concierge, would get a percentage of the fare. The consequences were evident: no one would tell the truth, and the Americans would not understand what had happened.

As he entertained that thought, Brunetti was momentarily deflected from his desire for a coffee and paused to consider whether he had perhaps stumbled upon some cosmic explanation of current world history. He smiled, making a note to repeat the idea to Paola that evening, or better yet, to tell it the following night, when they were invited to dinner at her parents'. He hoped that the Conte, who appreciated paradox, would be amused. He knew his mother-in-law would be.

He abandoned his reverie and continued down

the stairs of the Questura, eager for the coffee that would help him through the rest of the afternoon. As he approached the front door, the officer at the switchboard tapped on the window of his tiny cubicle and waved Brunetti towards him. When Brunetti was inside, the guard said into the telephone receiver, 'I think you should talk to the Commissario, Dottoressa. He's in charge.' He passed him the phone.

'Brunetti.'

'You're a commissario?'

'Yes.'

'This is Dottoressa Fabbiani. I'm the chief librarian at the Biblioteca Merula. We've had a theft. A number of them, I think.' Her voice was unsteady, the voice he had heard from victims of muggings or assault.

'From the collection?' Brunetti asked. He knew the library, had used it once or twice as a student but had not given it a thought for decades.

'Yes.'

'What's been taken?' he asked, preparing in his mind the other questions that would have to follow her answer.

'We don't know the full extent yet. So far, all I'm sure of is that pages have been cut from some volumes.' He heard her deep intake of breath.

'How many?' Brunetti asked, pulling a pad and pencil towards him.

'I don't know. I just discovered it.' Her voice tightened as she spoke.

He heard a man's voice from her end of the phone.

She must have turned away to answer him, for her voice grew indistinct for a moment. Then, silence from her end of the line.

He thought of the procedures he had gone through at the libraries in the city whenever he consulted a book and asked, 'You have records of the people who use the books, don't you?'

Was she surprised that a policeman should ask such a question? That he knew about libraries? It certainly took her some time to answer. 'Of course.' Well, that put him in his place, didn't it? 'We're checking on that.'

'Have you found who did it?' Brunetti asked.

There followed an even longer pause. 'A researcher, we think,' she said, then added, as if Brunetti had accused her of negligence, 'He had the proper identification.' He heard the response of any bureaucrat beginning to formulate a defence at the first whisper of an accusation of negligence.

'Dottoressa,' Brunetti began, using what he hoped was his most persuasive and professional voice, 'we'll need your help in identifying him. The sooner we find him, the less time he'll have to sell what he's taken.' He saw no reason to spare her this reality.

'But the books are destroyed,' she said, sounding anguished, as at the death of a loved person.

To a librarian, damage was as bad as theft, he imagined. Changing his voice to that of Authority, he said, 'I'll be there as soon as I can, Dottoressa. Please do not touch anything.' Before she could protest, he added, 'And I'd like to see the identification he gave you.' When there was no response, he replaced the phone.

Brunetti remembered that the library was on the Zattere, but the exact location eluded him now. He returned his attention to the guard and told him, 'If anyone wants me, I've gone to the Biblioteca Merula. Call Vianello and tell him to go over with two men to take fingerprints.'

Outside, he found Foa, arms folded, legs crossed at the ankles, leaning against the railing that ran along the canal. His head was tilted back, and his eyes were closed against the early spring sun, but when Brunetti approached, the pilot asked, 'Where can I take you, Commissario?' before opening his eyes.

'The Biblioteca Merula,' he said.

As if finishing Brunetti's sentence, Foa continued, 'Dorsoduro 3429.'

'How'd you know that?'

'My brother-in-law and his family live in the next building, so that has to be the address,' the pilot answered.

'I feared for a moment that the Lieutenant had made some new rule that obliged you to learn all the addresses in the city by heart.'

'Anyone who's grown up on boats knows where everything in the city is, sir. Better than a GPS,' Foa said, tapping his forehead with his finger. He pushed himself away from the railing and made towards the boat but stopped mid-stride and turned to Brunetti. 'You ever hear what became of them, sir?'

'Of what?' a confused Brunetti asked.

'The GPSs.'

'Which GPSs?'

'The ones that were ordered for the boats,' Foa answered. Brunetti stood still, waiting for the explanation.

'I was talking to Martini a few days ago,' Foa continued, naming the officer in charge of procurement, the man to consult to have a radio fixed or get a new flashlight. 'He showed me the invoice and asked me if I knew whether they were any good or not. The model that had been ordered.'

'And did you?' Brunetti asked, wondering where this conversation had come from.

'Oh, we all know about them, sir. They're crap. None of the taxi drivers wants them, and the only person I know who ever bought one for himself got so mad at it one day that he pulled it off the windscreen of his boat and tossed it over the side.' Foa walked towards the boat, then stopped again and said, 'That's what I told Martini.'

'What did he do?'

'What can he do? They're ordered by some central office in Rome, and someone there gets something for having ordered them, and someone else gets something for letting the order go through.' He shrugged and stepped on to the boat.

Brunetti followed him, puzzled that Foa had chosen

to tell him this, for he must have known that there was nothing Brunetti could do, either. That was how things worked.

Foa switched on the motor and said, 'Martini told me the invoice was for a dozen of them.' He stressed the amount.

'There are only six boats, aren't there?' Brunetti asked, a question Foa didn't bother to answer.

'How long ago was this, Foa?'

'Couple of months. Some time in the winter, I'd say.'

'You know if they ever got here?' Brunetti asked.

Foa tilted up his chin and made a clicking sound with his tongue: he could have been a street Arab, so much did his gesture remind Brunetti of the way they dismissed the ridiculous.

Brunetti found himself at a familiar crossroads, where he could go forward only to move backward, move sideways to move forward, or just close his eyes and take a comfortable seat and not move at all. If he spoke to Martini and learned that the GPS systems had been ordered and paid for but were nowhere in evidence, he would create trouble for himself. He could begin to look around privately and perhaps prevent further looting of the public purse. Or he could simply ignore it and get on with more important things or with things that might be remedied.

'You think this is the beginning of spring?' he asked the pilot.

Foa glanced aside and smiled: their agreement

could not have been more congenial. 'I think it might be, sir. I hope so. I'm sick to death of the cold and fog.'

As they completed their turn into the *bacino* and looked forward again, they both gasped. There was nothing theatrical about it, no attempt to make a scene or a statement. They did no more than express their human response to the otherworldly and impossible. Ahead of them was the stern of one of the newest, largest cruise ships. Its enormous rear end stared bluntly back at them, as if daring them to comment.

Seven, eight, nine, ten storeys. Was this possible? From their perspective, it blocked out the city, blocked out the light, blocked out all thought of sense or reason or the appropriateness of things. They trailed along behind it, watching the wake it created avalanche slowly towards the *rivas* on both sides, tiny wave after tiny wave after tiny wave, and what in God's name was the thrust of that vast expanse of displaced water doing to those stones and to the centuries-old binding that kept them in place? Suddenly the air was unbreathable as a capricious gust blew the ship's exhaust down on them for a few seconds. And then the air was just as suddenly filled with the sweetness of springtime and buds and new leaves, fresh grass and nature's giggly joy at coming back for another show.

They could see, scores of metres above them, people lining the deck, turned like sunflowers to the beauty of the Piazza and the domes and the bell tower. A vaporetto appeared on the other side, coming towards them, and the people on the deck, no doubt Venetians, raised their fists and shook them at the passengers, but the tourists were looking the other way and failed to see the friendly natives. Brunetti thought of Captain Cook, dragged from the surf, killed, cooked, eaten by other friendly natives. 'Good,' he said under his breath.

Not far along the *riva* of the Zattere, Foa pulled the boat to the right, flipped it into reverse and then neutral to let it glide to a stop. He grabbed a mooring rope and jumped up on to the pavement, bent and tied a quick knot. He reached down and grabbed Brunetti's hand to steady him as he made the jump to the pavement.

'This is probably going to take some time,' Brunetti told the pilot. 'You might as well go back.'

But Foa wasn't paying attention: his eyes were on the stern of the ship as it made its slow progress towards the dock at San Basilio. 'I've read,' Brunetti began, speaking Veneziano, 'that no decision can be made about them until all the agencies agree.'

'I know,' Foa answered, his eyes still on the boat. 'Magistrato alle Acque, Regione, junta of the city, Port Authority, some ministry in Rome...' He paused, still transfixed as the boat moved farther away, hardly diminishing in size. Then Foa's voice returned, and he named some of the men on these panels.

Brunetti knew many, though not all, of them. When Foa reached the names of three former city officials of the highest rank, he pounded on the pronunciation of each surname like a carpenter hammering the final nails into the lid of a coffin.

'I've never understood why they divided things up like that,' Brunetti said. Foa, after all, came from a family that had lived on and from the *laguna*: fishermen, fishmongers, sailors, pilots and mechanics for ACTV. They had everything except gills, the Foas did. If anyone were to understand the bureaucracy of the waters in and off which the city lived, it would be people like them.

Foa gave him the smile a teacher gives his dullest pupil: affectionate, poignant, superior. 'Do you think eight separate committees are ever going to reach a decision?'

Brunetti looked at the pilot as illumination came. 'And only a joint decision will stop the ships,' he said, a conclusion which caused Foa's smile to broaden.

'So they can consider and reconsider for ever,' the pilot said, in open admiration of the ingenuity of having divided the decision among so many separate governmental organizations. 'Getting their salaries, making inspection tours to other countries to see how things are done there, holding meetings to discuss projects and plans.' Then, mindful of a recent article in *Il Gazzettino*, 'Or hiring their wives and children as consultants.'

'And picking up small gifts that might fall from the table of the companies that own the ships?' Brunetti offered, though he knew as he spoke that this was not the sort of example he was meant to give to the uniformed branch.

Foa's smile warmed, but he said only, pointing along the narrow canal, 'Down there, just before the bridge. It's the green door.'

Brunetti waved his thanks for the ride and for the directions. A moment later he heard the motor spring to life, and when he turned he saw the police boat swinging out into the canal in a wide arc that would take it in the direction from which they had come.

Brunetti noticed that the pavement was wet, with large puddles against the walls of the buildings he passed. Curious, he walked back to the edge of the *riva* and looked down at the water, but it was more than half a metre below him. It was low tide, there was no *acqua alta*, and no rain had fallen for days, so the only way the water could have got there was by being washed up by a passing ship. And they were meant to believe, he and the other citizens the administration considered to be imbeciles, that these boats did no damage to the fabric of the city.

Weren't most of the men making these decisions Venetians? Hadn't they been born in the city? Weren't their children in the schools and university? They probably spoke Veneziano during their meetings.

He thought memory would return as he walked towards the library, but it all failed to become familiar to him. Nor could he recall whether the *palazzo* had been Merula's home when he lived in Venice: that was a job for the Archivio Storico, not the police, whose records did not go back a thousand years.

When Brunetti passed through the open green

door, he told himself it looked familiar, though what it really looked like was any of the Renaissance court-yards in the city, complete with outside steps leading to the first floor and a metal-capped well. He was drawn to it by the beautifully preserved carving, still safe inside these walls. Fat pairs of angels supported a family crest he did not recognize. The wings of some of the angels were in need of attention, but the rest of the carving was intact. Fourteenth century, he'd guess, with a garland of carved flowers encircling the well just under the metal lid: he surprised himself by having a strong memory of that, if of little else he saw there.

He started towards the remembered staircase, its broad marble handrail interspersed with the carved heads of lions, each the size of a pineapple. He climbed the stairs, patting the heads of two of the lions. At the top of the first flight, he saw a door and beside it a new brass plaque: 'Biblioteca Merula'.

He stepped inside, into coolness. By this time in the afternoon, the day had grown clement and he had begun to regret wearing his woollen jacket, but now he felt the sweat drying across his back.

In the small reception area, a young man with a fashionable two-day beard sat behind a desk, a book open in front of him. He looked at Brunetti and smiled and, when he approached the desk, asked, 'May I help you?'

Brunetti took his warrant card from his wallet and showed it. 'Ah, of course,' the young man said. 'You want Dottoressa Fabbiani, Signore. She's upstairs.'

'Isn't this the library?' Brunetti asked, pointing to the door behind the young man.

'This is the modern collection. The rare books are upstairs. You have to go up another flight.' Seeing Brunetti's confusion, he said, 'Everything was changed around about ten years ago.' Then, with a smile, 'Long before my time.'

'And long after mine,' Brunetti said and returned to the staircase.

In the absence of lions, Brunetti ran his hand along the bevelled marble railing smoothed by centuries of use. At the top, he found a door with a bell to the right. He rang it and, after some time, the door was opened by a man a few years younger than he, wearing a dark blue jacket with copper buttons and a military cut. He was of medium height, thickset, with clear blue eyes and a thin nose that angled minimally to one side. 'Are you the Commissario?' he asked.

'Yes,' Brunetti answered and extended his hand. 'Guido Brunetti.'

The man took it and gave it a quick shake. 'Piero Sartor,' he said. He stepped back to allow Brunetti into what looked like the ticket office of a small, provincial train station. A waist-high wooden counter stood to the left, on it a computer and two wooden trays for papers. A wheeled rack with what seemed to be very old books piled on it was parked against the wall behind the counter.

There might be a computer, which there had not been in the libraries he had used as a student, but the smell was the same. Old books had always filled Brunetti with nostalgia for centuries in which he had not lived. They were printed on paper made from old cloth, shredded, pounded, watered down and pounded again and hand-made into large sheets to be printed, then folded and folded again, and bound and stitched by hand: all that effort to record and remember who we are and what we thought, Brunetti mused. He remembered loving the feel and heft of them, but chiefly he remembered that dry, soft scent, the past's attempt to make itself real to him.

The man closed the door, pulling Brunetti from his reverie, and turned to him. 'I'm the guard. I found the book.' He tried, but failed, to keep the pride out of his voice.

'The damaged one?' Brunetti asked.

'Yes, sir. That is, I brought the book down from the reading room, and when Dottoressa Fabbiani opened it, she saw that pages had been cut out.' His pride was replaced by indignation and something close to anger.

'I see,' Brunetti said. 'Is that what you do, bring books down to the desk?' he asked, curious about what the duties of a guard might entail in this institution. He assumed it was his position as guard that made Sartor so unusually forthcoming in speaking to the police.

The look the man gave him was sudden and sharp and might as easily have been alarm as confusion.

'No, sir, but it was a book I'd read – well, parts of it – so I recognized it right away, and I didn't think it should be left on the table,' he blurted out. 'Cortés. That Spanish guy who went to South America.'

Sartor seemed uncertain how to explain this and went on more slowly. 'He was so enthusiastic about the books he was reading that he made me interested in them, and I thought I'd take a look.' Brunetti's curiosity must have been visible, for he continued, 'He's American, but he speaks Italian very well – you'd never know – and we got into the habit of chatting if I was on the desk while he was waiting for the books to come down.' He paused, and when he saw Brunetti's expression, went on. 'We have a break in the afternoon, but I don't smoke and I can't drink coffee,' he said, then added, 'Stomach. Can't handle it any more. I drink green tea, but none of the bars around here has it, well, not a kind that I'd drink.' Before Brunetti could ask why he was being told all of this, Sartor said, 'So I have a half-hour and don't much want to go out, so I started to read. Some of the people who come to do research mention books, and sometimes I try to read them.' He smiled nervously, as if conscious of having overstepped some sort of class barrier. 'That way I have something interesting to tell my wife when I get home.'

Brunetti had always taken a special delight in the surprising things he learned from people: they did and said the most unexpected things, both good and bad. A colleague had once told him how, when his wife was in the seventeenth hour of labour with their first child, he had grown tired of listening to her complain, and Brunetti had fought down the impulse to slap him. He thought of his neighbour's wife, whose cat was set free from the kitchen window every night to roam the rooftops of the neighbourhood, and who came home every morning with a clothes peg, not a mouse, in his mouth, a gift not unlike the interesting story Sartor took home to his wife.

Brunetti, interested in what he had to say, asked, 'Hernán Cortés?'

'Yes,' Sartor answered. 'He conquered that city in Mexico they called the Venice of the West.' He stopped and added, afraid perhaps that Brunetti might think him a fool, 'That's what the Europeans called it, not the Mexicans.'

Brunetti nodded to show he understood.

'It was interesting, although he was always thanking God when he killed a lot of people: I didn't like that very much but he was writing to the King, so maybe he had to say things like that. But what he said about the country and the people was fascinating. My wife liked it, too.'

He looked at Brunetti, whose approving smile to a fellow reader was enough to encourage him to continue. 'I liked how things were so different from how they are now. I read some of it, and I wanted to finish it. Anyway, I recognized the title – *Relación* – when I saw it in front of the place where he usually sits and brought it downstairs because I thought a book like that shouldn't be lying around up there.'

Brunetti assumed this unnamed 'he' was the man believed to have cut the pages from the book, so he asked, 'Why did you bring it down if he was working with it?'

'Riccardo, from the first floor, told me he'd seen him going down the stairs when I was at lunch. He never did that before. He always comes in soon after we open and stays until the afternoon.' He considered that for a moment and then added, sounding genuinely concerned, 'I don't know what he does about lunch: I hope he hasn't been eating in there.' Then, as if embarrassed to have confessed such a thing, he added, 'So I went up to see if he was coming back.'

'How would you know that?' Brunetti asked with genuine curiosity.

Sartor gave a small smile. 'If you work here for a long time, Signore, you learn the signs. No pencils, no markers, no notebook. It's hard to explain, but I just know if they're finished for the day. Or not.'

'And he was?'

The guard nodded emphatically. 'The books were stacked in front of where he had been sitting. His desk light was turned off. So I knew he wouldn't come back. That's why I took the book back down to the main desk.'

'Was this unusual?'

'For him it was. He always packed up everything and took the books back himself.'

'What time did he leave?'

'I don't know the exact time, sir. Before I came back at two-thirty.'

'And then?'

'As I said, when Riccardo told me he'd left, I went up to make sure and see about the books.'

'Is that something you'd normally do?' Brunetti asked, curiously. The guard had seemed alarmed the first time he asked this.

This time he answered easily. 'Not really, sir. But I used to be a runner – a person who brings books to the readers and puts them back on the shelves – so I sort of did it automatically.' He smiled a very natural smile and said, 'I can't stand to see the books lying around on the tables if no one is there, using them.'

'I see,' Brunetti said. 'Go on, please.'

'I brought the books down to the circulation desk. Dottoressa Fabbiani was just coming in from a meeting, and when she saw the Cortés she asked to look at it, and when she opened it, she saw what had happened.' Then, speaking more slowly, almost as if having a conversation with himself, he said, 'I don't understand how he could have done it. There's usually more than one person in the room.'

Brunetti ignored that and asked, 'Why did she open that particular book?'

'She said it was a book she'd read when she was at university, and she loved the drawing it had of that city. So she picked it up and opened it.' He thought a moment and then added, 'She was so pleased to see it, she said, after all these years.' Noticing Brunetti's expression, he said, 'People who work here feel that way about books, you know.'

'You said there were usually more people in the room?' Brunetti inquired mildly. Sartor nodded.

'There's usually a researcher or two, and there's a man who's been reading the Fathers of the Church for the last three years, sir. We call him Tertullian: that's the first book he asked for, and the name stuck. He's here every day, so I guess we've sort of begun to depend on him as a kind of guard.'

Brunetti forbore to ask about Tertullian's choice of reading matter. Instead, he smiled and said, 'I can understand.'

'What, sir?'

'That you'd trust someone who spent years reading the Fathers of the Church.'

The man smiled nervously, responding to Brunetti's tone. 'Perhaps we've been negligent,' he said. When Brunetti did not respond, he added, 'About security, that is. Few people come to the library, and after a while, I suppose we begin to feel as though we know them. So we stop being suspicious.'

'Dangerous,' Brunetti permitted himself to say.

'To say the very least,' a woman's voice said behind him, and he turned to meet Dottoressa Fabbiani.

2

She was tall and thin and, at first sight, had the look of one of those slender wading birds which were once so common in the *laguna*. Like theirs, her head was silver grey, its covering cut very close to the head, and like them, she leaned forward when she stood, back curved, arms pulled behind, one hand grasping the other wrist. Like those birds, she had broad black feet at the end of long legs.

She strode towards them, released her right hand and brought it forward to offer to Brunetti. 'I'm Patrizia Fabbiani,' she said. 'The Director here.'

'I'm sorry we have to meet in these circumstances, Dottoressa,' Brunetti said, falling back on formulaic courtesy, as he always found it best to do until he had a sense of the person he was dealing with.

'Have you explained things to the Commissario, Piero?' she asked the guard, using the familiar *tu* with him but as she would with a friend and not with an inferior.

'I told him that I brought the book to the desk but hadn't noticed that the pages were gone,' he answered, not addressing her directly and so not allowing Brunetti to discover whether this was a place where everyone was allowed to address the Director informally. It might be expected in a shoe shop, but not in a library.

'And the other books he was using?' Brunetti asked the Dottoressa.

She closed her eyes, and he imagined her opening them and seeing the stubs where once pages had been. 'I had them brought down after I saw the first one. Three more. One of them is missing nine pages.' He assumed she had done this without putting on gloves. Perhaps a librarian, in the face of books that might have been vandalized, was as incapable of leaving them untouched as a doctor at the sight of a bleeding limb.

'How serious is the loss?' he asked, hoping by her answer to get some idea of what was at stake in a crime such as this. People stole things because they had value, but that was an entirely relative term, Brunetti knew, unless a thief took money. The value of an object could be sentimental or it could be based on the market price. In this case, rarity, condition, and desirability would determine that. How put a price on beauty? How much was historical importance worth? He stole a look at the books on the rack against the wall but glanced away quickly.

She looked at him directly, and he saw, not the eyes of a wading bird, but the eyes of a very intelligent person who understood the complexity of any answer she might give to his question.

She took a few sheets of paper from the table next to her. 'We've started to assemble a list of the books he's consulted since he's been here, including the ones I saw today,' she said by way of answer, ignoring the books on the rack behind her. 'As soon as we know all the titles and examine them, we'll have an idea of what else he's taken.'

'How long has he been coming here?'

'Three weeks.'

'May I see the books you've already found?' Brunetti asked.

'Of course, of course,' she said. She turned to the guard and said, 'Piero, put a sign on the door saying we're closed. Technical problems.' She turned to Brunetti and with a bitter smile said, 'I suppose that's true enough.' Brunetti thought it expedient not to reply.

While Piero was writing the sign, Dottoressa Fabbiani asked the guard, 'Is there anyone still in the reading room?'

'No. The only other person who checked in today

was Tertullian, and he's left.' He took paper and a roll of tape from a drawer behind the counter and stepped over to the front door.

'*Oddio*,' Dottoressa Fabbiani said under her breath. 'I forgot all about him. It's almost as if he's part of the staff or a piece of the furniture.' She shook her head in exasperation at her own forgetfulness.

'Who's that?' Brunetti asked, curious to see if her explanation would match that of the guard.

'He comes here to read. It's been years,' she answered. 'He reads religious tracts and is very polite to everyone.'

'I see,' Brunetti said, deciding to ignore this information, at least for now. 'Would you tell me how a person gets to use your collection?'

She nodded. 'It's very straightforward. Residents have to provide their *carta d'identità* and proof of a current address. If they're not resident in the city and they want access to certain books, they have to give us a written explanation of their research project, a letter of recommendation from an academic institution or another library, and some form of identification.'

'How do they know that they can do their research here?' Seeing her confusion, he realized he had phrased his question badly. 'I mean, how do they know what's in your collection?'

Her surprise was too strong for her to disguise. 'Everything's online. All they have to do is search for what they want.'

'Of course, of course,' Brunetti said, embarrassed

that he had asked such a stupid question. 'The system was different when I was a student.' He looked around and said, 'Everything was different.'

'You came here?' she asked, curious.

'A few times, when I was in *liceo*.'

'To read what?'

'History, mostly. The Romans; sometimes the Greeks.' Then, feeling it proper to confess, he added, 'But always in translation.'

'For your classes?' she asked.

'Sometimes,' Brunetti said. 'But most often because I liked them.'

She looked at Brunetti, opened her mouth as if to say something, but then moved off towards what Brunetti calculated must be the back of the building.

Brunetti remembered his own university career and the eternities he had spent in libraries: find the title in the card catalogue, fill out the request form in duplicate (maximum three books), give the forms to the librarian, wait for the books to be delivered, go to a desk and read, give the books back at the end of the day. He remembered bibliographies and reading through them avidly in hopes that they would provide other titles on the subject of his research. Sometimes a professor would mention a few useful sources, but this was the rare exception; most of them hoarded what information they had, as if they believed that to give it to a student would be to lose control of it for ever.

'Was there some common element in the books requested by the American?' Brunetti asked.

'Travel,' she said. 'Venetian explorers of the New World.' She rustled the papers. 'At least that was the subject of his original requests. After two weeks, he started asking for books by writers who weren't Venetian, and then...' She broke off to consult the last of the pages in her hand. 'Then he began to ask for books on natural history.' Returning her attention to Brunetti, she said, 'They're all here.'

'But what did they have in common?' Brunetti asked.

'Illustrations,' she said, confirming what he already suspected. 'Maps, drawings of native species made by the explorers and the artists that went with them. Many of them were watercolours; done when they were printed.' As if surprised by what she had just said, the Dottoressa lifted the hand with the papers to cover her mouth and her eyes snapped shut.

'What is it?' Brunetti asked.

'The Merian,' she said, confusing him utterly. She stood stock still for so long Brunetti feared she was about to have some sort of seizure. Then he saw her relax: her hand fell to her side, and she opened her eyes.

'Are you all right?' he asked.

She nodded.

'What was it?' Brunetti asked, careful to make no move towards her.

'A book.'

'Which one?'

'A book of drawings by a German woman,' she

said, her voice slowly growing calmer. 'We have a copy of it. I was afraid he might have got his hands on that, but it's – I remembered – it's on loan to another library.' She closed her eyes and whispered, 'Thank God.'

Brunetti let a long time pass before he dared to ask, 'Do you have his application?'

'Yes,' she answered, smiling, as if she were glad of the change of subject. 'It's in my office. A letter from his university explaining his research with a recommendation, and a copy of his passport.' She turned and started across the room.

At the door she used the plastic sensor card she wore on a long lanyard around her neck to open it. Brunetti followed her inside and closed the door behind them. She led him into a long corridor illuminated only by artificial light.

At the end of the corridor, she used her card key again and let them into a vast room filled with rows of bookshelves so close together that only one person could pass through them at a time. Here inside, the scent was more pronounced: Brunetti wondered if the people who worked here ceased to smell it after a time. Just inside the door the Dottoressa took a pair of white cotton gloves from her pocket. While she put them on, she said, 'I haven't had time to check the other books he used, only the ones he left behind today. Some of them are here. We can do it now.'

She glanced at the top sheet, then turned left and went to the third row of shelves. Without seeming even to bother looking at the spines of the books, she stopped halfway along and reached down to pull one from the bottom shelf.

'Do you know where everything is?' he asked from the end of the aisle.

She came back and placed the book on a table beside him. She bent to open a drawer and pulled out a pair of cotton gloves and passed them to him. 'Almost. I've been here seven years.' She looked at the paper and again waved an arm towards the end of the same aisle. 'I'm sure I've walked hundreds of kilometres in these stacks.'

He was reminded of a uniformed officer in Naples he'd known when stationed there, who once remarked that, in his twenty-seven years on the force, he had walked at least fifty thousand kilometres, well over the circumference of the Earth. In the face of Brunetti's patent disbelief, he had explained that it worked out as ten kilometres each working day for twenty-seven years. Now Brunetti glanced down the aisle, attempting to estimate its length. Fifty metres? More?

He followed her for twenty minutes, going from room to room, his arms gradually filling with books. As time passed, he realized he was far less conscious of the smell of them. At one point, she stopped him beside the table and unpiled them before setting off again. She became his Ariadne, leading him through the labyrinth of books, stopping now and again to pass another one to him. Brunetti was quickly lost: he could orient himself only if a window looked across to the Giudecca: the nearby buildings he saw from the windows gave him no clues.

Finally, after giving him two more books, she flipped the list back to the first page, signalling to Brunetti that she was finished. 'We might as well look at them in here,' she said, leading him back to the table of books. He waited while she took the last books from his arms and stacked them on the table.

Standing by the first pile, the Dottoressa took the top book and opened it. Brunetti moved closer and saw the end sheet and flyleaf. She turned the page, and he saw, to the right, the title page. The missing frontispiece was present only as a stiff vertical stub. Though this small slip of paper looked like anything but a wound, Brunetti could not stop himself from thinking of the book as having suffered.

He heard her sigh. She closed the book and turned it to look at the bottom of the pages, no doubt searching for gaps in the thick paper. Hands made clumsy by the gloves, she set it on the table, removed the gloves, and started to page slowly through it. Soon enough, she came upon the stub of another sliced page, and then another, and then another, and then she was at the end of the book.

She set it aside and picked up another. Again, the frontispiece was gone, as were seven other pages. She closed the book and set it on top of the other. As she leaned forward to pick up another volume, Brunetti saw something drop on to the red leather binding, immediately turning it from rose to burgundy. She used the edge of her hand to blot at it. 'What fools we are,' she said to herself. Who did she mean? he wondered. The people who would do this or the people whose laxity allowed them to?

They stood side by side while she went through, by his count, another twenty-six books. All but two of them had pages sliced from them.

She placed the last book to one side and leaned forward, hands braced against the edge of the table. 'There are books missing, as well.' Then, reminding him of the way people often refused to accept even the most certain diagnosis, she added, 'But they might simply be mis-shelved.'

'Is that possible?' Brunetti asked.

Looking at the books spread out below her, she said, 'If you had asked me yesterday, I would have said none of this was possible.'

'What's missing?' he asked in open disbelief in the possible mis-shelving. 'Books he requested?'

'No, that's what's so strange. But they're the same kind of travel books.'

'What are they?' Brunetti asked, not that he thought there was any chance he would recognize them.

'A German translation of Ramusio's *Delle Navigationi et Viaggi* and a Latin edition of Montalboddo's *Paesi noua* from 1508.' She spoke as she would to a fellow librarian or archivist, assuming that he would know the books and have an idea of their value.

She saw his incomprehension and said, 'The

Montalboddo is a collection of different travellers' accounts of what they saw. Ramusio did the same thing, put together a collection of reports.'

Brunetti took out his notebook and wrote down the authors and what he thought the titles to be. Five-hundred-year-old volumes, and someone had simply waltzed into the place and walked out with them.

'Dottoressa,' he said, returning to the more immediate problem, 'I'd like you to show me the information you have about this man.'

'Gladly,' she said. 'I hope . . . I hope . . .' she began but forgot about the sentence and stopped.

'Can you see that no one else touches these books?' Brunetti asked. 'Some of my men will be here this afternoon to check them for fingerprints. If this comes to trial, we'll need that evidence.'

'If?' she asked. 'If?'

'We have to find him and we must have proof that he took them.'

'But we know he did,' she said, looking at Brunetti as though he had taken leave of his senses. 'It's obvious.'

Brunetti said nothing. The obvious was sometimes impossible to prove, and what people knew to be true was often of no use to a judge: not in the absence of proof. He did not want to have to say this to her. Instead, he put a mild expression on his face and waved a hand towards the door.

He followed her down the corridor and into her office. On the desk was a blue cardboard folder which she handed to him silently, then went to stand at one of the three windows that looked across at the Redentore. He wondered if anyone was going to be able to redeem these books for her. He opened the folder on the desk and began to read through it.

Joseph Nickerson, born in Michigan thirty-six years ago, currently living in Kansas. This much the passport told him; the photo told him that the man had light hair and eyes, a straight nose a bit too big for his face, and a small cleft in his chin. His expression was neutral and relaxed, the face of a man without secrets, someone you could sit next to on a plane on a short flight and talk about sports or how terrible things were in Africa. But not, he thought, about antiquarian books.

Nickerson could be any man of Anglo-Saxon or Northern heritage, could surely change his appearance by putting on a pair of glasses and letting his hair grow, perhaps adding a beard. So little was notable that it would be difficult to recall anything about him other than a vague memory of his direct, honest expression.

This suggested to Brunetti that the man was a professional and was possessed of that quality that the great confidence men had: the appearance of easy, innate honesty. He would never brag, never make a statement about right or wrong, but his manner, the trust he put in you, his undisguised interest in what you had to say and curiosity to learn more would make him irresistible. Brunetti had known two men who had that quality, and even while interrogating them, he had felt uncertain about what he knew to be true of both of them. He had, over the years, come to see it as a gift, the way great beauty is, or intelligence. It was simply there, and the possessors could do with it as they chose.

Touching the paper lightly on one corner, he slid it to the left and read the next. The letter of recommendation came from the Provost of the University of Kansas in Lawrence, Kansas, stating that Joseph Nickerson was Assistant Professor of European History with a specialization in Maritime and Mediterranean Trade History, which class he taught, and that he hoped the library would put their collection at the Professor's disposal. His name was typed below an illegible signature.

He took the letter by its top two corners and held it up to the light coming in from the window. The letterhead had been printed on the paper, perhaps by the same printer that generated the letter. Well, just about anyone could do that. Kansas, he believed, was in the middle of America somewhere; he had a vague memory of its being to the left of Iowa or at least near it, but definitely in the middle. Maritime and Mediterranean Trade History?

'I'll have to take these with me,' he said, then asked, 'Do you have an address for him, or an Italian phone number?'

Dottoressa Fabbiani turned away from her contemplation of the church. 'Not unless it's given there. It's required only for residents who use the collection,' she said. 'What happens now?' she asked.

Brunetti replaced the papers and closed the folder. 'As I mentioned, a team comes and takes fingerprints from the books and from the desk where he was sitting, and then we hope to be able to match them with prints in our files.'

'You make it sound very ordinary.'

'It is,' Brunetti said.

'To me, it sounds like the Wild West. Why aren't we being informed about these people? Why aren't we sent photos of them so we can protect ourselves?' she asked, not angry but surprised.

'I have no idea,' Brunetti answered. 'It might be that the libraries that are robbed don't want it to be known.'

'Why ever not?'

'Do you have patrons? Benefactors?'

That stopped her, and he watched while she put the two things together. Finally she said, 'We have three, but only the private one counts. The other money comes from foundations.'

'How would the private donor respond?'

'If she learned that we allowed this to happen?' she said, then held up a hand and closed her eyes for a moment. She took a deep breath, steeling herself for the truth, and said, 'Two of the books belonged to her family.'

'Belonged.'

She studied the pattern on the parquet floor before

looking at him and saying, 'They were part of a large donation. It must be more than ten years ago.'

'Which books?'

She needed only to name them, and he saw that she tried. She opened her mouth but could not speak. Instead, she looked again at the parquet, then back at him. 'One of the ones that's missing. The other's lost nine pages,' she finally managed to say. Then, before he could ask how she knew their origin, she added, 'The family's name is on the central listing in the catalogue.'

'What is it?' Brunetti asked.

'Morosini-Albani.' Then she added, 'They gave us the Ramusio.'

Brunetti did his best to hide his astonishment. That a member of this family should be a patron of any- thing would come as a surprise – even a shock – to any Venetian. Though the major branch of the family had given the city at least four doges, this offshoot had given it only merchants and bankers. While one side of the family ruled, this one acquired, a division that had gone on – if Brunetti had his lists right – until the reign of the last Morosini doge some time in the seventeenth century.

The Albani branch had then, in a sense, gone to ground, retreated to its *palazzo* – which they had chosen to build not on the Grand Canal, but in a part of the city where land was cheaper – and continued with the family passion of acquiring wealth. The current Contessa, a widow with three contentious stepchildren, was a friend of his mother-in-law. Contessa Falier had been at a private convent school with Contessa Morosini-Albani, at that time merely the younger daughter of a Sicilian prince who had gambled away the family fortune, her tuition paid by a maiden aunt. She had much later married the heir to the Morosini-Albani fortune, thus acquiring both his lesser title and his three children by a former marriage. Brunetti had met her a few times at dinner at the home of Paola's parents, met her and spoken to her and come away with the sense that she was well educated, intelligent and broadly read.

'Which of them gave you the books?'

'The Contessa,' she answered.

Like many foreigners – and anyone who was not born in Venice was equally foreign – Contessa Morosini-Albani had decided to become more Venetian than the Venetians. Her late husband had been a member of the Club dei Nobili, where he went to smoke his cigars and read *Il Giornale* while muttering vague things about the lack of respect shown to people of merit. She, in her turn, joined committees for the salvation of this and that, the protection of some other place or thing, attended the opening night of La Fenice without fail, and was a frequent and savage writer of letters to *Il Gazzettino*. That the family might have given away anything, let alone precious books, demanded of Brunetti the willing suspension of disbelief. The Morosini-Albanis were, or had always been, keepers and not givers; life had shown Brunetti precious little to suggest that people changed in profound ways.

But, he reflected, she was a Sicilian after all, and they were a legendarily profligate people, in the worst and the best sense. Her stepchildren were generally rumoured to be both thankless and feckless, so perhaps she had decided to spite them by giving it all away before they got their hands on it. Contessa Falier might know more. 'Do you have any idea how the Contessa will react to this?'

Dottoressa Fabbiani folded her arms and leaned back against the windowsill, legs straight and feet neatly side by side, just as those birds kept them. 'It depends, I suppose, on how negligent we are shown to have been.'

'My guess is that this man is a professional and does this on order.' He said this to suggest that negligence might not have been a major factor. 'He probably works for certain collectors who want specific items, which he gets for them.'

She made a huffing noise and said, 'Well, at least you didn't say he "acquires" them.'

'That would have been too much, I think,' Brunetti said, 'considering my job.' He risked a smile. 'Does she give the library money, as well?' he asked, not bothering to name the Contessa.

'A hundred thousand Euros a year.'

The Morosini-Albanis? When he recovered from his astonishment sufficiently to speak, Brunetti asked, 'How important is that for you?'

'We get yearly funds from the city and the region and the central government, but that's just enough to cover operating expenses. What the donors give us allows for acquisitions and restoration.'

'You said she gave you books. Were there many more?'

She turned her head away from his question but, finding nothing to look at, looked back at Brunetti. 'Yes. It was an important donation. I'm sure it was her doing: her husband was . . . a Morosini-Albani.' After some time, she said, 'She's promised the rest of the library to us,' before pausing to add, almost in a whisper, 'The family were the first patrons of Minuzio.' Something stopped her from saying more; superstition, perhaps. Talking of it might stop it from happening, and then the library would lose the family's hoard of the books of the greatest of printers of the greatest of printing cities.

When Brunetti was still a reluctant schoolboy, his mother used to encourage him to get out of bed by telling him that every new day would offer him some wonderful surprise. She might not have had the generosity of the Morosini-Albani in mind, but she certainly had been right.

'Don't worry, Dottoressa. I won't repeat this.'

Relieved, she added, 'Their collection is . . . extensive.' As if to make clear what she had said about the husband, she went on, 'The Contessa is the only one in the family who understands the real value of the books, and appreciates them. I don't know where she learned it – I never had the courage to ask her – but she knows a great deal about early books, and printing, and conservation.' She raised a hand in a broad sweep meant to encompass, perhaps, the Contessa's abilities, then paused briefly, as if uncertain how much she could say to Brunetti. 'I've asked her opinion about conservation a number of times.' Then, with the generosity he sometimes found in scholars, she said, 'She's got the gift, the feel.'

'"Feel"?' he asked.

She smiled. '"Love" might be a better word. As I told you, she's promised them to us.'

'Promised?'

She looked around the office. 'After this,' she began, as though the Vandals had just crashed out of the room, leaving nothing but devastation in their wake, 'she'll never trust us.'

'Couldn't it just as easily have happened to her in her own home?'

'You mean that someone could have tricked her?'

'Yes,' Brunetti answered.

'I can't imagine that anyone could trick her out of anything,' she said.

3

Brunetti smiled to show he was amused by the remark, which was certainly true, for it more or less mirrored his own opinion of the Contessa. Upon reflection, however, he realized that Dottoressa Fabbiani was expressing sincere appreciation of the Contessa's ferocity, a word that sprang to his mind when he tried to find one that would describe her character. Though he had met her only five or six times over the years, she had so often been the topic of conversation between his wife and her mother that he had formed an impression of a woman with inordinately strong opinions who was also – something he had always admired – a good hater. Even more admirably, she seemed to be a democratic hater, dealing out her contempt equally to Church and State, Left and Right. Paola adored her, and her mother thought of her as a close friend, yet more evidence of the inherent democracy of women.

'Dottoressa, I have to confess two things to you,' he said, hoping to turn them both back to the matter at hand.

She looked mildly alarmed but said nothing.

'There's my ignorance about the monetary worth of the missing books and about the market for the pages that have been taken.' He paused, but she had nothing to ask or say. 'Because of that, I think this is a case that should be handled by the Art Theft division, but they're in Rome, and . . .'

'And they have larger things to worry about?' she asked.

Neither of them saw fit to comment on the explosion of thefts from homes, churches, libraries, and museums – even from the library of the Ministry of Agriculture – that had taken place in recent years. Brunetti regularly read the circulars from the Art Theft police and from Interpol that announced the major thefts, not only of paintings and statues, but of manuscripts and books, either whole volumes or pages from them. Anything was fair game for the new book vandals, left to their own among the oldest collections in Europe.

'How many volumes do you have here, Dottoressa?' he asked.

She tilted her head to one side while she considered

his question. 'The total collection is about thirty thousand, but the bulk of that is downstairs, in the ordinary collection. Up here,' she said, waving her hand to include the rooms behind Brunetti, 'we have about eight thousand volumes: the manuscript collection contains about two hundred more.'

'Anything else?'

'We have a collection of Persian miniatures: a merchant brought them back from Iran at the turn of the last century. If anyone wants to see them, a member of the staff has to stay with them.'

That reminded Brunetti that someone had been with Dottor Nickerson for at least part of the time he was in the library, perhaps for a good part of it. 'This man you called Tertullian. Do you have his application on file?'

'What do you want with him?' she asked, sounding protective.

'I'd like to speak to him. You said he's been here so long he's like one of the staff. If that's true, then he might have seen something he thought was unusual.'

'I don't think there's any purpose in that,' she insisted.

Brunetti was tired of playing good cop. 'Dottoressa, I'm not sure the examining magistrate would see it that way.'

'What does that mean?' she asked, and he heard the hardening of her tone.

'That a magistrate would certainly issue an order that you give us his name and any information that

41

would help us locate him.' Then, before she could protest, he added, 'This is a library, Dottoressa, not a medical practice or a church. His name and address are not protected information, and there is every possibility that he was a witness to a crime. The only way to find out is to talk to him.'

'I think that might be,' she began, then paused in search of the right words. '… difficult for him.'

'Why?' Brunetti asked, this time more mildly.

'He's had problems.'

'Such as?' This time Brunetti drew on the infinite patience required to get people to say what they were reluctant to say.

He watched her weigh how much she would reveal. 'He might once have been a priest, or at least a seminarian.'

That would explain his interest in Tertullian, Brunetti thought. 'Might have been?' he asked. She gave him a confused look, and he added, 'Did he decide to stop being a priest, or stop studying to be one? Or was he forced to do so?'

'I don't know,' she answered. 'It's not something I could ask him.'

'But you have an idea?' he asked, his sensors activated by the uneasiness with which she had spoken.

'Why are we talking about him?' she demanded. 'All he did was sit and read. That's not a crime.'

'Seeing a crime being committed while you're sitting and reading and not reporting it is a crime, however,' Brunetti said, twisting the truth to his purpose.

'He's a good man,' she insisted. He knew from long experience that good men are not necessarily brave men, nor do they necessarily want to become involved in the lives of other people.

Brunetti had read something by the – he knew he was a lawyer and thought he was African – theologian ages ago, and he remembered not having warmed to him at all. He had never encountered anyone so opposed to pleasure as Tertullian, nor did he seem to have much good to say about life in general. Imagine the person who would want to read Tertullian.

'Will you show me his application?' he asked, refusing to be diverted.

'You really have to talk to him?' she asked.

'Yes,' Brunetti said.

'His name is Aldo Franchini, and he lives in Castello, down towards the bottom of Via Garibaldi.'

Brunetti took out his notebook and wrote the name and the location, then looked across at her, interested that she knew where he lived. 'How well do you know him?'

'Not well at all,' she said, going behind her desk to sit. She waved Brunetti to a chair, which he sat in, hoping this would lead to greater ease between them. 'But I do know his younger brother, who was at school with me. He called me about three years ago. He said his older brother had moved back to the city. He'd lost his job because of trouble with the Director, which meant he couldn't get a letter of recommendation. He wanted to come here to read, and his brother asked if I'd give my permission, even though he'd lost his job.'

'Which was?'

'Teaching theology at a private boys' school in Vicenza.'

'Theology?' Brunetti asked.

She gave him a level look and said, 'He was a priest then.' She sounded far more certain about him than she had been before.

'Then?'

'I didn't think that was any of my business,' she said, though without the huff of righteousness many people would have given.

'What did you do?'

'I told him that if his brother was resident here, then he didn't need a letter: all he had to do was come in with identification and apply for a reader's card.'

'You weren't interested in what he might have done?' Brunetti insisted.

She ignored his question. 'If he wants to read, it's his right. Nothing else about him is my business.'

'Did his brother say anything about him?'

'Is this part of your police work?' she asked. 'Or do you simply want to know?'

'Any man who would read Tertullian interests me,' Brunetti said, telling part of the truth, smiling when he said it.

'He told me his brother was a serious reader and needed a place where he could find books.' She seemed to relent, and in a softer voice added, 'He said it would help him, reading.'

'Did you ask why his brother might need help?' Brunetti asked, though he doubted she would have done so.

She smiled for the first time and all resemblance to a bird disappeared: she became a tall woman with a kind, intelligent face. 'I think he wanted me to ask, but I didn't. His word was good enough for me.'

'In the time he was here, did you find out anything about him?'

'No, not really. He read Augustine, Jerome, Maximus the Confessor, but he started by reading Tertullian, so that's the name we gave him.'

'Why would you do something like that?'

'Librarians are . . .' she began, thought about it, and then started again. 'Librarians are unusual people.' Brunetti was certainly willing to believe that. 'He was the first person any of us could remember who requested Tertullian and then actually sat and read him. Not for research for a university class but because he was seriously interested in the book.' Her praise was implicit in every word.

'How much contact have you had with him?'

'After some time, we would say hello to one another, and occasionally I'd ask him what he was reading.'

'And how did he seem when you spoke to him?'

She smiled, but this time Brunetti realized it was to warn him that her answer would not be a serious one. 'Do you mean do I think there's anything wrong with him?'

'Well, considering what he's been reading . . .'

She laughed. 'Yes, they seem like lunatics to some of us today, but perhaps he hoped to find . . .'

'Answers?'

She raised both hands as if to ward off his attempt to force his words on her, then said, 'I don't know what the Fathers of the Church have for us today. Comfort, perhaps.'

'You mean to a dying religion? Or from one?'

She looked across at the surface of her desk and then back at him. 'It is, isn't it?'

'Statistically, yes,' Brunetti answered. He was never sure just how he felt about that, but suspected he regretted it. 'Soon they may all be out of work,' he added. Then clarified. 'Priests, nuns, bishops.'

'It won't be that fast, I think,' she countered.

'No, probably not,' Brunetti agreed. Then, to move away from the mood that had been created, he said, 'Will you leave those books on the table, please?'

'What will your men have to do? Put black powder on them?' Her fear was obvious.

'That's only on television. They use lasers now, just shine a light on the pages and take a photo. It does no damage to the paper.' He saw how difficult she found this to believe, as would anyone who had grown up with films and television presenting the technicians with their brushes and black powder. 'Believe me, nothing will get on to the paper. You can be with them while they work if you want, and I promise they'll wear gloves.'

'When will they come?'

'They should be here today.'

She opened a drawer of her desk and took her card from it. He slipped it into his pocket without looking at it, thanked her and put out his hand.

'That's all?' she asked as they shook hands.

'For the moment,' he said and left the library.

4

Brunetti stopped on the way back to the Questura and finally had his coffee, but he drank it almost reluctantly, knowing it was merely a delaying tactic, not a pleasure. When he walked in, he decided to go directly to report to the Vice-Questore what had happened at the library. As he climbed the steps to his superior's office, he thought of a story, surely apocryphal, he had once heard about some American movie star – was it Jean Harlow? It was said that when she was given a book for her birthday, she unwrapped it and looked at it, then said, 'A book? I have a book.'

Thus Vice-Questore Giuseppe Patta, he was sure. When he entered the small office where Signorina

Elettra usually sat, he saw that her chair was empty and her computer wasting its sweetness on the desert air. In recent weeks, she had often been absent from her desk. Vice-Questore Patta, who was her direct superior, had either not noticed or – far more likely – was afraid to ask. Because she was not his secretary, Brunetti thought it was not his place to inquire and so said nothing. This time her absence meant he would be exposed to the Vice-Questore's mood with no preparation. Was he a man or a mouse? Brunetti went to the door and knocked.

'*Avanti*,' he heard and entered.

Dottor Giuseppe Patta, the finest flower of Palermitano manhood, sat behind his desk, caught in the act of folding his handkerchief into the breast pocket of his jacket. Brunetti was glad to see that the handkerchief was white – linen, perhaps – and bleached to the colour of dinosaur bones in the Gobi, the uniform of the umpires at Lord's, a child's first tooth. Patta would never concede to modern liberties of dress, would see himself dragged through the streets before he would put a coloured handkerchief in the breast pocket of his suit. In some things, usually those related to fashion, Patta was a man of stalwart principle; it was an honour to be in the same room with him.

'*Buon giorno*, Vice-Questore,' Brunetti said, resisting the impulse to tug at his forelock.

Patta gave the handkerchief a final prod and turned his attention to Brunetti. 'Is this important?' he asked.

'It might be, Dottore,' Brunetti said easily. 'I thought you should know about it before it's reported to the press, as I'm sure it will be.'

Had the handkerchief caught fire, Patta could have been no more energized. 'What is it?' His look of mild displeasure had been upgraded to that of defender of the nation.

Brunetti approached the desk and stood behind one of the chairs. He placed his hands on the back and said, 'We had a call from the Biblioteca Merula, reporting a combination of vandalism and theft.'

'Which is it, vandalism or theft?' Patta demanded.

'Someone sliced pages from more than twenty books, Dottore. And books are missing, probably stolen.'

'Why would anyone do that?' Patta asked.

Brunetti breathed a silent prayer to Saint Monica, that emblem of patience. She was the patron saint of the abused, so Brunetti could invoke her for either function, depending upon the ferocity of Patta's behaviour. 'Books, as well as pages from rare books, are very popular with collectors, sir, and have a certain value.'

'Who did it?'

'The books were all used by a Doctor Joseph Nickerson, who was there with a letter of reference from the University of Kansas and gave them an American passport as identification.'

'Is it valid?'

'I haven't contacted the Americans yet, Vice-

Questore.' He looked at his watch and realized it was hopeless to try to do anything else that day.

Patta gave him a long look and said, 'It doesn't sound like you've done very much at all, Brunetti.'

Brunetti again consulted Saint Monica. 'I've just got back, and I wanted you to know about it in case it's necessary to deal with the press.'

'Why should that be necessary?' Patta asked, as though he'd been channelled the information that Brunetti was deliberately hiding something he should be told about.

'One of the patrons of the library is the Contessa Morosini-Albani. In fact, it was she who donated at least one of the books that are missing. They're concerned about what her reaction will be.'

'She'll probably take back anything else she's given them. That's what any sensible person would do.'

It certainly sounded like what Patta would do, though Brunetti would need more than the help of the saints to believe that the Vice-Questore would ever donate a book to a library.

Then, abruptly, Patta asked, 'Is this what you meant about the press? That they'll be interested in her?'

'I think it's possible, sir. Her family is very well known in the city, and their appetite has certainly been whetted by her stepson.'

Patta's look was fierce as he replayed Brunetti's remark, scanning for criticism of the higher orders. Brunetti ironed all emotion from his face and stood, attentive, neutral, waiting for his superior's response.

'Do you mean Gianni?' Patta asked.

'Yes, sir.'

Brunetti watched as Patta's memory, which was elephantine for scandal of any sort, flashed across the photos and headlines that had filled the gutter press for years. Brunetti's favourite was '*Gianni paga i danni*', for the rhyme between his name and the damages he had had to pay after destroying the sound equipment of a band whose music he had not enjoyed in a club in Lignano. '*Nobile ignobile*' had followed his arrest for shoplifting from an antique dealer's in Milano, and then the delightful headline in the British press, 'No-account Count', after he was stopped trying to steal from a shop in New Bond Street. As Brunetti recalled, he had been serving as an attaché of some sort to the Italian embassy in London at the time, and so he could not be arrested, only declared *persona non grata* and expelled from England.

Though Gianni was in no way, at least to the best of Brunetti's current knowledge, involved with the library or the theft, the mention of the family name would be enough to work the Miracle of San Gennaro on the press: give it a good shake, and the blood would flow afresh. The young man – who was no longer young and not much of a man – had so saturated the press that any combination, no matter how accidental, of his name and a crime of any sort would quickly become a headline; the Contessa would hardly want to see the family name exposed to the public eye in this fashion.

'Do you think . . .?' Patta began.

Brunetti waited, but his superior left the question unasked.

Patta shifted his attention, and Brunetti saw the very moment when the Vice-Questore remembered that Brunetti had, by virtue of his marriage, slithered in among the nobility. 'Do you know her?' Patta asked.

'The Contessa?'

'Who else have we been talking about?'

Brunetti, instead of correcting him, said only, 'I've met her a few times, but I can't say I know her.'

'Who does?'

'Know her?'

'Yes.'

'My wife and my mother-in-law,' Brunetti answered reluctantly.

'Would one of them talk to her, do you think?'

'About what?'

Patta closed his eyes and sighed deeply, as one does when forced to deal with lesser intellects. 'About how she might answer the press, should they find out about this.'

'And how should that be, sir?'

'That she has no doubt that this will be resolved quickly.'

'By the hard work and intelligence of the local police?' Brunetti suggested.

Patta's eyes blasted away at Brunetti's sarcasm but his voice said only, 'Something like that. I don't want the public institutions of this city to be the victims of criticism.'

Brunetti could only nod. Citizens have complete faith in the police. Libraries that allow theft should not be criticized. He wondered if Patta believed this amnesty should be extended to all public institutions in the city. And in the province? The country?

'I'll see my mother-in-law at dinner tomorrow evening, sir, and I'll mention it to her,' Brunetti said, reminding Patta which of them it was who would sit down to dinner with Conte e Contessa Orazio Falier, and who it was who would some day live in Palazzo Falier and look across at the façades of the *palazzi* on the other side of the Grand Canal.

Patta, fatuous but not a fool, backed away from this by saying, 'I'll leave it to you, then, Brunetti. See what the Americans can tell you.'

'Yes, sir,' Brunetti said, pushing himself back from the chair.

Signorina Elettra had returned to her desk, which now held a large vase. In this she was adjusting dozens of bright red tulips. The windowsill held the same excess of daffodils, the two colours in competition for the viewer's attention. Brunetti turned his, instead, to the creator of this floral exuberance. Given that she was today wearing an orange woollen dress and shoes so narrow with heels so high that either they or the toe could have delivered a mortal wound, this was not hard to do.

'And what was it the Vice-Questore had to say to you, Commissario?' she asked amiably.

Brunetti waited until she was seated before leaning against the windowsill that had no vase. 'He asked where the flowers came from,' he answered, straight-faced.

It was rare that Brunetti had the pleasure of surprising her, but this time he obviously had, and so he decided to continue with it. 'It's Monday, so there's no market at Rialto, and that means you bought them in a florist's.' He put on a stern face and said, 'I hope the office expenses can cover the cost.'

She smiled, a glow to match that of the flowers. 'Ah, but I'd never abuse that account, Dottore.' She let three beats pass and added, 'They were sent to me.' The glucose level of her smile soared and she asked, 'And what *was* it the Vice-Questore had to say?'

Brunetti waited for a few seconds to acknowledge his defeat and then smiled to show her he appreciated it. 'I told him about a robbery – quite a few of them – at the Biblioteca Merula.'

'Books?' she inquired.

'Yes, and a lot of maps and title pages cut from others.'

'Might as well steal them, then,' she said.

'Because they're ruined?' he asked, surprised to hear her repeat what he now thought of as Dottoressa Fabbiani's opinion.

'If you break the nose off a portrait bust, you've still got most of the face, haven't you?' she asked.

'If you cut a map out of a book,' he said right back, 'you've still got all of the text.'

'But it's ruined as an object,' she insisted.

'You sound like the librarian,' Brunetti said.

'I hope so,' was her response. 'They spend their lives working with books.'

'So do readers,' Brunetti said.

This time she laughed in return. 'Do you really mean that?'

'That the missing page doesn't change the book?'

'Yes.'

He lifted himself up by his hands until he was sitting on the windowsill, legs dangling down. He studied his feet, waved one and then the other. 'Depends on how you define "book", doesn't it?'

'Partly, yes.'

'If its purpose is to present a text, then it doesn't matter if you pull out the maps.'

'But?' she asked.

He wanted to show her that he could see the other side of the argument, so he said, 'But if it's an object that captures information about a particular time – the way the maps are drawn, for example – and representative of . . .'

Patta's door opened and the man appeared. He shot a glance at Brunetti, sitting as casually as a schoolboy on a flowery bank, and then at his secretary, seen consorting with the enemy. The three people in the room froze.

Finally Patta said, 'Could I see you for a moment, Signorina?'

'Of course, Vice-Questore,' she answered, getting smoothly to her feet and sliding her chair back in place.

Wasting no words on Brunetti, Patta turned back to his office and disappeared. Signorina Elettra did not look at Brunetti as she followed him into the room. The door closed.

Brunetti hopped down and, looking at his watch, saw that it was justifiably time to go home.

5

The children were interested in the story of the theft and tried to come up with explanations of how it could have happened. Brunetti gave a vague estimate of the sizes of the pages and stressed that it was essential to the thief that they not be wrinkled or damaged in any way. Raffi, who had been given a Mac Air by his grandparents for Christmas, went to his room and brought it back. He opened it, set it aside, and pulled a few pages from last week's issue of *l'Espresso*. He folded them neatly, placed them on the keyboard and closed the lid, then looked around the table for approval.

Chiara pointed to the slivers of paper visible at one side. 'If I had the one with the larger screen, you wouldn't see the edges,' Raffi insisted.

Without asking, Chiara went down the hall to Paola's office and returned with the battered leather briefcase her mother had not carried for a decade but could not bring herself to throw away. She took the magazine from Raffi and pulled out a few pages herself, placed them into the curve of her left palm, then gently lowered the thicker edge of Raffi's computer on to them. When she closed her hand, the pages nestled tight against the sides of the computer without reaching the top. Gently, she worked it into its padded case and zipped it closed along the top, then slid the case into the briefcase. 'That's how I'd do it,' she said. Then, to stifle any doubts, she walked around the table and let them all look inside the briefcase, where all they could see was the top of the innocent computer safe in its case.

Brunetti stopped himself from pointing out that guards would have long since learned about those tricks.

'And the other people in the library would just sit and watch you do it, and then applaud?' Raffi asked, irritated that her suggestion was as good as his own.

'If there was no one else in the room at the time, they wouldn't,' she said.

'And if there was someone?' Brunetti asked. He had not mentioned the stolen books but did not want to initiate another round of demonstrations.

'It would depend on how intent they were on what they were reading,' Paola broke in to say. Brunetti knew, from decades of experience, that Paola would fail to notice Armageddon itself, were it to occur when she was reading – and for the seven hundred and twelfth time – the passage in *The Portrait of a Lady* where Isabel Archer realizes Madame Merle's betrayal. Had she reached that point, kidnappers could enter the house and remove the three of them, kicking and screaming, and she would read on. And on.

Chiara having shown her expertise at a skill Brunetti hoped she would never use, they went back to their fusilli with fresh tuna and capers and onions. Talk turned to other subjects, and it was not until Paola and Brunetti were sitting in the living room, drinking coffee, that he thought to mention the ecclesiastical reader.

'Tertullian?' Paola asked. 'That creep?'

'The real one or the one who's been reading in the library?'

'I have no idea who the reader in the library is,' she said. 'I mean the real one, what was he, third century?'

'I don't remember,' Brunetti admitted. 'But about then.'

She placed her empty cup on the saucer and set them on the low table in front of the sofa, then leaned back and closed her eyes. He knew what she was going to do, and even after decades with her, it still astonished him when she did it: it was all in there, behind her eyes, and she had only to concentrate sufficiently to bring it up from he had no idea where. If she had read it, she remembered the sense and general meaning; if she had read it carefully, she remembered the text. At the same time, she was hopeless with faces and could never remember having met someone, although she would remember the conversation they had had.

'"You are the gateway of the devil; you are the one who unseals the curse of that tree, and you are the first one to turn your back on the divine law; you are the one who persuaded him whom the Devil was not capable of corrupting . . ."' She opened her eyes, looked at him, and gave him a shark's smile.

'Or, if you'd like more about women, there's my special friend Augustine.' Again she slipped into trance mode and, after a moment, said, '"How much more agreeable it is for two male friends to live together than for a man and a woman."' Coming back to the present, she asked, 'Isn't it time all these guys came out of the closet?'

'That's an extreme position,' he said, though he had pointed this out to her countless times and treasured her because she defended so many such positions. 'I think he was talking about conversation in that passage, that men speak together more easily than they do with a woman.'

'I know that. But it's always seemed strange to me that men can say things like this about women – dare one call it holding "extreme positions"? – and yet become saints.'

'That's probably because they said a lot of other things, as well.'

She shifted towards him on the sofa and said, 'I've

also found it strange that people can be made saints for what they say, when what we do is so much more important.' Then, with one of those sudden changes of subject that still managed to surprise him, she asked, 'What are you going to do?'

'I'll call the Americans tomorrow and see if it's a real passport. And ask Signorina Elettra to contact the other libraries in the city to see if this Nickerson has paid any of them a visit. Call this university in Kansas to see if he really worked there. And I'll see if I can locate Tertullian.'

'Good luck. I'm curious about a man who would read him.'

'So am I,' Brunetti said, wondering if there might be a copy of Tertullian in the house and whether he should take it to read in bed. Because that would mean putting aside his current book, *The White War*, an English history of the war in Alto Adige, a war in which his grandfather had fought, Brunetti resisted the not very strong temptation. He decided to return to the rocklike stupidity of General Cadorna, he of the eleven futile battles of the Isonzo, the man who returned to the Roman idea of executing every tenth man in any battalion that retreated, the general who led half a million men to their deaths for little purpose and no gain. Would Paola be comforted, Brunetti asked himself, by the fact that almost all of the victims of Cadorna's savagery had been men, not women? Probably not.

*

As he walked to the Questura the next day, Brunetti reflected on the press and began to wonder if he had been precipitate in mentioning it to Patta. Dottoressa Fabbiani was certainly not going to notify them, and he suspected that Sartor was sufficiently loyal to keep his mouth closed. Only Dottoressa Fabbiani and Sartor were certain about what had taken place in the library, and only they had seen the papers with the names of all of the books Nickerson had consulted, although she and Brunetti were the only people who had seen all of the vandalized books. It was in her best interests to keep this quiet until she found some way to inform the Contessa. Brunetti was a public official and could imagine how the press would treat this, so he saw no reason to inform them of the thefts. The authorities had been alerted: the press could go to hell.

The first thing he did when he got to his office was call Dottoressa Fabbiani, who told him, not at all to his surprise, that Dottor Nickerson had not returned to the library that morning. He thanked her and called the American embassy in Rome, identified himself, then explained his need to verify Nickerson's passport, saying only that the man was a suspect in a crime and the passport the only identification they had. He was transferred to another office, where he again explained his request. They told him to wait, after which he found himself speaking to a man who did not identify either himself or his office, although he asked Brunetti to give his name. When Brunetti offered to give his phone number, he was told that was not necessary, and they would call him back. Twenty minutes later, he received a call on his *telefonino* from the secretary of an undersecretary at the Italian Foreign Office, asking if he was the man who had called the Americans. When he said he was, the man thanked him and was gone. Soon thereafter he received a call from a woman speaking excellent Italian with the slightest of accents, who asked his name. When he identified himself, she said that the United States government had issued no such passport, and did he have any further questions? He said he did not, they exchanged polite monosyllables, and he ended the call.

They still had his photo. Nickerson – for want of a better name – might well look different by now and could very likely be out of the city, even out of the country entirely. But what had prompted his sudden departure?

Piero Sartor had said the man spoke excellent Italian: perhaps he would not waste that talent by going to some other country. Besides, Italy was rich in museums and libraries, public, private, and ecclesiastical, all providing an endless field in which he could work. Brunetti was not unaware of how grotesque his use of that word was to describe what the man was doing.

He took the photocopy of Nickerson's passport and went down to Signorina Elettra's office. It was only a little after ten, far too early for Patta to have arrived. She was behind her computer today, wearing a pink angora sweater, the sight of which caused him immediately to revise his low opinion of both the colour and the wool.

'The Vice-Questore expressed his concern about the theft at the library, Commissario.' He wondered if the Vice-Questore had also expressed his concern about summoning the Eumenides of the press down upon their heads.

'I've checked with the Americans, and the passport is fake,' he said, putting the photocopied page on her desk.

She studied the photo. 'That was to be expected, I suppose.' Then she asked, 'Shall I send this to Interpol and the art theft people in Rome and see if they recognize him?'

'Yes,' he said, having come down specifically to ask her to do this.

'Do you know if the Vice-Questore has talked about this to anyone else?' Brunetti asked.

'The only person he talks to is Lieutenant Scarpa,' she said, pronouncing 'person' as if she weren't quite sure it applied. 'I believe neither of them would consider the theft of books a serious crime.'

'I was concerned about the press,' he said, turning his attention to the tulips on her desk and telling himself it would be nice to take some home that evening. He reached across to move one slightly to the left and said, 'I doubt that the Contessa would enjoy the publicity.'

'Which contessa?' Signorina Elettra inquired mildly.

'Morosini-Albani,' Brunetti answered, his attention still on the flowers.

She made a noise. It was not a gasp and it was not a word, merely a noise. By the time he glanced at her, she was looking at the screen of her computer, her chin propped on and covered by her left hand. Her face was impassive, her eyes on the screen, but the colour of her face more nearly approached that of her sweater than it had a moment ago.

'I've met her a few times at my parents-in-law's,' Brunetti said casually, moving another tulip into place in front of the broad leaf that had been hiding it. 'She's a very interesting woman, I'd say.' Then, oh so casually, 'Have you ever met her?'

She hit a few keys with her right hand, chin still propped on the left. Finally she said, 'Once. Years ago.' She turned her attention from the computer and looked at Brunetti with an expression devoid of emotion. 'I once knew her stepson.'

Brunetti, curious, was silent, then finally thought to say, 'She's the major donor to the library. I don't know how many of the books that were vandalized were once hers, or if they were part of the original collection, but she gave them one of the books that were stolen, and one that was vandalized. It's hardly news that would please a major donor.'

'Ah,' she said in a tone meant to display little interest in the matter.

He pulled out his notebook and opened it to the

page where he had written the names Dottoressa Fabbiani had given him. 'There's an edition of Ramusio and a Montalboddo,' he said, quite proud of the ease with which he named them.

She murmured something appreciative, quite as if she were familiar with them.

'Do you know the books?' he asked.

'I've heard their names,' she answered. 'My father's always been interested in rare books. He owns a few.'

'Does he buy them?' Brunetti asked.

She turned to him and laughed outright, banishing whatever tension had been in the room. 'You sound as though you think he might be stealing them. I assure you he's been nowhere near the Merula for months.'

Brunetti smiled, in relief that her good humour had returned after her strange response to the Contessa's name. 'Do you know much about rare books?'

'No, not really. He's shown me some of them and explained what makes them special, but I'm a disappointment to him.'

'Why?'

'Oh, I think they're beautiful enough – the paper, the bindings – but I can't get excited about them.' She sounded genuinely displeased with herself. 'It's collecting: I don't understand it, or I don't feel it.' Before he could ask, she continued, 'It's not that I don't like beautiful things: I just don't have the discipline for collecting in a systematic way, and I think that's what real collectors do: they want one of everything in the classification they're interested in, whether it's

German postage stamps with flowers on them or Coca-Cola bottle caps or . . . or whatever it is they've decided to collect.'

'And if you don't feel the enthusiasm . . .' he began.

'Then there's no way you'll ever feel their excitement,' she said. 'Or even really understand it.'

Her mood had softened somehow and so he asked, 'And the Contessa?'

Signorina Elettra's look was suddenly austere. 'What about her?' she asked.

He danced about mentally, searching for a task that would justify his having brought the Contessa back into the conversation. 'I'd like you to see what you can find out about the gift she made to the library: it was about ten years ago. Anything you can find about the terms and conditions of the donation might help,' he added, thinking of Patta's suggestion that the Contessa might ask for the return of the books.

Her head was lowered over the notebook as she wrote down his request. 'I'd also like you to see if there's anything you can find about Aldo Franchini, who lives down towards the bottom of Via Garibaldi and taught in a private school in Vicenza until about three years ago. He has a younger brother who was at school with the Director of the library, who's probably in her late fifties. So he's certainly not a young man.'

'Anything else?'

'You might check on his involvement with the Church.'

She looked up at him and smiled. 'We live in Italy, Commissario.'

'Which means?'

'That, like it or not, we are all involved with the Church.'

'Indeed,' was the first thing he could think of to say. 'But even more so in this case: he used to be a priest.'

'Ah.'

'Indeed,' he said and turned to leave.

As he started to walk away, she asked, 'What sort of thing are you looking for about this Aldo Franchini?'

'I don't know,' Brunetti confessed. 'It seems that he was sitting in the same room for at least some of the time that the thefts were taking place.' She raised her eyebrows at this. 'For the last three years, he's been reading the Fathers of the Church.'

'How much time does he spend there? Reading.'

'I didn't ask. But it must be a great deal. The librarian said he'd become a piece of furniture, almost one of the staff.'

'And he said nothing to them about what was going on?' she asked.

'He might not have noticed anything.'

'So enraptured with the ravings of the Fathers of the Church?'

'Or his chair might have faced in the other direction.'

She allowed a few seconds to pass and then asked, 'Could he have been interested or involved in what was happening?'

Brunetti shrugged. 'Involved would mean sitting

and reading the Fathers of the Church for three years, or pretending to read them: I don't know which is worse. Can you imagine the level of greed that would induce a person to do that?' Before she could answer, he added, 'Besides, if he's been reading the Fathers of the Church seriously, then it's unlikely he'd be involved in anything like this.'

She looked away from him and at the now-empty screen of her computer for so long that he thought she had nothing to say, but finally she asked, 'Do you really believe that?'

'Yes.'

'Remarkable,' she said, then added, making no attempt to hide her own surprise, 'So do I.'

6

Brunetti paused on the stairs to reflect on the strangeness of their joint assumption that a person who spent his time reading the Fathers of the Church was likely to be honest. There were many reasons why Franchini could have been reading them: interest in rhetoric, history, the minutiae of theological disagreement. Yet both Brunetti and Signorina Elettra had automatically assumed he could not have been involved in the thefts, nor even aware of them, as if the mantle of the Fathers' presumed sanctity had covered Franchini as well.

Brunetti did not remember what the historical Tertullian had to say about theft, but he could hardly have been made a Father of the Church unless he had condemned it, or what use was the Commandment? Was it the fourth? Coveting came later in the list, he knew, a sin that Brunetti had always seen as the antipasto to Orwell's Thought Crime. In fact, he thought it quite normal to covet someone else's wife or goods. Why else were movie stars famous and why else build the Reggia di Caserta, buy a Maserati or a Rolls-Royce unless covetousness and envy were in our bones?

Back at his desk and forgetful of the time difference, he decided to call the office of the History Department of the University of Kansas. He dialled the number and, after five rings, got a recording saying that the offices were open from 9 a.m. until 4 p.m. Monday to Friday and please press 1 to leave a message. He switched to English and explained that he was a commissario of the Italian police and would like someone to call him or email him. He gave his name, phone number, and email address, thanked the machine, and hung up. He looked at his watch again and worked out on the fingers of both hands that it was still the middle of the night in Kansas. Always uneasy when reliant upon the combination of technology and office workers, he turned on his computer and found the email address of the Department of History. He wrote a more detailed explanation of his request, gave Nickerson's name and area of study as well as the name of the person who had signed the letter, and asked for the courtesy of a quick response because this concerned a criminal case.

He read quickly through his emails, finding nothing

that interested him, however insistent the demands for responses. He brought up the Questura's file of people arrested in the last ten years, typed in the name Piero Sartor, then added Pietro, just to be sure. His request brought up two possibilities, one for Piero and one for Pietro. But their ages, the first more than sixty and the other only fifteen, excluded them *a priori*. For purposes of exclusion, he entered the name of Patrizia Fabbiani, but it was not in their files.

While he was doing this, he thought he might as well duplicate Signorina Elettra's search and typed in the name of Aldo Franchini. 'Well, well, well,' he muttered as the system listed a man of sixty-one, living at Castello 333. Brunetti didn't know where it was exactly, but he knew it was somewhere beyond the end of Via Garibaldi.

Franchini had been questioned, though not arrested, six months earlier in connection with an incident in Viale Garibaldi that had sent him to the hospital with a broken nose. A man sitting on a bench along the Viale had told the police that he noticed Franchini on another, a book in one hand, talking to a woman who was standing in front of him. Some time later, he heard an angry voice and looked up to see a man standing where the woman had been. With no advance warning, the man pulled Franchini to his feet and hit him, then walked away.

The assailant, who was quickly identified and arrested, had a record of petty theft and the receiving of stolen property and was under court order to remain at least one hundred metres from his former companion, whose life he had threatened. She turned out to be the woman who had been talking to the victim.

Franchini, however, refused to press charges against the assailant, saying that he had stood up when the man shouted at him and must have tripped and broken his nose when he fell.

Brunetti entered the name of the assailant, Roberto Durà, into the computer and discovered a string of arrests for minor crimes that had never sent him to jail, usually because of lack of witnesses or sufficient evidence or because the prosecuting magistrate had decided the case was not worth pursuing. He discovered that Durà was currently in jail in Treviso, sentenced three months ago to four years for armed robbery and assault.

Brunetti looked out the window and saw blue sky, clouds huffing and puffing towards the east, a perfect day for a walk down to Castello to have a look around. He stopped in the squad room on his way out, where he saw Ispettore Vianello at his desk, bent forward and speaking into his *telefonino*, one hand shielding the phone to trap the sound of his voice. Brunetti stopped a few metres from him and watched his face: Vianello's eyes were closed, his face intent, as though he were urging a racehorse to win, win, win.

Brunetti had no wish to distract Vianello from the call, so he went to the desk Alvise shared with Riverre and found the former busy writing in a small note-book. When he approached, however, he saw that it was a crossword puzzle: Sudoku was perhaps too taxing for Alvise. So intent was he on the words that he did not sense the approach of his superior. Alvise actually jumped to his feet when Brunetti spoke his name.

'*Sì, Signore,*' he said, raising to his forehead the hand that held the pencil and putting his eye at risk.

'When Vianello's finished, would you ask him to come down to the bar?'

'Of course, Commissario,' Alvise said and, using his pencil, made a note in the margin of his puzzle book.

'Thanks,' Brunetti said, failing for once to find a way to engage Alvise in easy conversation. He left the Questura and went along the *riva* to the bar. Bambola, the Senegalese who now all but ran the place for its owner, smiled when Brunetti came in and poured him a glass of white wine. Brunetti took it, grabbed up that day's copy of *Il Gazzettino*, and went to the booth at the far end, near the window, so he could see Vianello arriving. He opened the paper to the centre page. Idly, he looked at his watch: the time made him suddenly aware of how hungry he was. He took out his *telefonino*, thinking he'd send Paola an SMS to apologize for having forgotten about lunch, but he pushed away cowardice and called her.

She grumbled, but since she didn't name the dishes he had missed, he knew her heart wasn't in it. He promised to be home on time for dinner, said he loved her beyond measure, and hung up. He called over to Bambola and asked him to choose three *tramezzini* for him and three for Vianello, then turned to the open pages.

There was the usual political chaos, but Brunetti had vowed not to read anything to do with politics until the end of the year or the arrival of the Philosopher King. Fifty acres of farmland filled with toxic waste in Campania, complete with photos of the poisoned sheep who had had their last meal there. Guardia di Finanza blitz on the offices of the political party that had ruled Lombardia for the last decade. Well, that was politics, wasn't it? Award of the city's highest civic honour to the man who wanted to build a tower of surpassing ugliness on the mainland that would be visible from everywhere in Venice. Brunetti sighed and flipped back to the front page, where he saw the photo of the former Director of the MOSE project – seven billion Euros already spent to block the waters of the *laguna* – now arrested and charged with corruption. Brunetti smiled, raised his glass in a sardonic toast, and took a long sip.

'Alvise said you wanted me to come down,' Vianello said, setting down the plate of *tramezzini* and a glass of white wine. Before Brunetti could say anything, the Inspector went back to the bar and returned carrying two glasses of mineral water. He set them on the table and slipped on to the bench opposite Brunetti.

Brunetti nodded his thanks and picked up a sandwich. 'You get any fingerprints from those books?' he asked, not having had time to speak to Vianello before now.

Vianello took a sip of his wine and said, 'I've never seen those two lab guys so close to tears, both of them.'

'Why?' Brunetti asked, and took a bite of his egg and tuna.

'You ever think of how many people touch a book in a library?' Vianello set his glass down and picked up a sandwich.

'*Oddio*,' Brunetti said. 'Of course: there'd be scores of them.' He sipped at his wine, then asked, 'They take prints of the people who work there?'

'Yes,' Vianello said. 'They kept saying there'd be hundreds of prints in a book, but they were cooperative when we said we had to have them.'

'Even the Direttrice?' Brunetti asked.

'She's the one who told them just to do it. Even volunteered to give her own.'

This surprised Brunetti, who had seldom found people in positions of authority cooperative with requests that the police made of them. 'Good for her,' he said and took another sandwich. 'I'm going down to Castello to talk to someone, and I thought you might like to come along.' Ham and artichokes, and he suspected Bambola must have scraped off some of the mayonnaise before putting it on the plate.

'Sure,' Vianello said and picked up a second

sandwich. 'You want me to be the good cop or the bad one?'

Brunetti smiled in return and said, 'No need for it today. We can both be good cops. I just want to talk to him.'

'Who?'

Brunetti explained the theft and vandalism at the library, mentioned the connection with the Morosini-Albanis, and then described Signorina Elettra's strong response to the family name.

'She knew the stepson?' Vianello asked. 'What's his name? Giovanni? Gianni?' He picked up another sandwich, then sipped at his wine.

Brunetti's curiosity was rekindled. Gianni Morosini-Albani was a poster boy for the eradication of the nobility: dishonest, a well-known consumer of illegal substances. He and Signorina Elettra? The very idea.

He muted his desire to defend her and said only, 'She didn't seem pleased to hear his name.'

'He has a reputation of being very charming,' Vianello said with a complete lack of conviction.

'Yes, many people seem to like him,' Brunetti offered.

Vianello dismissed that. 'Years ago, I had to go along when he was arrested. Well, brought in for questioning. Must be fifteen years ago. He was very pleasant, invited the Commissario in, offered us all coffee. There were three of us, including the Commissario.' Vianello did not smile at the memory.

'Who was it?'

'Battistella.' Brunetti remembered him: a fool who had drifted his way to early retirement and could still occasionally be seen in the bars, talking about his illustrious career as a defender of justice. Over the years, Brunetti had noticed, he was no longer offered drinks but seemed willing to buy them for anyone who listened to him, which guaranteed him a constant audience.

'He was thrilled, of course, Battistella. Here was the son of one of the richest families in the city, the heir, the ladies' man, inviting us in for a coffee,' Vianello said, his voice growing even harder. 'Battistella fell in love with him, I think. If he'd wanted to escape, Battistella would have helped him, probably would have given him his gun and held the door for him.'

'Why was he being brought in?'

'A young girl, only about fifteen, sixteen. She'd ended up in the hospital with some sort of overdose the night before. She'd been at a party at the *palazzo*, but she was found – it was never explained how – at the side entrance to the hospital.' Vianello paused and, voice even harder, corrected himself. 'She said she was at the *palazzo*, but none of the people she said were there remembered seeing her.'

'What happened to her?'

Vianello gave an eloquent shrug. 'She was a minor, so the record was sealed. She spent the night in the hospital, and the next morning she was allowed to go home. And when she finally told her parents about what had happened, they called us.'

'And that's why you went to see him?' Brunetti reached for another sandwich but saw that Vianello had eaten the last one. He finished his wine.

'The magistrate called him and said he wanted to speak to him about what had happened at the party, but Gianni said he was too busy, and what party was he talking about, anyway?' Vianello picked up his glass, but there was none left, and he set it down again.

'After the call, the magistrate sent us over to bring him in for a conversation.'

'To see if he could remember the party? Or the girl.'

'Exactly.'

'Was it Rotili?' Brunetti asked, naming a particularly aggressive magistrate whose successes had earned him a transfer to a small town on the border between Piemonte and France, where he could concern himself with the theft of skis and barn animals.

'Yes, and this was probably the thing that led to his transfer. Gianni's father was still alive then, and he refused to believe his son could do anything wrong.'

Brunetti had never met the late Count, but he knew his reputation and the extent of his power. 'So Rotili went to Piemonte?'

'Yes,' Vianello answered without comment.

'And how did the story of the girl end?' Brunetti asked.

'She named four people she said had been there. All of them were at least fifteen years older than she was,' Vianello added. 'Including Gianni.'

'And none of them had been at a party and they had never seen the girl in their lives?'

'Yes. And two of them were women,' Vianello said, unable to hide his disgust.

'How did Battistella behave?'

'I was only a patrolman then, and I had the sense to keep my mouth shut, but it was pretty awful.'

'Meaning?'

'Meaning he was a man of about fifty who kow-towed to someone who couldn't have been much more than thirty, who'd been arrested in at least two other countries by then, and who was known as a drug user, probably a dealer who sold them to his rich friends.' Vianello leaned forward, bracing his weight on his forearms.

'He told Battistella the girl must be crazy, to invent a story like that. When Battistella agreed with him, Morosini said it was probably because of drugs, and he thought it was terrible, the way people didn't discipline their children.'

Vianello shifted back in the bench with no warning, as if trying to get away from his words or from the memory of the scene. 'I'd had some experience by then, so I didn't say anything, just did my best to stand there and look stupid.'

'Battistella always liked that,' Brunetti permitted himself to observe. 'What happened?'

'It was a nice day, as I remember, so the two of them walked to the Questura together, chatting like the best of old friends.' He paused, then added, 'I'm surprised they didn't hold hands.'

'And you?'

'Oh, I walked behind them, and I made it obvious that I wasn't interested in what they said. I walked next to the other guy – I don't even remember who it was any more – and we occasionally said something to one another. But I listened to a lot of their conversation.' After a moment, he said, 'It was hard not to hear it.'

'About?'

'About young girls.'

'Ah,' Brunetti said. 'It's not a terribly long walk from their *palazzo* to the Questura, so you didn't have to listen to much of it, at least.'

'As my grandmother often told us, God's mercy is everywhere.' Vianello got to his feet and they started down towards Castello.

7

They walked because not to do so would be to throw away the joy of this waning day. It had grown warm enough to encourage the wisteria buds to flex their muscles, like athletes who scrape their feet on the ground prior to a sprint or a leap: they'd begun their yearly creep over the brick wall of the garden on the opposite side of the canal they were passing, Brunetti noticed. Within a week, their panicles would be suspended over the water, and after another their lavender eruption would take place overnight, hurling scent across to every passer-by, enough to make anyone who caught a whiff wonder what in heaven's name he or she was doing going to work on a day like this, staring at a computer screen, when outside, life was starting all over again.

For Brunetti, springtime was a succession of scent memories: the lilacs in a courtyard over by Madonna dell'Orto; the bouquets of lily of the valley brought in by the old man from Mazzorbo, who each year sold them on the steps of the church of the Gesuiti and who had been coming for so many years that no one dared to question his right to set up shop; and the smell of fresh sweat from clean bodies pressed together on the now-crowded vaporetti, a welcome relief after a winter of the musty smell of jackets and coats worn too many times, sweaters unwashed for too long.

If life had a smell, it was to be found in springtime. There were times when Brunetti wanted to bite at the air to try to taste it, impossible as he knew that to be. It was too soon to start ordering a spritz, but his desire for rum punch had disappeared with the last cold day.

As had happened to him since boyhood, Brunetti felt a surge of directionless goodwill towards everything and everyone around him, as at the end of a period of emotional hibernation. His eye approved of all it saw, and the possibility of a walk was an intoxication. Like a sheepdog, he guided Vianello the way he wanted to go, leading him past S. Antonin and out to the *riva*. San Giorgio stood opposite them, the view of it filtered through the tall-masted boats moored along the side wall that faced them.

'It's days like this that make me want to quit,' Vianello surprised him by saying.

'Quit what?'

'Work. Being a policeman.'

Brunetti exercised his will and remained calm. 'And do what?' he asked.

Both of them knew it would have been shorter to go the back way and over the bridge in front of the Arsenale and then along the Tana, but the chance to look at that open expanse of water had lured them, and they had proved incapable of resisting its force.

Vianello stood for some time, looking across at the church and the waves that flopped about in the *bacino*, then turned left and started towards Via Garibaldi. 'I don't know. Nothing interests me as much as work. I like what we do. But it's these first spring days: they make me want to run away and join the Gypsies, or sign up on a freighter and sail to – oh, I don't know – Tahiti.'

'Can I come along?' Brunetti asked.

Vianello laughed and made a huffing noise to voice his disbelief that they'd ever, either one of them, find the courage to do such a thing. 'It would be nice, though, wouldn't it?' he asked, taking Brunetti's cowardice for granted.

'I ran away once,' Brunetti said.

Vianello stopped and turned to him. 'Ran away? Where to?'

'It was when I was about twelve,' Brunetti said, letting the memory start to seep back. 'My father had lost his job, and there wasn't much money, so I decided to try to find a job so I could bring something home.' He shook his head at his youth or his desire or his folly.

'What did you do?'

'I took the vaporetto to Sant'Erasmo and started asking the farmers in the fields – there were a lot more than there are now – if they'd give me some sort of job.' He waited but Vianello started walking again, and Brunetti hurried to catch up with him. 'Not a real job; just for the day. It must have been a weekend because I don't have any memory that I was staying away from school.'

He put himself on the outside, nearer the water. 'Finally one of them said all right and handed me the fork he was digging with and told me to finish turning over the earth in that field.' Brunetti's steps slowed, and Vianello slowed his own to keep pace with memory.

'I started out too fast and dug too deep, so he stopped me and showed me how to do it: dig it in at an angle, push it in with one foot, flip the earth over and smash the clod open with the back of the tines, and then dig it in again.' Vianello nodded.

When Brunetti said no more, Vianello asked, 'What happened?'

'Oh, he left me working for the rest of the afternoon. By the time I was finished, I had bloody blisters on both hands, but I kept at it because I wanted to be able to take something home to give my mother.'

'Did you?'

'Yes. After I'd turned over about half the field, he told me it was enough, and he gave me some money.'

'Do you remember how much it was?'

'It might have been two hundred lire. I don't remember at all. But it seemed like a lot to me then.'

'I can imagine.'

'He took me back to his house so I could wash my face and hands and clean off my shoes. His wife gave me a sandwich and a glass of milk – I think it came straight from their cow. It was sensational; I've never had anything so good since then – and I walked up to the *imbarcadero* and took the vaporetto back.'

'And your mother?'

Brunetti stopped again. 'I went in and up to the apartment. She was in the kitchen, and when she saw me, she asked me if I'd had fun playing with my friends. So I guess it must have been the weekend.'

'And then?'

'I put the money on the table and told her it was for her. That I'd earned it working. She saw my hands then and turned them over. She put iodine on them and bandaged them.'

'But what did she say?'

'She thanked me and said she was proud of me, but then she said she hoped I'd seen how hard a person had to work if all they had to work with was their body.' Brunetti smiled, but there was little humour in it. 'At first I didn't understand her. But then I did. I'd worked all day, well, it seemed like it had been all day to me, though I suppose it was only a few hours. And all I had for it was enough for her to buy some pasta and some rice and maybe a piece of cheese. So I understood what she meant: if you work with only your body, all you'll do is work for enough to eat. Even then I knew I didn't want to spend my life like that.'

'Well, you haven't, have you?' Vianello asked with a broad smile. He clapped Brunetti on the upper arm and started again towards Via Garibaldi. As they turned into the broad street, Brunetti saw evidence in support of his belief that this was one of the few areas of the city still filled primarily with Venetians. It was enough to see the beige woollen cardigans and short, carefully permed hair to know the older women were Venetian; those children with their skateboards were not there on vacation; and most foreign men did not stand so close to one another during a conversation. The shops, too, sold things that would be used in the city where they were purchased, not wrapped up and taken home to be shown off as some sort of prized acquisition, like a deer hunted and shot and tied to the top of a car. Here, people bought things they needed in the kitchen: they bought toilet paper, and they bought T-shirts in plain white cotton that were going to be worn as underwear.

At the bottom, where the street ran into Rio di S. Ana, they stayed left, Brunetti leading the way. He had found the number in *Calli, Campielli e Canali*. It was in Campo Ruga, and he let his memories take him there: left, right, to the canal and over the bridge, down to the first left and then into the *campo*.

The house was on the opposite side of the *campo*, a narrow building much in need of new plastering and, from the look of it, also in need of new gutters. Water streaks had dined for years on three places in the plaster and were now starting on the bricks for dessert. The sun had turned the paint on the shutters of the windows of the first- and second-floor apartments a tired, dusty green. Any Venetian could read the greyish blisters the way an archaeologist can read earth strata to determine the length of time since the last human habitation. The apartments had been empty for decades.

The shutters on the apartment on the third floor were open, though they seemed not in much better condition than the ones on the floors beneath. There were three bells beside the door, but only the top bell had a name attached: 'Franchini'. Brunetti rang it, waited, rang it again, this time attentive for any fugitive sound that might come down from above. Nothing.

He looked around the *campo*, which seemed curiously inhospitable. There were two leafless trees, apparently uninterested in the arrival of springtime, and two park benches as faded and stained as the shutters of the house. Though the *campo* was large, no children played there, perhaps because of the canal running along one side, which had no wall.

He had not bothered to write down the phone

number, but Vianello, who had a smartphone, found the directory online and then the number, which he dialled. This time, the tiny, tinny sound of a ringing phone came down to them. It rang ten times and then stopped. They both backed off from the building and looked up at the windows as if waiting for a man to fling them open and sing his first aria. Nothing.

'The bar?' Vianello asked, pointing with his chin to the far end of the *campo*. Inside, the place appeared as run-down as the shutters had, everything, including the barman, old and tired and in need of being wiped with a damp cloth. He looked at them when they came in and gave what he must have thought was a welcoming smile.

'Sì, *signori?*'

Brunetti asked for two coffees, which arrived quickly and were surprisingly good. A sharp clang came from the back of the bar and, turning, they saw a man sitting on a high stool in front of a slot machine: the noise came from the coins trickling into the tray in front of him. He slipped a few from the tray and began to feed them into the machine, then tapped at the brightly coloured buttons. Whizz and clink and lights. Nothing.

'Do you know Aldo Franchini?' Vianello asked the barman, speaking Veneziano and tilting his head backwards in the general direction of the building.

Before he answered, the barman looked over at the man playing the slot machine. 'The ex-priest?' he finally asked.

'I don't know,' Vianello answered. 'All I know is that he studied theology.'

The barman considered this for as long as he thought necessary and said, 'Yes, he did,' then asked, 'Strange, isn't it?'

'That he'd study theology? Or stop being a priest?' Vianello asked.

'It's not as if it matters any more, is it?' the barman asked. His tone was not in the least disapproving. If anything, it held the same sympathy he'd express if he'd been told that someone had devoted part of his life to learning how to repair typewriters and fax machines.

Vianello asked for a glass of mineral water.

'Do you know anything else about him?' Brunetti asked.

'You police?'

'Yes.'

'Is this about that guy who broke his nose? He out of jail?'

'No,' Brunetti assured him. 'He's got some time still.'

'Good. They should keep him there a long time.'

'You know him?'

'We went to school together. He was a violent, nasty kid, and now he's a violent, nasty man.'

'Any reason for that?' Brunetti inquired.

The barman shrugged, saying, 'Born that way.' Tilting his head, he indicated the man who was still feeding the machine. 'Like him. He can't help himself:

it's like a disease.' Then, as if the simplicity of his own answer had disappointed him, he asked, 'Why are you looking for Franchini?' When neither of them answered, he said, again nodding in the direction of the man at the machine, 'You think he . . . ?' but the last part of the question was drowned out by a rivulet of coins, and Brunetti wasn't sure what he had said. Nor, apparently, had Vianello heard him.

'We'd like to talk to him. It's about something he might have seen. All we want to do is ask him a few questions.'

'I've heard the police say that before,' the barman said in a weary voice.

'All we want to do is talk to him,' Brunetti repeated. 'He hasn't done anything wrong, just been at a place where someone else did.'

The barman started to say something but stopped himself.

Brunetti smiled and urged, 'Say it.'

'That usually doesn't make much difference to you guys,' the barman risked saying.

Vianello looked at Brunetti, leaving it for him to respond. 'This time all we want is information.' Brunetti could see the man fight down his curiosity.

'I saw him yesterday morning. He was in here about nine for a coffee. Haven't seen him since.'

'Does he come in often?'

'Often enough.'

Brunetti turned when there was a sudden burst of noise from the back of the bar. The man at the slot machine was pounding the palm of his hand against the front of the machine.

'Stop it, Luca,' the bartender shouted, and the noise ceased. He turned to Brunetti and Vianello and said, 'See? I told you: it's a disease.' Brunetti waited to see if he meant this as a joke, but it seemed he did not. 'They shouldn't be allowed. It's too easy for them to gamble everything away.' His indignation seemed genuine.

Brunetti waited for Vianello to ask the obvious question, but when the Inspector said nothing, Brunetti took out his wallet and removed one of his cards. He wrote his *telefonino* number on the back and handed it to the barman. 'When he comes in again, would you give him this and ask him to call me, please?'

Brunetti took two Euros from his pocket and set them on the counter. As they turned to leave, they heard a burst of obscenity from the man in front of the slot machine, but the closing door cut it off.

8

They agreed to walk to the Questura, but the way back was far less pleasant, the warmth having fled the day while they were in the bar. He might as well have sent a uniformed officer to look for Franchini, but Brunetti had given in to his urge to be outside and moving and thus had wasted two hours. Wasted? He'd had a pleasant conversation with Vianello, had remembered a bit of his youth, and had his conviction that some people were simply born bad confirmed by a neutral source. All in all, his time had been far more productive than if he had spent the afternoon at his desk, reading files.

This belief was strengthened by his spending the late afternoon doing just that: transcriptions of interrogations, regulations concerning the correct treatment of female suspects by male officers, a new three-page form to be used in the case of an injury experienced while at work. The only relief came from his computer, which brought him an email from the Department of History at the University of Kansas, telling him that there was no one named Joseph Nickerson on the faculty, and the university offered no class in Maritime and Mediterranean Trade History. Nor had the Provost, whose name appeared to be on the letter referred to by Mr Brunetti, ever signed such a document.

Brunetti had been prepared for this, would have been surprised if Dr Nickerson had proved to be a real person. He dialled Signorina Elettra's number to see what she had learned, but her phone rang unanswered. Though it was only six-thirty, he let her absence be an overture to his own and went home.

As he closed the door, he heard Paola call his name urgently from the back of the apartment. When he entered their bedroom, the last light was disappearing in the west, and silhouetted against it he saw his wife, bent to one side, as if in the grip of pain or frenzy. One arm was wrapped across her throat, the elbow pointing in his direction. Only half of her other arm was visible. He thought of swift-striking disease, a ruptured disc, a stroke. As he moved towards her, heart chilled, she turned her back, and he saw that the fingers of both hands were joined at the zipper of her dress.

'Help me, Guido. It's stuck.'

It took him a few seconds to conjure up the appropriate husbandlike behaviour. He reached to take her hands from the zipper and bent his head to see a thin slip of grey cloth caught by one side of it. He pinched the cloth above it and tried to move the zip, first up and then down. After a few tugs, he freed the cloth and pulled the zip to her neck. 'That's fine now,' he said and kissed her hair, saying nothing about the punch his lungs had taken.

'Thanks. What are you going to wear tonight?'

Years ago, he had once suggested that he wear the same suit he had worn to work that day, only to have Paola stare at him as though he'd suggested he initiate the dinner conversation with an indecent proposition to her mother. Since then, to prevent her thinking him some untutored youth, unlearned in the world's false subtleties, he always named the suit he believed she would find most suitable. 'The dark grey one.'

'The one Giulio had made for you?' she asked, her tone suggesting her guarded opinion of his old friend Giulio. They'd been to school together, when Giulio had been sent to live with an aunt in Venice for the six years his father was a guest of the state. The fact that he was Neapolitan had not affected Brunetti's instant liking for the boy: ingenious, industrious, thirsty for learning and pleasure and, like Brunetti, the son of a man of whose behaviour many people did not approve.

Once again like Brunetti, Giulio had gone on to study criminal law, although he had chosen to use his knowledge the better to defend criminals, not to arrest them. Surprisingly, this in no way affected their friendship. Giulio's acquaintances and friendships – to make no mention of his enormous and well-connected family – had provided Brunetti with a protective halo during the years he worked in Naples, a fact Brunetti had appreciated as much as he had tried to ignore it.

Some months before, Brunetti had returned to Naples to interview a witness and had met Giulio for dinner on the first night in the city. In the five years since they'd last seen one another, Giulio's hair had turned entirely white, as had the moustache under his long pirate's nose. Because his olive colouring had resisted the attempts of time to age it, the contrast with the white hair had succeeded only in making him look younger.

Rashly, Brunetti had begun by complimenting his friend on the suit he wore, charcoal grey with an almost invisible black stripe. From the inside pocket of his jacket, Giulio pulled out a notebook and a gold fountain pen, wrote a name and phone number, ripped out the paper and passed it to Brunetti. 'Go see Gino. He'll make you one in a day.' Brunetti frowned. Giulio took another bite of San Pietro: the owner had assured them it had been caught that morning. Suddenly Giulio set down his fork and took one of his phones from where they lay beside his plate; he typed in a short message, then looked up at Brunetti with an enormous, pleased smile and returned to the serious business of dinner.

They had talked, as they always did, about their families and, from long habit, did not discuss current events or politics. Their children matured, and their parents aged, sickened, and died; the world beyond their families did not exist as a subject of conversation. Giulio's oldest boy had left Bocconi Business School and joined a rock band, and his daughter, who was eighteen, had an unsuitable boyfriend. 'I try to be a good father,' Giulio said. 'I want them to be happy and have happy lives. But I see where they're going, and there's nothing I can do about it. All I want is to keep them safe.'

Brunetti recognized his own heart's desire in what his friend said. 'What's wrong with her boy . . .' Brunetti started to ask but was interrupted by the arrival of a short, bald man who came to their table and said good evening to Giulio. Giulio stood and shook his hand, thanked him for coming at such short notice, or at least that was what Brunetti thought he said, for the men spoke in Neapolitan that might as easily have been, for all Brunetti understood, Swahili.

After a few moments, the man turned and looked at Brunetti, who stood and shook his hand. The man ran his eye up and down his body, then moved around behind him. Brunetti, disconcerted, stood stock still, as he would at the first sign of a threat.

Speaking in Italian suffused with the perpetually

inserted sh sound, g's used in place of c's, final syllables hacked off as if they were the heads of traitors, the other man told him not to worry, that he just wanted a look at his back. He rested a hand on the table and went down on one knee, and it was then that Brunetti realized that this man must be Gino, which surmise was confirmed when the man pinched the hem of the right leg of his trousers and gave it a sharp pull.

Nodding and muttering to himself, Gino stood, reached out to shake Brunetti's hand, then Giulio's, and said it would be ready by noon.

'But I can't,' Brunetti said.

'You can pay for it,' Giulio said, smiling. 'Be at peace with your conscience. Gino will do it for you at cost, and I promise you I won't give him anything extra.' He looked at Gino, who smiled, nodded, and held up both hands as if to block the very thought. Before Brunetti could speak, Giulio said, 'You'll dishonour me if you don't accept.' Gino put on the face of tragedy and Giulio asked, 'All right?'

Giulio, although a lawyer, never lied; at least not to his friends. Brunetti nodded. He went to see Gino the following afternoon: hence the suit 'Giulio had made for you'.

Paola turned away and opened a drawer to hunt for a scarf to put over her shoulders. She'd wear a coat on the street, but once they were inside, there was no certainty about what the heating system in an eight-hundred-year-old building would decide to do.

Brunetti removed his suit and hung it in the ward-robe, put on a clean shirt, then took the trousers of the suit – Gino's suit – from the hanger and put them on. He chose a red tie: why not? Slipping his arms into the sleeves of the jacket, he was overcome with a sense of physical delight. He pulled it up by the lapels and rolled his shoulders until the fit was perfect. Only then did he look in the full-length mirror. It had cost him more than 800 Euros: God alone knew what Gino's clients paid. Gino had provided no receipt, nor had Brunetti asked him for one. 'I am at peace with my conscience,' he told himself and smiled.

It took them only a short time to walk to the *palazzo*. No one they passed on the street seemed at all in a hurry: springtime was sinking in, forcing people to remember pleasure and ease and the end of the working day. At the top of the steps in the courtyard, a young man opened the door for them and took Paola's coat, telling them the Count and Countess were in the small salon.

Paola led the way through what Brunetti knew would one day be hers. He allowed himself to wonder how many people it took to keep it running: how did you keep a place this size clean? He had never managed to count the rooms and would not permit himself to ask Paola. Twenty? More, surely there must be more. And to heat it? And what about the new tax on houses? His salary would probably not be sufficient to maintain it, and he'd find himself working to support a house, not his family.

By Its Cover

His reflections were cut short by their entrance into the salon. Conte Orazio Falier stood by the window, looking across at Palazzo Malipiero Cappello; Contessa Donatella sat on the sofa, a glass of prosecco in her hand. Brunetti knew it was prosecco because the Conte had once delivered an attack on French wines, saying he wouldn't have them in the house. Furthermore, his vineyards in Friuli produced one of the best proseccos in the region, which Brunetti had to confess was better than much of the champagne he'd tasted.

The Conte had suffered a slight heart attack some years before, and ever since that, he had greeted his son-in-law with two kisses instead of a formal handshake. His manner had softened in other ways: he was both more affectionate and more indulgent with his grandchildren, less ready to poke fun at what he called Brunetti's 'crusades', and the uxorious warmth with which he had always treated the Contessa had grown more noticeable.

'*Ah, bambini miei,*' he surprised Brunetti by saying when he saw them. Did this mean that, after more than two decades, he was ready to accept Brunetti as his son? Or was it nothing more than an affectionate formula?

'I hope you don't mind if we have dinner alone,' the Conte added, coming towards them, hands outstretched to place first on Paola's shoulders and pull her close to kiss, and then on Brunetti's. He led them over to his wife, whom they both bent to kiss.

Paola plunked herself down next to her mother, kicked off her shoes, and tucked her feet up under her. 'If you'd told me we were going to be alone with you, I wouldn't have worn this dress.' Then, pointing towards Brunetti, 'But I would still have made Guido wear that suit. It's beautiful, isn't it?'

His father-in-law gave Brunetti an appreciative glance and asked, 'Did you have it made here?' What was it, Brunetti wondered, that told the Conte that the suit had been made for him and not bought in a shop? It was one of those secret Masonic powers men like the Conte had; that and the possession of perfect social pitch that let him speak to the postman or his lawyer with the same correctness, never offending by too much formality or too much familiarity. Perhaps eight centuries of good manners taught a man that.

'You both look wonderful,' the Contessa said in her accent-less Italian. She'd lived in Venice most of her life, yet not a whisper of its speech had penetrated her own. She pronounced every 'l', did not refer to her daughter as '*la*' Paola: no cadence drove her sentences up and down. 'The suit's perfect, Guido. I do hope your superior sees you wearing it some time.'

The Conte was beside them, carrying two flutes of prosecco. 'It's last year's,' he said as he handed them the glasses. 'What do you think?'

Brunetti took a sip and thought it was delicious, but he left it to Paola, who knew the jargon, to pass judgement.

While she sipped and rolled it around on her

tongue, Brunetti studied his parents-in-law. The Conte's face was more lined, his hair whiter, but he still stood straight, though Brunetti realized he was no longer as tall as he once had been. The Contessa seemed the same as ever, her hair now a blonde that hinted at whiteness. She had had the sense, decades before, to declare the sun her enemy, and her face, as a result, was unlined and unblemished.

Paola interrupted his thoughts by saying, 'It's still young and a bit rough on the back of the tongue, but next year it will be perfect.' She looked at Brunetti and said, 'So next year we have to visit more often.' Saying that, she leaned aside and patted her mother on the thigh, then started to tell her about Chiara's latest scholastic triumph.

The Conte drifted back to the front window, and Brunetti, who could never see enough of the view, joined him. Looking down at the water two floors below, the Conte said, 'I used to swim there when I was a boy.' He sipped at his wine.

'So did I. But not here. Down in Castello,' Brunetti said. Then, after imagining the water, 'It's a terrible thought, isn't it? Doing it now, I mean?'

'Many things have become terrible here,' the Conte said, tilting his glass in the direction of one of the *palazzi* on the other side of the Grand Canal. 'The third floor of Palazzo Benelli is a bed and breakfast. The heir's Brazilian companion runs it and that gives him enough to keep him in cocaine.' He leaned forward and pointed up the Canal on their side. 'Two doors down from here, the owner had his friends appoint him an inspector for the Fine Arts Commission and is now available for consultations about permits for restorations.'

'"Consultations"?'

'That's what they're called. An English acquaintance wanted to gut the *piano nobile* of a *palazzo* near the Rialto, but to do it he had to take down a wall that had frescoes from the sixteenth century. He had his consultation, and then he had his permits.'

'How is that possible?' Brunetti asked out of real curiosity, having no intention to pursue it professionally.

'The frescoes had been hidden by a fake wall, probably for centuries, and weren't discovered until his workers started removing that wall, so they were never registered. The workmen were all from Moldavia and didn't much care what they did. So he had his consultation, and the wall came down.'

'He's Venetian, isn't he?' Brunetti asked unnecessarily. He knew whom the Count was talking about and had heard other stories about building permits and how to be sure to get them, but something perverse in him needed confirmation.

'They're all Venetian,' the Conte said, speaking the word as though it were 'paedophile' or 'necrophiliac'. 'The men who decide that the cruise ships can continue to shake the city to pieces and pollute it as though it were Beijing, and the men who insist that MOSE is going to work and let's see how much more we can get out of it, and the people who run the only *casinò* on the planet that loses money.'

Brunetti had been hearing the same things – and saying them – for years, and now he said the same thing he often asked himself: 'What are you going to do about it?'

The Conte looked at him with real affection. 'I'm so glad we finally talk to one another, Guido.' He sipped, then set his glass down on a table. 'The only thing I can do is what I've been doing for the last five years.'

'Which is?'

'Move my money out of the country. Invest in countries that have a future, invest in countries where there is the rule of law.' He stopped, all but inviting Brunetti to ask.

'Which ones are those?'

'The Northern ones. Even the United States. Australia.'

'Not China?'

The Conte made a face and said, 'The rule of law, Guido. I don't want to go from the frying pan into the fire. I don't want to go from a country where the law is hopeless and the political system corrupt to one where there is no law, and the political system is even more corrupt.'

Brunetti ran his mind around the globe, seeking some other place where the rule of law prevailed and where – his father-in-law's concern – money would be safe. Searching for safety on that green, blue, and beige ball suspended in space, Brunetti realized that people tended to be physically safe in the countries where money was also safe. Or had the Conte's capitalism infected him during these past years, and he'd got it backwards and it was actually that money was safe in places where people were safe?

It was delicate, proceeding here. Could he ask Conte Orazio what money it was? Could he ask if he were investing in companies there or relocating his own to other countries? The Guardia di Finanza dealt with this sort of thing, checking for irregularities; in the tangled skein of Italian law, there was always a way to find irregularities of one sort or another. 'Make the laws for your friends, impose them on your enemies.' How many times in his life had people explained that rule of survival to him?

'I hope your plans are successful,' was all he could think of to say.

'Thank you,' the Conte said, with a smile and a nod that acknowledged Brunetti's right to avoid engagement with this subject. 'And you? What are you doing?'

It was not necessary for Brunetti to ask the Conte not to repeat what he was told. His father-in-law had not achieved his position in the country by being a blabbermouth. 'We were called about a robbery at the Biblioteca Merula. Someone who was using the library for research sliced pages from books. Others are missing.'

'How did he get in?' the Conte asked. 'Didn't they check him or check his application?' Then, after a pause replete with feigned patience, he added, 'If they make people fill out applications, that is.'

'He filled one out. But he had a fake passport and a fake letter of recommendation from an American university.'

'No one noticed they were fake?'

Brunetti shrugged. 'They believed him to be a member of the community of scholars.'

This was greeted by a wild hoot of derision from Paola, who had apparently diverted her attention from her mother long enough to eavesdrop on their conversation. '"Community of scholars",' she repeated. 'It would make the chickens laugh.'

Mildly, her mother said, 'We sent you to all those famous schools, dear, and now you speak badly about your colleagues. Couldn't you be a little bit kinder?'

Paola leaned to the side and put her arm around her mother's shoulders. She kissed her cheek, then kissed it again. '*Mamma*, you are the only person on the planet who would consider the riff-raff I'm at university with to be scholars.'

'You went there and you're one, please don't forget,' her mother said, still mildly.

'*Mamma*, please,' Paola begged. But before she could say more, the young man who had greeted them on their arrival appeared in the doorway and said that dinner was ready.

Brunetti extended his hand to the Contessa, who placed hers on it, as light as a feather, and got

effortlessly to her feet. Paola stood up, far less grace-
fully, put on her shoes, and took her father's arm.

Brunetti accompanied the Contessa to the small
dining room. 'It always troubles me to hear Paola
speak so badly of her colleagues,' her mother said
as they entered the room.

'I've met a few of them,' Brunetti limited himself
to saying.

She gave him a quick look and smiled. 'She is a
rash woman.'

'Your daughter?' Brunetti said in feigned shock.

'Oh, Guido, I think you provide encouragement
sometimes.'

'She needs none, I suspect,' was all Brunetti said.

They sat at a round table, Brunetti facing Paola,
with the Contessa on his left, the Conte on his right.
A young woman appeared and placed an enormous
ceramic platter in the middle of the table, covered
with a seafood antipasto sufficient to sate the appe-
tites of the people at the table, in the kitchen, and
probably in the adjoining *palazzi* as well.

The conversation was the normal talk of families:
children, relatives, mutual friends, ailments – there was
more of that with each passing year – and then on to the
condition of the world, which they all agreed was dire.

Later, when the maid was removing the plates that
had held *capesante al cognac*, Paola asked, 'Did you
tell *Papà* about the library?'

The Conte answered, 'Yes, he did. It's starting
here now, as well.' He shrugged and took a drink

of mineral water. None of them found it necessary to mention the Girolamini Library in Naples, one of the most illustrious in the country, which had been subject to the depredations of its own director, now in prison. Because the catalogue of holdings, such as existed, was believed to have been altered, there was no way to know what was missing: estimates ranged from 2,000 to 4,000 volumes, some of which had surfaced in Munich, Tokyo, in the shops of respectable book dealers and in the libraries of politicians who, of course, expressed astonishment at the presence of those volumes. In MY library? Heavily laden cars were reported to have been seen driving out of the library's courtyard in the night, groaning under their weight of paper. How many volumes were missing? Who knew? Manuscripts, incunabula, gone, gone, gone.

'Friends of mine have had things stolen from their libraries,' the Conte interrupted his own reverie by saying.

'May I ask . . . ?' Brunetti said and immediately regretted having spoken.

The Conte looked at him and smiled. 'I think they'd be happier if you didn't know their names, Guido.'

Of course, of course: no one wanted the authorities to know what was in their homes. What happened if and when the government slapped a tax on private possessions? If they could reimpose a tax on your house, or houses, what was to stop them from putting a tax on what was in them?

'They didn't report it?' Brunetti inquired.

The Conte's smile was indulgent, but he did not bother to answer.

'At least I stopped the man who was doing it at the university,' boasted a self-satisfied Paola.

No one commented on this. None of them had wanted dessert, so they were drinking coffee while waiting to see what would appear in response to the Conte's request for '*una grappina*'.

To break the silence that still lingered after Paola's remark, Brunetti turned to his mother-in-law and said, 'Contessa Morosini-Albani's a patron of the Merula, so she'll have to be told about the thefts. How do you think she'll react?'

'Patron? Elisabetta?' the Contessa repeated. 'How remarkable.'

'Why is that?'

'Elisabetta can be so tight-fisted at times, you'd think she was born here,' she said, and Brunetti marvelled that Paola's father let his wife loose among his Venetian friends. In a more reflective, sadder, voice, his mother-in-law continued, 'She's mad to be accepted into society, so perhaps being a patron of something is one of the prices she's willing to pay.'

'If she's been here, with you,' Brunetti said, waving toward a Moroni portrait of one of the Conte's ancestors, 'then she's accepted into society, isn't she?'

'Oh, she's here because she's one of my oldest friends,' the Contessa said with a warm smile. 'But most people won't have her.'

'But you do?'

'Of course. She was very good to me when we were at school together. She's two years older than I, and she protected me. And so I try to do the same now, where I can and when I can.' She thought for a moment, placed her coffee cup to the side and said, 'I never thought about it before, but it's much the same situation. I was an outsider, and the older girls, the richer girls, bullied me terribly for that. Once Elisabetta – she was the daughter of a prince, after all, even if her family was ruined and the *palazzo* a shambles – became my friend, I was accepted.'

'It doesn't sound as if that's happened here,' Paola interrupted to say.

'You know Elisabetta,' the Contessa said. 'She's outspoken and judgemental and not an easy person. And she's got those unfortunate stepchildren.'

Paola nodded. Brunetti, thinking of Signorina Elettra's response, asked, 'Unfortunate for themselves or for her or for other people?'

'For all of them, I'd say,' the Conte answered.

The Contessa couldn't hide her surprise. 'You know her stepchildren?'

'I've done business with Gianni,' he answered. 'And I've met his two sisters. They tried to get some money back.'

'From you?'

'From an investment he made for them in one of my companies.'

'What happened?' interrupted Paola. 'What company?'

'Oh, it was a small thing, a wind farm in the Netherlands, and it wasn't really very much money they were talking about.'

'How much?' Brunetti inquired, curious to know what sum 'wasn't much'.

'Oh, half a million Euros, perhaps a bit more. I don't remember now. It was about six years ago.'

'What happened?' Paola asked.

'It was a well-run company, but Gianni decided to pull out too soon, and when he came to me, the stock had gone down about fifty per cent. He said he needed money. First he tried to borrow it from me, but I refused. Then he offered to sell me the stock.' The Conte looked at his wife, but the arrival of the grappa saved him from having to continue with the story.

He picked up his grappa and opened his mouth to pass judgement on it but was interrupted by the Contessa, who asked, 'What was his offer?'

Brunetti, who had lacked the courage to ask that question, was curious about the answer. The Conte toasted his wife with his tiny glass of grappa and took a sip. He set the glass down in front of him and tilted his head to one side, as if acknowledging that he had no choice but to answer his wife's question.

'He said he'd accept a lower price for the stock if I'd give him a receipt with an even lower price he could show his sisters, and he'd give me half the difference in cash. The stock was owned by all three of them in common, but he was the administrator, and they didn't have any real understanding of business.' Then, significantly, he added, 'They trusted him. At the time.'

'What did you do?' Paola asked.

'I refused. I told him he was free to sell the stock any way he chose but that I wasn't interested.' The Conte took another sip; irritation seeped into his voice as he said, 'He was very insistent, and I had to be curt with him. He left.' Then, after some time, 'The sisters came to me a month later and demanded that I make good their loss.' The Conte sighed. 'Gianni had told them I'd cheated him – cheated them all.'

'You never told me this, Orazio,' the Contessa interrupted.

'Elisabetta's your friend, my dear. I didn't want to trouble you.'

'What did you tell them?' she asked, visibly troubled by what he had just said.

'I told them they would have to ask their lawyer to speak to mine, and he'd explain what had happened.'

'Did you tell them what Gianni had tried to do to them?'

'I don't think that would have been correct, my dear. He's their brother.'

'Did they do it? Did their lawyer get in touch?'

'Yes. Arturo explained the sale to them.'

'Did the lawyer tell them what Gianni had tried to do?'

'I never told Arturo about that,' the Conte said and finished his grappa.

'What will happen to Gianni?' the Contessa asked.

The Conte shrugged and rose from his chair. 'I have no idea. I know only that he is not as clever as he thinks he is and that he is unable to resist his impulses – of any kind. So he will always fail at anything he does.'

9

They walked back to the apartment hand in hand, a desire brought on by the advent of spring or perhaps by Paola's lingering admiration for Brunetti's suit. 'I've always considered her a friendly dragon,' Brunetti said, believing Paola would understand.

'Elisabetta?' It was a request for confirmation, not a question.

'Certainly not your mother.'

After some thought, Paola said, 'I can see that: she is, and she isn't.'

'The times I've seen her at your parents', she hasn't been breathing smoke and fire from her nostrils, but she's never much seemed to care if people like her or not, and she certainly doesn't hesitate to express her opinion.'

'With us, she knows that she's with people who like her.'

'Am I included in that?' Brunetti asked.

Paola turned to look up at his face, surprised. 'Of course you are. Goose. Because you're one of us, she doesn't pretend to be anything except what she is.'

'Which is?'

'Intelligent, independent, impatient, lonely.'

Brunetti, who had observed the first three qualities in the Contessa, had not considered the fourth. 'What do you make of her giving that money to the library?'

'I agree with my mother: it's the price she thinks she has to pay in order to be accepted into society.'

'You don't sound as if you believe she'll succeed.'

'I know these people, Guido. For God's sake, I'm one of these people. Remember that. She's got pedigrees, both on her father's side and her mother's, that date to long before the titles of the noble families here. But she's Sicilian, and she's not a principessa – even if her father was a prince – so she's never going to be let in. Not fully.'

'Even though she married a Venetian?' he asked.

Paola surprised him by saying, 'Perhaps that's the reason why.'

'You see how crazy all this is?' Brunetti asked in a level voice.

'I've seen how crazy it is since I was six, but that's not going to change it one whit.' She stopped on the top of the bridge leading to San Polo and leaned on the parapet. ' I wish she'd just forget about it, but I don't think she's capable of that. The wiring is too strong, or too old, and that's the only world she knows, so it's the world she has to be accepted into.'

Brunetti asked, 'Do you think she'd talk to me?'

'Elisabetta?'

'Yes.'

'I suspect she would. I told you, she thinks of you as one of us. And she likes you.' Then, from habit, she added, just as he put his key in the front door, 'I think.'

The next morning, Brunetti waited until ten-thirty to call the Contessa at the number Paola had given him. This gave him time to check both *Il Gazzettino* and *La Nuova* for any report of the theft at the library, but neither newspaper mentioned it.

He dialled the Contessa's *telefonino* number, and after only two rings a woman's voice answered, 'Morosini-Albani.'

'Contessa,' Brunetti began. 'This is Guido Brunetti, Paola Falier's husband.'

'I recognize you by your own name, Commissario.' It was a jest, not a provocation.

'I'm complimented by that, Contessa,' he said. 'We so seldom speak during the dinners.'

'I've always considered that a pity.' Her voice bore only the most minimal trace elements of her Sicilian origins.

'Then perhaps we might speak today, if you have time,' he said, having decided it would be best to be straightforward with the Contessa.

'About?' she asked, and he was reminded of Dottoressa Fabbiani's reluctance to tell him about the bequest.

'The Biblioteca Merula,' he said.

A long pause followed. 'Dottoressa Fabbiani told you about my involvement with the library?' she finally said.

'I'm afraid she had no choice, Contessa.'

'People always have choices,' she said instantly.

'Perhaps fewer, when the police are involved,' he answered mildly.

'Unfortunately, yes,' she said, apparently displeased at the idea. 'Is this an official request for information?' she asked, immediately adding, 'Not that I have any to give you.'

'I want to talk to you about books, Contessa. I know little.'

'But we've talked about books, Commissario.'

She sounded so disingenuous that he laughed. 'I mean rare books.'

'The sort people would steal?'

'Have stolen, in this case,' Brunetti risked saying.

'Does this mean you're in charge of the investigation?'

'Yes.'

'Then you'd better come here and we can talk about it.'

*

He knew where the *palazzo* was: he used to walk past it on his way to middle school, and he and Paola usually passed by if they chose to take the long way home after having dinner at Carampane. Its four floors loomed over a small *campo* in San Polo, the water door at the side providing access to one of the canals that ran perpendicular to Rio San Polo. The windows on the ground and first floors were protected by iron bars. During the decades he had seen them, Brunetti had always thought about fire and how the residents would have to leap from the second floor if one broke out. There were no graceful arabesques, no suggestion of filigree, no interest in beauty on these grilles: as straight as the lines on a crossword puzzle, the bars had been soldered together centuries before at the points where the verticals and horizontals intersected. Nothing except reaching hands had passed through those bars since then.

The grilles had rusted over the centuries and scoured long dark trails down the façade. They reminded Brunetti of the signs of age on the front of Franchini's building.

He switched his briefcase to his left hand and rang the bell; after a short time a dark-skinned woman in a white apron opened the door for him. She might have been Thai or Filipina. 'Signor Brunetti?' she asked. When he said he was, she gave something that, in a former age, would have been called a curtsey. Brunetti forced himself not to smile. She stepped aside, said the Contessa was expecting him, and let him enter the vast open *androne* that extended all the way back to the canal, where he saw more of the barred windows.

She closed the door, which appeared to cost her some effort, then turned and led him across the room and to a flight of steps that rose to the first floor. The door at the top was a vast slab of walnut squares, and into the centre of each was carved a rose in full blossom. The handle was brass, in the shape of a lion's claw.

Inside, she led him down a central, windowless corridor and into a large sitting room that looked out on the *campo*. Telling him to make himself comfortable, she said she would go and fetch the Contessa and disappeared through a set of double doors on the other side of the room.

He had no idea how long he would have to wait, but he did not want to be found sitting when she came in. He went and studied the first painting on his left, a large hunting scene of a boar being pulled to earth by a pack of slavering hounds, two of whom appeared to have abandoned the hunt in order to roll on the ground together. An enormous Great Dane was savaging the boar's ear, and another had him firmly by a back leg. Brunetti recognized the style from a still life the Conte had in his study and thought the painting might be a Snyders, but even the painter's name could not make him like the painting.

There were six portraits of men and women on the wall that received what little light came in from the *campo*. He detected a resemblance between one of the men and the boar; the expression on the face of another did not differ much from that of the dog dragging on the boar's back leg. He wondered if they were family portraits.

His observations were interrupted by the arrival of the Contessa. She wore a simple grey sweater and a darker woollen skirt that fell to slightly below her knees. Brunetti remembered that she had good legs, and a quick glance confirmed this. She wore strings of tiny linked gold circles, each smaller than the head of a pin, the delicate Manin link that had been the dream of his mother and her friends. They aspired to own one chain; the Contessa must have been wearing thirty.

He knew she was two years older than his mother-in-law, but she looked at least a decade younger than that. Her skin was unblemished and seemed to be composed of cream and roses, though Brunetti gave himself a mental shake when he heard himself using those terms.

She came quickly across the room to greet him, extended her hand and seemed not at all surprised when he bent to kiss it. She led him to a chair and asked, 'May I offer you a coffee, Commissario?'

'That's very kind of you, Contessa, but I had one on the way. You've already been very generous by agreeing to speak to me.'

He waited until she had taken the chair opposite him before he sat. Perched upright, she looked so perfectly placed as to cause him to doubt that her back had ever touched that of a chair. Her profile, he had realized the first time he saw her, was perfect, with a straight nose and high forehead that spoke, in a way he did not understand, of optimism and energy. Her eyes, as close to black as eyes could be, were exaggerated by her pale skin.

Brunetti placed his briefcase on the floor. 'I'd like to thank you for finding the time to speak to me, Contessa,' he said.

'Books that once belonged to me have been damaged and stolen, and you're going to try to find the person responsible. I hardly feel that I am being generous with my time if I speak to you.' She smiled to soften the remark.

Unsure if he had been reproved or thanked, he said, 'I hope I don't sound venal, but I'm here chiefly to speak about the financial loss to the library and, if you have enough time to spare, to learn more about books. Dottoressa Fabbiani said you know a great deal.'

He caught the surprise that flashed across her face, and said, 'She was very complimentary.'

'I'm flattered,' the Contessa replied, sounding as though she meant it.

'She said you have a feel for books,' he told her. She smiled at this and raised a hand as if to push away the compliment, and Brunetti continued. 'I know very little, really, about the world of books, well, books of this quality. That is, I understand the theft, but not why they chose to steal what they did or what happens after: where the pages can be sold, or their value.'

'What a pity we never talked about this at Donatella's dinners,' she said.

'I try to go there as Paola's husband, not as a policeman.'

'But you're here as one today?'

'Yes,' he said. Brunetti opened his briefcase and removed a notebook and pen. 'One of the books that was stolen,' he began, 'was a gift from you to the library. Dottoressa Fabbiani said it was a Ramusio, but I have no idea of its value.'

'What importance does that have?' she asked.

'It gives me an idea of the seriousness of the crime,' Brunetti answered.

'There's no question of its seriousness,' she said severely. 'It's a rare and beautiful book.'

Brunetti shook his head to ward off confusion. 'I'm afraid mine is a policeman's vision, Contessa. The monetary value of the book affects the way we treat the crime.'

He watched her consider this, certain that the idea offended her. She said, 'The prices paid for them would be in the family records.'

'But wouldn't those prices be out of date?' he asked, though he knew they must be. Then, thinking this would help calculate a more current price, he asked, 'Was the Ramusio insured?'

'My father-in-law,' she began with a small smile, 'once said that he had considered buying insurance for the things in the *palazzo*.' She let that remark sit alone for three long beats and then added, 'But he told me he found it cheaper to make sure that there was always at least one servant in the house.' Her glance was as cool as it was level.

'Yes, that would no doubt be cheaper,' Brunetti agreed.

'It was, then,' she said. Having established the social position and wealth of her husband's family, she added, more practically, 'One way to discover their recent price would be to check the online lists of sales and auctions.'

Brunetti had suspected that such lists must exist and said, 'I'll have someone do that.' He, too, had servants to do things for him.

'What else is missing?' she asked.

'I don't think they know yet,' Brunetti said. 'The man who cut the pages never requested or received the two books that are missing.'

'But she's sure they're gone?' she asked.

'Yes.'

After a moment, the Contessa asked, 'Does this mean there's more than one thief?'

'It would seem so.'

She made a noise that, in a person who did not have a title, would be called a snort and said, 'I thought they'd be safe in a library.'

Brunetti had the wisdom not to speak.

'This man was there for three weeks,' she continued, 'and no one saw anything?'

He heard the harshness but still said nothing.

'She told me he was an American,' the Contessa said, adding, 'Not that it makes any difference.'

Brunetti bent down and took the file from his brief-case. 'His name is Joseph Nickerson,' he read, glancing at her to see if it meant anything to her. It obviously did not, so he gave her the rest of the information: the University of Kansas, Maritime and Mediterranean Trade History, letter of introduction, passport.

'Do you have his photo?' she asked.

'Yes,' Brunetti said, passing her the photocopy of his passport pages.

'He looks like an American,' she said with mild disdain.

'It's what he told them at the library.' Brunetti reached to take the paper back and studied the face again. The people who had spoken to Nickerson had done so in Italian and had heard his accent: in that case, he could as easily have been English or perhaps from some other country. His Italian was fluent. It came to Brunetti to wonder if it was the accent that had been learned and not the language, and the man was perhaps Italian. If the passport was fake, why believe anything on it?

He took a fresh look at the photo, darkened the hair, let it grow a bit longer. Yes, he supposed it was possible. It was a pity Nickerson hadn't left a sample of his handwriting, even if only a few words: that was a far more certain sign of origin than accent or appearance.

The Contessa was silent for a long time, while Brunetti's mind remained on the idea of handwriting. Had not Nabokov written somewhere that he had consciously stopped putting the crossbar on the number 7 when he moved to America as a public declaration that he had left the Old World behind? How had Nickerson requested books if not by filling out a form? Or was that now computerized, too?

The Contessa interrupted his thoughts. 'What am I meant to call you, by the way? "Commissario"? "Dottore"? "Signore"?'

'Paola's husband's name is Guido,' he said. 'Would it be an imposition to suggest you use that?'

She tilted her chin to one side and stared at him, subjecting Brunetti to a scrutiny that succeeded in making him uncomfortable. Even though he rested, in a way, under the protective wings of the Falier family, he was not sure she saw them when she looked at him.

'Yes, it is, isn't it? Now, what was it you wanted to know about books?' she asked, not calling him anything and repeating the formal *lei* with which he had addressed her.

It took him a moment to digest her rejection of grammatical intimacy and return his thoughts to the crime. *Cui bono*? Who would profit from the theft, and how was that profit measured? If the thief and the future owner were not the same person, how did each of them profit? They would want the books or pages for different reasons, one venal and one . . . he couldn't think of the right word here, perhaps because he didn't understand the desire.

His thoughts were interrupted by the Contessa, who cleared her throat in a sign of impatience.

'You're known to be a collector,' he began. 'An intelligent collector.' He paused to see if she would respond to this compliment, but she simply waited, face impassive.

He had no choice but to continue. 'I don't understand the desire to have rare books.' Seeking clarity, he added, 'That is, a desire so strong as to steal them or have them stolen.'

'And so?'

'And so I'd like you to help me understand why someone would do this. And what kind of person would do it.'

She surprised him by smiling. 'Donatella's told me a little about you,' she said, still addressing him formally.

'Should I worry?' Brunetti asked lightly.

Her smile did not change. 'No, not at all. She's said you want to understand things.' Before Brunetti could thank her for the compliment, for he had taken it as such, she continued, 'But that's not going to help you here. There's nothing to understand. People steal them for the money.'

'But . . .' Brunetti began, but she talked over him.

'That's the only reason that animates the thieves. Forget the articles about the men who suffer a mad passion for maps and books and manuscripts: that's all romantic nonsense. Freud in the library.' She leaned forward and raised a hand, though it was hardly necessary to catch his attention. 'People steal books and maps and manuscripts, and they cut out single pages or whole chapters because they can sell them.'

It cost Brunetti no effort to believe in greed as a motive for human crime, so he asked calmly, 'And who buys them?'

'I've heard talk,' she said. 'Dealers, gallerists, auction houses are willing to buy things without asking questions.

'Do the thieves steal to order?'

'So long as there's no library stamp and they're rare enough, they'll sell them.' Then, with savage emphasis, 'To the better class of client, that is.'

Brunetti remained silent, then finally asked, 'Who are?'

She gave him a long look, as if assessing how much she could tell him. 'Those people who want beautiful things but want them at cut-rate prices.'

'Are you talking about people you know?'

'I'm probably talking about people you know,' she answered.

10

'What can you tell me about the market for these things?' Brunetti asked.

'Books and pages?' she asked, almost as if she believed that hearing the words would keep her anger hot. Then, in a more temperate voice, she went on. 'I don't think there's much else to tell you,' she said neutrally. 'Professionals go in and steal them, and they sometimes do it to order.'

'Who buys them?'

'Collectors buy the important things,' she said and then stopped. 'Please understand that I'm merely telling you what I've inferred from what I've heard and overheard during the years.'

'And the rest?'

'Small things – individual pages from a book about birds or flowers or mammals – they can be sold to small shops.' She turned her attention to the windows on the other side of the *calle*. 'It's possible, even likely, that the person buying it for his shop isn't sure it's stolen.' She didn't sound completely convinced of this, nor was Brunetti, who knew how easily people persuaded themselves into whatever they wanted to believe. But he let it pass without question.

'And I suppose a person who buys it in a shop,' she went on, 'would have little reason to suspect that it might be stolen.' Brunetti looked at her and nodded, then returned his eyes to his notebook.

'There are shops that do framing, street markets and fairs: these places buy as well as sell, so it's easy for the thief to unload the pages there.'

'Let's come back to the complete books,' he said. 'They're the most valuable.'

'Ah,' she began, drawing the sound out for a long time, 'they're much harder to hide or disguise. If they come from a library, they'll have the library stamp on certain pages. Every library uses a different system, but they all stamp multiple pages.' He nodded: eager that she should not think him completely ignorant about the subject. 'Once the seal is on the pages, they might as well have "Stolen" embossed on the cover.'

'Then why bother to buy them?' Brunetti asked.

She moved farther back in her chair, as if to afford herself a better view of him. Folding her hands in her lap, she said, 'You are not a credit to your wife's family, you know.'

'I haven't heard that for years,' Brunetti said and smiled.

She laughed. It was something like a smoker's cough and surprised him so much that he started to get out of his chair to go to her aid, but she raised a hand to pat the air and, with the gesture, sent him back to the chair. When the noise stopped, she said, 'I mean that you seem to lack the proper Venetian acquisitive impulse.'

He shrugged, suspecting this was a compliment, although not entirely sure.

'Many want the books so that they can boast about them, at least with certain friends, show them their impressive new acquisition and know no questions will be asked,' she said. 'That they have a Galileo codex or a first edition of this or that. Something rare. A survivor from the sixteenth century. A piece of culture.' Her voice had darkened, as if she were a magistrate reading out the list of charges. 'It suggests they're more sophisticated than the person who buys a Ferrari, I suppose.' Her contempt was withering.

He nodded, understanding – but not feeling – the desire.

'I like the fact that it makes no sense to you,' she said with another smile, though this one ended in a grimace. She pointed to something behind him. Brunetti turned and saw a portrait of a hook-nosed man wearing a dark brown velvet jacket. Sixteenth

century, he'd guess, probably from central Italy somewhere: Bologna perhaps?

'How much is that painting worth?' she asked.

He put his notebook in his pocket and got to his
feet, walked over to the painting and took a closer
look. The painter certainly had the gift: one look at
the subject's hands revealed that. Brunetti could have
reached out and stroked the velvet, and because he
was on a height with the man, he saw the clear intelligence in his eyes, the power of his jaw and the heft
of his shoulders. He would be a good friend and a
fierce enemy.

'I have no idea,' Brunetti said, his eyes still on the
man. 'All I can say is that it's a beautiful painting,
wonderfully done.'

When he turned to her, he saw that she was smiling
again. 'If I told you it was one of my ancestors, then
would you agree that it's worth more to me than to
you or to anyone else?' she asked.

'Other than to someone else in your family,' he said.

'Of course.'

Brunetti went back to his chair and sat again to
face her. 'What should I know about collectors? And
about value?'

She had clearly been waiting for this question or
for one like it. 'They're very strange people, most of
them. Almost all are men, and most of them like to
show off.' He nodded to tell her he knew both things,
and she went on. 'With watches or cars or houses,
it's easy for your friends to find out what they cost:

so they'll swoon at your new Lamborghini or your Patek Philippe. But not many people understand what books are worth.'

'So why bother to collect them?' he asked. 'And why bother to steal them? Or have them stolen? All it does is make you a higher class of thief.'

She smiled at the turn of phrase. 'If their friends are thieves, too, then it's reason for more boasting.'

Brunetti had not considered this. Had we sunk so low? He thought for a moment of some of the politicians in whose libraries stolen books had been found. Yes, we *had* sunk this low.

'Some people collect books because they love them and see them as part of our history and culture,' she said. 'You hardly need me to tell you that.'

'Was this the case with your husband's family?' he asked.

Again, she laughed, and again he thought she sounded like a heavy smoker. 'Good God, no. They acquired them as investments. And they were right. They're worth a fortune now.'

'You're going to give them all to the library, aren't you?' he asked.

'I probably will,' she said. 'I'd rather see them safely in a library, where people who are interested in them can read them, than think of them falling into the hands of those who see them only as repositories for money.'

As if she sensed his reaction, she abruptly asked, 'Do you have other questions?'

'How much damage does cutting out a page do to a book?'

'It's irreparable. Even if the pages are found. The book isn't the same object any more.'

Brunetti thought it sounded like the idea of female virginity that had been current in his youth, but he thought it prudent not to voice the comparison.

'And the effect on the . . .' he hesitated over what word to use. Finally he decided on 'price?'

'It's greatly decreased, even by half, if just one page is missing. The book is corrupted.'

'And if the text is untouched?'

'What do you mean?' she asked.

'If it's intact. If the text of the book is all still there to be read?'

She couldn't stop her mouth from contracting in a moue of disapproval. 'We aren't talking about the same thing,' she said. 'I'm talking about a book, and you're talking about a text.'

Brunetti smiled and slipped the cap on to his pen. 'I think we're both talking about the same thing, Contessa: books. We're just defining them differently.' He got to his feet.

'Is that all?' she asked, surprised.

'Yes,' Brunetti said. 'You've been generous with your time and your knowledge, Contessa.'

He closed his notebook and put it into the inside pocket of his jacket. She handed him back the papers, taking one last look at Nickerson's passport photo. He slipped them into his briefcase.

She watched him snap it closed. He got to his feet, and she rose from her chair and moved towards the door.

'Again, thank you for your time, Contessa,' he said, pausing at the door.

She put her hand on the handle but made no move to press it down. Instead, she looked at him and smiled. 'If you want to know what texts are worth, Guido,' she said, calling him by name and using the familiar *tu* she had denied him all during their conversation, 'take a walk over to Rio Terà Secondo.' He raised his eyebrows but said nothing. 'You'll find the building where Manutius' printing press was. You don't need me to tell you it is the most important printing press in the history of the Western world.

'There are two plaques on the wall of the building. One of them announces that it is the site of the Aldine Press, "which returned the splendour of Greek literature to civilized people". It was put there by the School of Greek Literature. In Padova. On the ground floor, on the right, there's an abandoned shop, and on the left there's a shop selling tourist junk. The day I found it, I asked in four shops nearby, but no one knew who Aldus Manutius was.'

'How did you find it?' Brunetti asked.

'I called a friend and asked. She found it in Wikipedia and called me back. San Polo 2310, in case you want to go and see it.'

She extended her hand, and again he bent over it to give an invisible kiss. Oh, if only his mother could see her boy now, kissing the hand of a contessa. Her *palazzo* wasn't on the Grand Canal, but Brunetti was certain his mother would not mind that in the least: it was still a *palazzo*, and the woman who had offered him her hand was still a contessa.

11

He and Paola had lunch alone that day, lasagne with sausage and *melanzane*. Chiara had gone to Padova on a school trip and Raffi for a ride on a friend's boat. 'He'll catch his death,' Paola said. 'Out there on the *laguna* in an open boat for hours. What happens if it starts to rain?'

Brunetti glanced out the kitchen window and saw a sky so blue it could have been cut from the Madonna's mantle. He had stepped out on to the terrace before lunch and been deafened by the chirping of birds in the pine trees in the courtyard of the house on the other side of the *calle*. Spring had clambered atop Juggernaut, and nothing would prevent its advance. In two months, they'd all be whining about the heat.

'I understand what you mean about the Contessa,' he said, ignoring her remarks.

At the possibility of something akin to gossip, Paola jettisoned her concern for her firstborn and asked, 'Which thing that I meant?'

'That she has something less than a gossamer touch in social situations or in disguising her opinions.'

'Oh, that,' she said. 'Yes, she can be outspoken, but she was raised as a favourite child and treated like a princess – although she was only a vicontessa – so I suppose it's understandable.'

'Forgivable?' Brunetti asked.

'Good heavens, no,' she said instantly. 'It's more important to understand people than to forgive them.'

Brunetti wondered if his wife had just discovered why Freud had replaced Christ but did not intend to spend time discussing this possibility with her, not when he wanted more information about the Contessa.

'She has little sympathy for people who collect things,' Brunetti said.

'Good for her,' Paola said, suddenly alert.

They were on the sofa in her study, the room happy with the return of the sun. Instead of wine with lunch, both had wanted the coffee that sat in front of them. Paola sipped at hers, swirled up the last sugar and emptied the cup.

Recalling his conversation with Contessa Morosini-Albani, Brunetti said, 'She makes a distinction between people like herself, who understand and love beautiful things, and people who simply want pretty things to put on the walls.' Even though he had tried to temper it, his uneasiness was audible, even to himself.

Paola set her cup down without making a sound and turned to him. 'If I make a distinction between the careful reading you give to Roman history and a journalist who refers to the court of the Emperor Heliogabalus as a parallel for the current situation in Rome while having no idea who Heliogabalus was, would you call that a spurious distinction?' Her voice was mild, but Brunetti heard the rustle of her tail in the underbrush as she prepared to strike. 'Or if I refer to my own benighted profession and suggest that my reading of *The Portrait of a Lady* might be more nuanced than that given in a Hollywood film, is *that* a spurious distinction?'

He lowered his head and studied the remains of his own coffee, then set his cup on the saucer beside hers. 'I suppose it depends on how visible you make your contempt for Hollywood,' he said.

'All contempt for Hollywood should be made as visible as possible.' That said, she smiled brightly and added, 'You know she's a snob. We all are. But she might have reason on her side.'

'Perhaps,' Brunetti said, making it clear it was concession and not agreement. He glanced at his watch, saw that he still had half an hour before he had to start back to work, and decided to ask Paola: she read everything and thought about what she read. 'You ever read science fiction?'

'Henry James wrote so little,' she said with a laugh.

'I'm serious,' he said.

'Yes. Some. But no more.'

'You ever read the one about burning books?' he asked. If she had, he knew it would be in there, packed away.

'No, not that I remember. Can you tell me more?'

'I don't recall the title, but it talked about a world where books had been outlawed by the state, and the firemen – this was very clever – the firemen went around burning any books that were found. If you had a book, you were killed.'

'I'm sure my students would all want to move there,' Paola said, straight-faced.

'They wouldn't like it because some people memorized entire books: they *became* the book. It was the only way to preserve them.'

She turned to stare at him. 'What made you think of it?'

He shrugged and glanced at the table in front of them, covered with books in all stages of reading: dog-eared; cellophane-covered still; open and face down; kissing each other face to face to mark the page in both; pages spread open and staring at the ceiling. 'I should have mentioned it to the Contessa.' He doubted the Contessa's familiarity with the genre and suspected she might not find his reference very compelling.

'If you get rid of all the books, you get rid of memory,' he said.

'And culture, and ethics, and variety, and any argument that opposes what you choose to think,' Paola said, as if reading from a list. Then, because he hadn't answered, she repeated her question, 'What are you thinking about?'

'Something she said. It's as if she thinks the prettiness of books as important as the text.'

'To some people it is. Or they wouldn't steal them, I suppose.' Then, after a moment's reflection, she added, as if conceding, 'The physical object can tell a lot about the culture, and they have historical importance. And think of all those natural history books where the facts are wrong and the drawings perfect.'

'We didn't agree,' Brunetti said.

'You voted for the text, I hope,' Paola said, turning to him.

'Of course.'

'Good,' she said. 'Divorce would be so troublesome.' Brunetti huffed and shook his head. 'Goose.'

After a long pause, she said, 'One thing you told me still makes no sense.'

'What?'

'That he bolted.'

'Excuse me?'

'That this Nickerson left the library in a hurry, leaving the books on the table.' The sun had been crawling across the floor as they sat there, and it now touched the soles of her feet stretched on the table in front of the sofa. She slid down and stretched them farther, wiggling them in the sunlight. 'Oh, that feels good,' she sighed.

'Is it warmer?' he asked.

'Not physically,' she answered. Then, back to the original topic, she added, 'Why would he do that?'

'He saw someone watching him,' Brunetti said, remembering Tertullian.

'Or someone could have warned him,' Paola suggested.

'How?' Brunetti asked.

'People can take their *telefonini* into the building, can't they?' she asked.

'I would assume so. People take them everywhere.'

'Then he could have had a call or an SMS.'

'That would require an accomplice,' Brunetti added.

'The fact that he managed to have a false American passport suggests a more sophisticated organization than the local troop of Boy Scouts gone to the bad,' she answered, but defanged the remark with a smile and added, 'It seems we agree that something frightened him.'

Brunetti allowed himself to sink into the sofa's embrace. He closed his eyes and tried to remember what Sartor had said about the American. Something about being led by Nickerson's enthusiasm for the books he was reading to read the same volume of Cortés.

Brunetti pulled out his *telefonino* and called Signorina Elettra's office number, hoping she would be there.

She picked up on the second ring. '*Sì*, Dottore?' she answered.

'I have a favour to ask. Can you look at the Merula catalogue and see how many copies they have of the book by Hernán Cortés? It's called *Relación* Something or Other.

'Would you like me to do this now, Dottore?' she asked.

'If it's no trouble.'

'One moment, then,' she said.

. He wedged the phone between his shoulder and his ear and leaned his head back. He heard a page turning beside him: Paola obviously had kept some text secreted about her person or under the cushion where she sat, left there in the event that life presented her with the necessity of spending three minutes with nothing to read. He didn't bother to look at her, merely counted the pages she turned.

After the fourth, Signorina Elettra was back on the line. 'Their catalogue lists a copy of *Segunda Carta de Relación*, printed in Seville in 1522, one copy of *Carta tercera*, same city, one year later, and another of the *Quarta relación*, by Gaspar Avila of Toledo, that's been removed for conservation.

'There is also a version that was printed here in 1524, by Vercellese, translated into Italian by Nicolò Liburnio.'

She allowed a long moment to pass and then inquired, 'Anything else, Dottore?'

'No, thank you, Signorina. I applaud you and I thank you.'

'*Dovere*,' she said and replaced the phone. Brunetti laughed out loud and switched off his *telefonino*.

'What did she say?' Paola asked, looking up from her book.

'That she was only doing her duty.' He laughed again. 'She's Patta's secretary, not mine, yet she's always willing to drop what she's doing to help me. And she says it's her duty.'

'You have a weakness for irony,' she said.

He placed his hand on her knee and shook it a bit. 'And you don't?'

Brunetti decided to stop at the Biblioteca Merula on his way back to the Questura and called Vianello to ask him to meet him at the Accademia Bridge so they would have time to talk while walking to the library. He chose to walk to the bridge, enjoying the rare freedom to pass through relatively empty streets. In two months, it would be impossible to walk through San Polo towards the bridge at this hour. He corrected himself: it would be possible, but it would be unbearable. When had this happened, he wondered; when had the city become unpleasant for so much of the year? But when he came down the bridge into Campo San Barnaba and saw three women sitting at a table in front of a café, their babies' pushchairs parked at their sides, faces tilted upwards to catch the sun as they sat and chatted with one another, his grumbling was swept away in a riptide of euphoria.

At the Accademia, he saw Vianello standing at the back of the *edicola*, watching the owner play chess with a friend. Approaching him, Brunetti said, 'I didn't know you played.'

'I don't, really,' Vianello said. 'I know how the pieces move and all that, but I'm no good at tactics or strategy.'

Brunetti chose not to comment on this. That so fine a predator should fail to recognize his talent surprised him, but perhaps pursuing criminals was different from capturing rooks and bishops.

Falling into step, they turned away from the water. 'I want to talk to the guard at the library. And I'd like you to come along and tell me what you think of him.'

'What are you going to talk to him about?' Vianello asked.

'He told me something when I spoke to him, and I want him to tell me more.'

'What?'

'I'd rather you heard it from him.'

Vianello turned to face him as they walked and asked, 'You suspect him?'

'No, I don't think I do. He seems an honest man.'

'But you never know?' the Inspector asked.

'Exactly.'

When they got to the library, Brunetti went to the desk on the first floor and told the same young man that he would like to have a word with Signor Sartor. He watched the emotions cross the younger man's face: curiosity, concern, fear.

'I'll go and find him,' he said, getting up from his chair.

A few minutes later, the two men emerged from the door that led to the collection of modern books. Recognizing Brunetti, Sartor came towards him, extending his hand, but when he saw the man standing next to Brunetti, his hand dropped to his side. 'Good afternoon, Commissario,' he managed to say, his eyes moving between the two men.

'Signor Sartor,' Brunetti said, 'this is my colleague, Ispettore Vianello.' Sartor shook hands with both men but said nothing.

'I'd like a few minutes of your time,' Brunetti told him. Then, looking around them, he addressed both Sartor and the young man. 'Is there some place where we can talk?'

Sartor looked at his colleague but said nothing.

'You could use the staffroom, Piero,' the young man suggested.

'Ah, yes,' Sartor said after a moment. 'Of course.' He turned towards the door to the staircase, leaving it to Brunetti and Vianello to follow him. This time he went downstairs. When they reached the courtyard, Sartor led them along the pavement on one side and turned left, heading for a door at the end. Brunetti did not understand why he didn't simply cut diagonally across the courtyard, but perhaps there was some prohibition about walking on the new grass. Nor did he understand why Sartor made sudden, awkward movements as they walked, as though he'd developed cramp in one leg, but then he realized he was avoiding stepping on the cracks between the paving stones. They passed under a large lilac bush that Brunetti noticed was in bud and stopped in front of steps leading to the wooden door with a double-glazed window.

Sartor reached into the pocket of his jacket; when he took out his key ring, it pulled with it a number of brightly coloured cardboard rectangles, which fluttered to the ground. Vianello bent quickly and picked up three or four, saying, as he saw them, 'Ah, *Gratta e Vinci*.' He smiled and said, 'My wife buys them: one a week. The best she's ever won is fifty Euros, and I don't want to think of what it's cost her to win that.'

Sartor hurried to pick up the rest of the cards and took the ones Vianello held out for him, then stared down at them as if they were a hand at poker and he had to decide what to bet on them. Finally he said, 'I get them for mine, too. But she's never won anything.' He shrugged this off, muttered, 'Gambling's for fools: *roba da donne*,' to express his disapproval of this weakness of women, and stuffed them back in his jacket pocket. He climbed the steps and opened the door. 'It's where we come for our breaks if we want, or to change our clothes.' He stepped back to let them enter before him.

Brunetti was pleased to find it so warm and welcoming, and so large. There was a sink, a fridge, even a small stove, everything spotlessly clean. Two windows at the back, giving on to a canal, allowed light into the white-walled room, as did the window in the door, which Sartor closed behind them.

'They had it all raised when the restoration was done, so the *acqua alta* can't come in,' the guard said, pulling two chairs away from the wooden table, and then a third. 'Not unless it's over 140, that is.' The unstained walls proved that to be true.

A row of metal lockers with padlocks stood on one side of the room; a coat and a few jackets hung from hooks on the opposite wall. At the far end, three rather battered but equally comfortable easy chairs were arranged in a rough circle between the windows.

'I can make coffee, it you like,' Sartor said, playing host, his hand nervously slipping into and out of his pocket to assure himself that the cards were still there.

Brunetti lied and said they'd just had one and went to one of the chairs at the table; Vianello did the same. The three men sat.

'When we spoke two days ago, Signor Sartor,' Brunetti began without introduction, 'you told me that Dottor Nickerson had spoken so much and so well about a book he was using in his research that you read it.'

Sartor looked back and forth between the two men, almost as if he were searching for some sign of reprimand for having read one of the library's books. Finally he nodded. 'Yes, I did.'

'Could you tell me again what book that was?'

Sartor's mounting confusion was written clearly on his face. 'But I told you that, sir: Cortés.'

'In Italian?' Brunetti asked.

'Of course. It's the only language I know.'

'Was it a separate volume or was it collected as part of another one?'

'It was a separate volume, Signore, the one that I found on Dottor Nickerson's table the other day.' He nodded emphatically. 'Same book.'

'You're sure?' Brunetti asked.

As if searching for the trap, Sartor glanced aside at the silent Vianello, who was following the conversation with an interest he did nothing to disguise. 'Yes, I'm sure. It was the same book. I know because it had a stain on the front cover, upper right corner. It might have been ink, but it was very old.'

'I see,' Brunetti said. 'Thank you.'

Sartor relaxed visibly. 'Could you tell me what this is about, sir?'

'Let me ask you one more question,' Brunetti said, ignoring the one he had been asked.

Sartor nodded, and his hand patted the cards in his pocket from outside.

'That morning, did you see Dottor Nickerson when he came in?'

'Yes, I did.'

'Is the morning your usual shift?'

'It is now, sir, for the first two hours every day. It has been for the last two months.'

'Why is that?' Brunetti asked.

'Manuela – she's the librarian who's usually at the desk and accepts the requests – she's going to have a baby and doesn't come in now until eleven. So Dottoressa Fabbiani asked me if I'd take over the desk for two hours.' He smiled and added, 'Manuela refuses to tell us whether it's a boy or a girl, but I'm betting it's a boy.'

Ignoring that remark, Brunetti asked, 'Were you on the desk all the time that Dottor Nickerson was using the library that day?'

'Yes, sir.'

'I see,' Brunetti said. 'And did you talk to him every morning?'

'Oh, no, only if there were no other people or if the runners took a long time to bring the books.' Again Brunetti recalled his student days and suspected there would have been plenty of time for the two men to talk.

'What sort of things did you talk about?' Brunetti asked casually, as if to pass the time until he could get back to his real questions.

'Fishing, for one,' Sartor surprised him by saying.

'Fishing?'

'I don't remember exactly how it started, but we were talking about the weather one day, and I said how eager I was for the season to start again.' Sartor looked at Vianello, as if asking if he understood this desire. The Inspector smiled and nodded.

'Did he fish?' Brunetti asked.

'Yes, he did. Not in the sea, though. He said that,

where he came from, there were only lakes, but some of them were very big.'

'Anything else?'

'Not much, really, just the sort of things you talk about when you have time to kill.'

'You said it was his enthusiasm that made you read the Cortés?' Brunetti said with a smile, one reader to another.

Sartor gave him a long look, then glanced at Vianello. Finally he answered. 'When I asked him, for politeness, what he was working on, he told me he was reading about European travellers in the fifteenth and sixteenth centuries. I told him the only one I'd read – we had to, in school – was Marco Polo, and he said his book was very good, and then he named a few more, saying they were just as interesting.'

Sartor pushed his chair back from the table and crossed his legs. Apparently Vianello's presence had calmed him sufficiently for him to ask, 'Are you sure you want to hear all of this?'

'Yes,' Brunetti said.

Sartor sighed and crossed his arms over his chest. 'When he told me the names of the explorers he was interested in, the only one I recognized was Cortés.' He cleared his throat a few times, then continued, 'I wanted to take a look at it and . . . and surprise him by saying I was reading it.' He paused to look back and forth between them, perhaps nervous about confessing his desire to impress the foreign professor.

'And so?' Brunetti prompted him.

'So I read some of the first volume, as I told you. And then, the other day, when Dottor Nickerson came in, I told him how I'd enjoyed reading Cortés.'

'Was he pleased?' Brunetti asked in an easy voice. When Sartor didn't answer, Brunetti asked, 'Did he say anything when you told him?'

Sartor looked away, as if suddenly puzzled by his memory of the conversation. 'That's strange,' he said in a low voice.

Brunetti was as quiet as a lizard on a rock. He permitted himself a small nod.

'He seemed surprised at first. But then he said he was glad I'd liked the book, and then he went up to the reading room.'

'Did you say anything else to him?'

'Only how eager I was to read the next volume.'

12

Brunetti smiled and got to his feet. Sartor looked back and forth between him and Vianello a few times for signs of what was going to happen, before he stood. Brunetti reached across the table and shook his hand, saying, 'You've been very helpful, Signor Sartor.' He tried to make his voice as reassuring as possible.

The guard gave a weak smile. He pushed his chair back in place and turned towards the door.

As if the idea had just come to him, Brunetti asked, as Sartor was opening the door, 'You said Dottor Nickerson spoke Italian very well. Did it ever occur to you that he might really be Italian?'

Sartor let them pass in front of him and down the stairs into the courtyard, then turned to lock the door.

He left his hand on the key for a long time before putting it into his pocket. He came down the steps and stopped in front of Brunetti. 'I never thought of that before, but he might be. He said he was American but that he'd gone to school in Rome when he was a boy. I figured that would explain why he didn't have much of an accent.' He was silent for a while then started across the courtyard, stopped and turned to them. 'Maybe I heard it because I thought it had to be there. Is that possible?'

Vianello spoke for the first time. 'Eyewitnesses often remember seeing things that didn't happen and people who weren't there.'

'Crazy, isn't it?' Sartor asked of no one in particular.

He started to walk towards the door to the *calle*, but Brunetti stopped him by saying, 'I'd like to have a word with Dottoressa Fabbiani.'

'Of course, of course,' Sartor said and turned back and headed towards the main steps. At the top, Brunetti noticed that the sign announcing 'technical problems' was still taped to the door. Sartor opened the door, then closed and locked it after them. 'If you gentlemen will wait here, I'll tell her you'd like to see her,' he said and walked towards what Brunetti thought was the back of the building.

'It's possible, isn't it, that he imagined the accent?' Vianello asked.

'People have done stranger things,' Brunetti answered. He went to the counter and looked down at the papers in the letter trays. He read the top sheets:

a request for an interlibrary loan, a list of books on sale in an upcoming auction in Rome, and a letter of inquiry about the possibility of working as an unpaid intern at the library.

Hearing footsteps, he moved away from the counter and sat in one of the chairs. Vianello did the same, leaned back, and crossed his legs.

The door opened and Dottoressa Fabbiani entered, Sartor visible just behind and holding the door for her.

'Thank you,' she said, and added, smiling, 'You can go back and plan for the Formula Uno.' Sartor left, closing the door behind him.

Though it was none of his business, Brunetti asked, getting to his feet, 'Formula Uno?'

She smiled. 'Piero's mad for it and for all sports. I don't know how his wife puts up with it: all he thinks about is calculating the odds and winning.' Then, seeing Vianello, she stopped.

'This is my colleague, Ispettore Vianello,' Brunetti said.

Ease and informality gone, she suggested they come back to her office. She led them through the stacks so quickly that Brunetti lost all orientation. After a time, she opened a door at the end of a long corridor lined with wooden bookshelves and ushered them into her office. Her desk held a computer, a telephone, and one manila folder: no other papers were in evidence, nor pen, pencil, paperclip. The surface of the desk was a smudgeless slab of black glass.

Four walls, four prints he recognized as being from Piranesi's *Carceri*, cheerless and lifeless, regardless of their quality. Diamond-patterned parquet, two windows looking across to the Giudecca. She sat in a straight chair and indicated that they should sit near her.

'What can I help you with, Commissario?' she asked.

'I'm curious about the financial loss to the library and wonder if you've had time to calculate it,' he said.

She studied one of Piranesi's ruins before answering. 'The Montalboddo sold at auction earlier this year for 215,000 Euros. The Ramusio was only one volume of three, but it was a first edition.'

'How does that affect the price?' Brunetti asked.

'Although it was volume two, strangely enough it was printed last,' she said.

'I'm sorry, Dottoressa, but that doesn't help me understand.'

'Ah, of course,' she said, running the fingers of her right hand through her hair. 'One thing it means is that the thief was probably sent to get it for someone who needed it to complete his set.' When neither Brunetti nor Vianello said anything, she continued. 'If so, now he'll have all three volumes and the total value will be much more than the total price of the separate single volumes.' Both of them nodded.

'Excuse me, Dottoressa,' Vianello interrupted, speaking as though he could not contain his curiosity, 'but how does that affect the value of your set?'

She looked at him in surprise, perhaps not having considered inspectors capable of thought. 'It destroys it,' she shot back. Then, immediately, with a weary smile, 'No, that's an exaggeration. It lowers it a great deal. But that's not the point.'

'Of course not,' Vianello agreed with a sympathetic look. 'You're a library, not a bookshop.'

Her look grew more attentive and she said, 'You're right: we're not. The financial loss isn't what's important to the institution.' She returned her attention to the Piranesi.

'How could someone have managed to take books from the library?' Vianello asked, his voice filled with concern.

Again, she ran her hand through her hair. 'I don't know. Someone is always at the desks, both for the modern and the rare books collections. They check people's bags on the way out.' Brunetti wondered how thorough a check was made, especially of someone with whom you'd chatted about your shared love of fishing.

'Only that?' Brunetti asked.

'We've begun a system of tagging,' she said. Seeing their incomprehension, she went on, 'Computer chips. They're being put into the spines of all of the volumes, at least the ones up here. A sensor – like the thing you walk through at the airport – will detect it if you try to carry one through without checking it out.'

Brunetti, who had seen no sign of such a thing near the desks on either floor, asked, 'Is it installed?'

She closed her eyes and took a deep breath. 'We ordered it six months ago, which is when we started inserting the chips.' She opened her eyes and looked at Brunetti.

'But?' he prompted.

'The machine that was delivered had been designed to respond to chips that used a different program. Or at least that's what we were told.'

'What happened?'

'The company took it back, but they haven't delivered the new one yet.'

'Have they said when they'll deliver it?' Vianello asked.

Voice tight, hard, she answered, 'No.'

Brunetti asked, 'You told me you have eight thousand books here, Dottoressa. How many of them will you put chips into?'

'All of them,' she answered with a wave around them to indicate this floor of the library, then added, 'And in the manuscripts.'

'How long will that take, do you think?'

She gave him a sharp look and asked, 'What has this got to do with the theft, Commissario?'

'I hope this won't offend you, Dottoressa, but I was thinking about future thefts.'

Her face froze. Brunetti wondered if she was going to tell them to leave. She folded her hands in her lap and began to work at a loose piece of cuticle on her left thumb. She looked at Brunetti. 'It's already happened.' She took a long breath and tried to steady

By Its Cover

her voice. She started to speak, failed, tried again and finally managed to say, 'There are more.'

A silence fell on the room. Brunetti and Vianello did not move. More than a minute passed, and finally Brunetti asked, 'More what, Dottoressa?'

'More books,' she said.

'Missing?'

She lowered her eyes and scratched at her thumb. Soon she gave up on that and looked at Brunetti. 'Yes. I wanted to be sure nothing else was gone, so I printed out every tenth page of the first hundred pages of the catalogue and looked to see that the books listed were either checked out or still on the shelves.'

'How many books did that include?' Brunetti asked.

He watched her consider his question and saw when she realized the sense of it. 'More than a hundred and forty,' she answered.

Brunetti saw no reason to waste time and asked directly, 'How many are missing?'

'Nine,' she said, glancing at Vianello and back at Brunetti.

'It's getting worse,' she added in a voice suddenly grown loud with anger. 'I hear it from colleagues everywhere, not only in this country. Nothing's safe any more.' Brunetti saw her hands, locked together now, one crushing the other. Then, in a calmer voice, she said, 'I don't know what to do. We can't stop people coming. Scholars need what we have here.' She looked down at her hands and pulled them free of one another.

'Have you completed the list of the books that Nickerson requested?' Brunetti asked.

'Yes.'

'How many books were . . . ?' Brunetti failed to find the correct word.

'He vandalized thirty-one of them,' she answered, using the proper word, then added, 'That we've found so far, that is.'

'And the loss?' he asked, hoping she'd understand he was again trying to determine their financial value and certain she would appreciate his failure to ask how this could have gone on unobserved.

She shook her head as at the inability of someone to understand a simple thing. 'The books are ruined, at least as far as our standards are concerned. They might have kept a part of their value – one of them had only one map removed, so it's worth only half as much – but they're no longer the same things they were, and the ones he took more pages from are virtually worthless.' Convinced that they finally understood, she went to her desk and came back with the folder. Opening it, she handed Brunetti a set of papers, kept one for herself. She sat back down.

'These are the books that we know he vandalized and the prices we paid for the ones we bought.' She leaned forward and pointed to the first column of numbers. 'The rest were donated to the library, so all we can provide is their last price at auction. We haven't had time, and I'm afraid I lack the ability to estimate what they might be sold for today.' Then, after a moment's reflection, she added, 'I don't know if it's worth finding out.'

'Why?' Brunetti asked.

'We'll never have enough money to replace them.'

'But the insurance?'

Her laugh was bitter and dismissive. 'We don't have it. Because we're a public institution, the government is supposed to cover us. But that's worthless.' Before they could ask, she said, 'We had water damage from a burst pipe about eight years ago, and we're still waiting for them to send an inspector to look at the books.'

As if that weren't enough, she said, 'They don't pay for anything that was a donation.' She saw their astonishment and explained, 'They maintain that, if we didn't pay for the books, then we've suffered no loss.'

She allowed some time to pass so that they could absorb what she had just said, then leaned towards Brunetti and tapped at the numbers in a column on the right. 'Those are the last auction prices for two of the pages that are missing. They're the only ones we could find.'

'Excuse me, Dottoressa,' Vianello said, 'is it common for people to collect separate pages?'

'Yes,' she answered.

'So people just *do* it?' Vianello asked. He must have seen her confusion, for he added, 'I mean, if there are auction prices for these pages, then some of the books have already been . . . damaged.'

'It's a common practice,' she said austerely. 'Once a single page is removed, many people decide they might as well cannibalize the whole thing and sell the individual pages. Until there's nothing left. If it's privately owned, there's no one to stop them from doing it.'

Into the silence that spread out from that, Brunetti asked, 'Did you ever meet him?'

'You mean Nickerson?'

'Yes.'

'We spoke to one another a few times, but no more than to say hello.' She opened the folder again and pulled out a stack of index cards. 'These are his request forms,' she said. 'We still had them.'

Seeing Brunetti hesitate, she said, 'Your men took prints from all of them, so you can touch them.'

Brunetti glanced at Vianello, who nodded.

Brunetti handed half of them to Vianello and began to examine the handwriting on the cards one by one; Vianello did the same. After less than a minute, they looked up from the cards, and their eyes met. 'He's Italian, isn't he?' Vianello asked.

'I suspect so,' Brunetti agreed.

Brunetti's phone rang. He pulled it out and looked at the number. 'Excuse me,' he said and got to his feet. With no explanation, he went to the door and stepped back into the room that held the books, pulling the door closed behind him.

'Brunetti,' he said.

'It's Dalla Lana, Commissario,' he heard one of the new officers say.

'Yes?'

'There's been a death, Signore,' he said, paused, then added, 'Violent.'

'If you mean murder, Dalla Lana, just say it, all right?'

'Yes, sir. I'm sorry, but this is my first one, and I didn't know whether to use that word.'

'Tell me what you know,' he said.

'A man called – it was about ten minutes ago – to say he's at his brother's apartment, and his brother's been killed. He said there's a lot of blood.'

'Did he give his name?' Brunetti asked, noting that it had taken Dalla Lana ten minutes to call him. Ten minutes.

'Yes, sir. Enrico Franchini. He lives in Padova.'

Brunetti raised his eyes and looked at the rows and rows of books, survivors from former ages, witnesses to life. 'Did he tell you his brother's name?' he asked in a very cool voice.

'No, sir. All he said was that he was dead, and then he started to cry.'

'In Castello?' Brunetti asked, but it really wasn't a question.

'Yes, sir. Do you know him?'

'No.' Then, more practically, 'Did you send someone?'

'I've been trying to find you, sir. I called your office, but you weren't there. No one could give me your *telefonino* number. But then . . .'

'You have it now,' Brunetti said. 'Call Bocchese and

tell him to get over there with a crew. Did the man who called give you his phone number?'

'No, sir,' Dalla Lana said, and then, in a much smaller voice, 'I forgot to ask him for it.'

Brunetti realized his fingers were white around his phone. He relaxed his grip and said, 'The phone there, in your office, lists the numbers that have called. Find the last one and call him back and tell him, if he's still in the apartment, to leave it, go outside, and wait for the police. He doesn't have to go outside the building, but I want him out of the apartment. Do you understand that?'

'Yes, sir.'

'Call Foa, either on his phone or on the radio, and tell him to stop whatever he's doing and go to the end of La Punta della Dogana. I'll meet him there in ten minutes.'

'If he can't come, sir?'

'He'll come.' Brunetti broke the connection.

He opened the door and went back into the room. 'I'm afraid I have to return to the Questura, Dottoressa,' he said, voice striving for calm. She seemed not to find this unusual, but Vianello got to his feet and moved towards the door.

'Thank you for your time,' Brunetti said. Without waiting for her response, he turned and left the room and started down the steps, folding the papers she had given him and putting them into his pocket.

'What's wrong?' Vianello asked, one step behind him.

Brunetti hurried down to the courtyard, then out on to the street, turning left on the *riva* and towards the Punta della Dogana. 'Franchini's dead,' he said. Vianello stumbled but quickly regained his footing.

'His brother called from the apartment and said he was dead. There's a lot of blood.'

'What else did he say?'

'I didn't talk to him. He called the Questura: they called me.'

Blind to everything around them, the two men walked, almost running. 'Bocchese's coming, with a team. I told Dalla Lana to call the brother and tell him to get out of the apartment.'

'Where are we going?' Vianello asked as he suddenly realized where they were walking. The *riva* ended at a point that led only to water, and there was no boat stop, no chance to do anything except circle back towards the vaporetto at La Salute or flag a passing taxi.

'I told Foa to meet us up there,' Brunetti said. They passed a woman out walking two dogs. One of the dogs chased after them, barking wildly, though from fun and not in menace, and how, Brunetti asked himself, did he know that?

'*Bassi, smettila,*' the woman called after the dog, which gave up the chase and doubled back towards her.

As they reached the open triangular space at the end of the island, Brunetti saw the police boat moored at the very point. 'Foa,' he called. The pilot came to the side of the boat and put out his hand. Brunetti, and then Vianello, jumped on board; Foa flipped the rope from the stanchion and revved the motor. He pulled away from the *riva* and to the left, doubling back towards Castello.

They stayed on deck with the pilot, almost as if they believed that being able to see the buildings streaming by would shorten the trip. Neither spoke, and Foa, sensing their mood, said nothing. He did not use the siren: noise was for novices. Instead, he put on the blue light and weaved in and out of what traffic there was until he turned into the canal of Sant'Elena. He slowed to a more moderate speed, snaking past moored boats as he moved into the ever smaller canals of Castello. Ahead of them, a large flat-decked transport boat stuck its nose into the canal, but Foa blasted it into sudden reverse with one short bleat of his siren.

Foa slowed again when he entered Rio di S. Ana and told them to duck their heads as they went under a bridge; he turned left and glided up and stopped behind another police launch that was moored on the right side of the canal. He hadn't even grabbed the rope before Brunetti and Vianello leaped up to the *riva* and started across the *campo*.

They saw a man on one of the benches who seemed unaware of anything around him. He sat slumped over, legs apart, looking at the ground between his feet. He held a white handkerchief in his left hand, and as they approached him, he wiped at his eyes and blew his nose, then looked down again, his forearms propped on his thighs. Brunetti saw his shoulders rise and fall and heard his choked sob. The man wiped his eyes again but didn't look up at the sound of their approaching footsteps.

Brunetti heard a humming sound, and then the man sobbed again. His hands were coiled into tight fists, the handkerchief crushed between his fingers. Brunetti approached the bench and stopped a metre from the man. 'Signor Franchini,' he said in a normal voice. The humming noise continued, and the man wiped at his eyes again.

Brunetti squatted down, bringing his eyes level with the other man's. 'Signor Franchini,' he said again, this time raising his voice a little.

The man gave a sudden start, looked at Brunetti, pulled himself upright, and pressed himself against the back of the bench. Brunetti held up a hand, palm towards him. 'We're police officers, Signore. Don't be frightened.'

The man stared at him, silent. He appeared to be in his late fifties, dressed in a woollen suit, his tie neatly knotted, as though he had come here from his office. His thin grey hair fell across a narrow forehead. His eyes were brown, swollen in the aftermath of tears, his nose long and slender.

'Signor Franchini?' Brunetti said again. His knees began to hurt, and he leaned forward and pressed one hand against the ground. He pushed himself to his feet, careful to rise very slowly, though he felt it in his knees as he did.

'Can we help you in any way?' he asked, turning to Vianello, who had stopped a few metres away, then motioning him to come closer. Vianello was careful to move very slowly as he came to stand near his superior, leaving a space big enough for a man to dash through between them.

'Who are you?' the man asked. He sniffled, blew his nose, let his hands fall to his lap.

'I'm Commissario Guido Brunetti, and this is Ispettore Vianello. We just heard about your brother, so we came here.' He half turned and indicated the two police boats moored one behind the other, as if that would prove he was telling the truth.

'Have you seen him?' the man asked.

Brunetti shook his head. 'No. We've just got here.'

'It's very bad, you know,' the man said.

'You're his brother?' Brunetti asked.

The man nodded. 'Yes, the baby brother.'

'Me, too,' Brunetti said.

'It's not easy,' Franchini said.

'No, it's not,' Brunetti agreed.

'They're never careful enough.' Franchini stopped, surprised at what he had just said, and raised the handkerchief with both hands to press it against his eyes. He gave a single, short sob, before lowering his hands.

'Do you mind if I sit?' Brunetti asked. 'My knees can't do that any more.'

'Please, please,' Franchini said and moved to the left to make room for him.

Brunetti sat down with a sigh and stretched his legs in front of him. He made a motion with his head, and Vianello started walking towards the house. The other man paid no attention to him.

'You came from Padova?' Brunetti asked casually.

'Yes. Aldo and I always speak to each other on Tuesday nights, and when he didn't answer his phone last night, I decided I better come and see what was wrong.'

'Why did you think something was wrong?' Brunetti asked in an entirely conversational voice.

'Because we've spoken to each other every Tuesday night, at nine o'clock, for sixteen years.'

'I see,' Brunetti said and nodded to confirm the good sense of Franchini's decision to come. He turned to face the man, as in a normal conversation, and saw that, although he was a thin man, a double chin hung incongruously beneath his face. He had large ears.

'And you came this afternoon?'

'I had to work today. We don't get out until three.'

'Oh, what do you do?'

'I'm a teacher. Latin and Greek. In Padova.'

'I see,' Brunetti said. 'Those were my favourite classes.'

'Really?' Franchini turned to ask him, unable to contain his pleasure.

'Yes,' Brunetti said. 'I liked the precision of them, especially of Greek. Everything had the right place.'

'Did you keep it up?' Franchini asked.

Brunetti shook his head, his regret real. 'I got lazy, I'm afraid. I still read them, but in Italian.'

'It's not the same,' Franchini said, then quickly added, as though afraid of hurting a student's feelings, 'But it's good that you still read them.'

Brunetti let a long time pass and then asked, 'Were you and your brother close?'

After an even longer time, Franchini said 'Yes.' Another pause, then he added, 'And no.'

'Like me and my brother,' Brunetti offered, waited a few moments and asked, 'How were you close?'

'We studied the same things,' Franchini said, glancing aside to look Brunetti in the face. 'He preferred Latin, though.'

'And you Greek?'

Franchini shrugged in assent.

'How else?'

He could see Franchini start to fold his handkerchief into a neat square, as if the apparent normality of the conversation had eliminated the need for tears. 'We were raised as believers. Our parents were very religious.'

His father having been a savage atheist, Brunetti nodded to suggest a common experience.

'Aldo was more interested than I.' Franchini looked away. 'He answered his vocation and became a priest.' He was still folding the handkerchief, which was now reduced to the size of a packet of cigarettes.

'But then he lost it. He told me once that he woke

up one morning and it was gone, as if he'd put it somewhere before he went to bed and couldn't find it when he woke up.'

'What did he do?' Brunetti asked.

'He left. He stopped being a priest, so they fired him from his teaching job. They couldn't do that, not legally, so they had to make it seem like he retired early, and they gave him a pension.'

'How did he manage to live here?' Brunetti asked, knowing Franchini would understand he was asking about money.

'The apartment belonged to my parents, and they left it to us. So he moved here, and I stayed in Padova.'

'Is your family there?' Brunetti asked.

'Yes,' he said but did not elaborate.

'And you called him every Tuesday?'

Franchini nodded. 'Aldo changed when he lost his job: it was like he'd lost everything that was important to him. Except for Latin. He spent his time reading.'

'In Latin?'

'I helped find him a place here where he could read. He said he wanted to read the Fathers of the Church,' Franchini said.

'To find his faith again?' Brunetti asked.

He heard the cloth of the other man's jacket rub against the back of the bench as he shrugged. 'He didn't say.' Then, before Brunetti could speak, he added, 'And I never asked.'

'So he spent his time reading the Fathers of the Church,' Brunetti said, half statement, half question.

'Yes,' Franchini said. 'And then this,' he added, raising the hand that was not holding the handkerchief and waving it vaguely at the building behind them.

13

From that same building, as if in response to the waving of Franchini's hand, came the sound of a window being opened, and then a voice called down, 'Commissario.'

Brunetti stood and turned to face the voice, angry that his peaceful colloquy with Franchini had been interrupted so sharply. A uniformed officer stood at the window, leaning out and waving, as if he thought Brunetti did not know they were in the apartment. Brunetti raised his hand and made a rolling gesture, hoping the man would understand he was on his way, or would be soon.

When he looked back at Franchini, he saw that he had bent forward again and was staring at the pavement, hands together, forearms resting on his thighs. He seemed unaware of Brunetti, who took out his phone and dialled Vianello's number. When the Inspector answered, Brunetti said, 'Can you send someone down to stay with Signor Franchini?' and hung up before Vianello could speak.

A few minutes later, Brunetti was relieved to see Pucetti emerge from the front door of the building.

When Pucetti reached the bench, Brunetti bent down to Franchini and said, 'Signore, Officer Pucetti will stay here with you until I get back.' Franchini looked at him, then at Pucetti. The officer gave a small bow. Franchini returned his gaze to Brunetti, then to the pavement. Brunetti patted the younger man's arm but said nothing.

Inside, an officer he recognized, whose name he thought was Staffelli, stood in the corridor beside an open door on the third floor. He saluted Brunetti, then pressed his lips together and raised his eyebrows in an expression that could signify anything from surprise at human behaviour to acceptance of the way the world functioned. Brunetti raised a hand to acknowledge his salute as well as whatever message he was trying to transmit. There was no sign of Vianello.

Inside, he saw Bocchese, the head of the scientific team, dressed in his white paper suit and shoes, standing in an open doorway, looking into a room from which came the occasional flash of light.

'Bocchese,' Brunetti said.

The technician turned and looked at him, raised a hand in greeting, then turned back just as another quick series of flashes shot past him. Brunetti took a few steps, but was stopped by a hiss from Bocchese. The technician reached into his pocket for two transparent plastic envelopes. 'Put these on,' he said, handing them to Brunetti.

Familiar with Bocchese's rules, Brunetti backed out into the hall. He held the railing with one hand while he slipped the paper coverings over his shoes, then put on the plastic gloves. He handed the empty envelopes to Staffelli and went back into the apartment.

Bocchese was no longer in the doorway, so Brunetti took his place there. Men's voices filtered towards him from some other place in the apartment: one of them sounded like Vianello's. Two white-suited technicians were moving their camera equipment to the other side of the room, away from the man's body that lay against the wall.

So that was Tertullian, he thought, looking across at the surprisingly small sprawled form. Had there not been so much blood, he could have been a drunk who had passed out in his home while trying to find his way to bed or lost his balance and slithered down to lie with his head and one shoulder resting against the wall. This could have been the case, indeed, had not the alternative scenario been drawn on the wall behind him. Three bloody right-hand prints climbed the wall, as if the man had braced himself as he got to his feet, but a descending red hand-streak had cancelled them as it raced to the floor, like the central red brushstroke at the heart of a Shiraga.

The dead man lay with one shoulder lodged against the wall, his arms spread open, head at an unlikely angle, one knee bent under his other leg. Had there been a sign of life, any person seeing him would have acted on pure animal instinct and shifted him away from the wall to free his neck and straighten his trapped knee. A moment's reflection, however, would have convinced even the most optimistic that there was no life left in this inert, diminished thing.

Brunetti had observed the same phenomenon more times than he liked to recall, how the spirit seemed to take mass and substance with it when it fled the body, leaving behind a smaller being than the one it had inhabited. This man had been young once, had been a priest, a believer, a reader, and now he was a twisted form with a blood-streaked face and a jacket bunched under his shoulders. The sole smiled loose from his left shoe: above was a dark grey sock and above that a slice of the pasty white skin of an old man.

Two pools of dried blood darkened the parquet a metre from the body. One of them had been squashed by a foot, and from it three partial bloody footprints, all of the right foot, came directly towards him. There was no fourth.

A flash burst, and Brunetti shied away from it, instinctively raising one hand in surprise. He turned to the two technicians. 'Who's coming?'

'Probably Rizzardi,' the taller of them answered but did not explain his uncertainty.

'When did you get here?' Brunetti asked.

The man shoved up the sleeve of his white suit with the edge of a gloved hand. 'About twenty minutes ago.'

'What else is there?' Brunetti asked.

'He was in the other room,' the second one interrupted, shifting the tripod that held their camera a bit to the left.

'Why do you say that?'

He clicked a few photos. Brunetti, accustomed to the flash now, did not bother to shield his eyes. Shifting the camera further left, the technician said, 'Take a look, Commissario,' pointing towards the door to his left. 'You'll see what I mean.'

Brunetti walked to the door and looked into the room, curious about what story he would read there. An easy chair covered in dark green corduroy sat in one corner, behind it a reading lamp with a white glass shade. Beside the chair stood a round table with a smaller lamp. Both lamps were turned on, and beside the one on the table a book lay face down, as though the person reading it had been momentarily interrupted and had placed it there while he went to answer the phone, or the door. Behind the chair stood a large bookcase with every shelf filled.

An acoustical trick carried the men's voices, now recognizable as Vianello's and Bocchese's, to him. 'You taking prints in every room?' Brunetti heard

Vianello ask. 'Of course,' Bocchese answered, but then they must have moved because their voices grew muffled and indistinct.

Brunetti turned back to the first room and saw Dottor Rizzardi, the pathologist, at the door. They exchanged quiet greetings. Tall, slender, his hair greyer than the last time Brunetti had seen him, Rizzardi looked at Brunetti but could not keep his attention from drifting to the broken package that had once held Franchini's life.

Rizzardi was already wearing plastic booties and was just pulling the second glove on to his left hand. He walked over to the corpse and stood above it for some time, and Brunetti wondered if he were saying a prayer for the man's spirit or wishing him peace on his journey to the next world, until he remembered that Rizzardi had once said he couldn't believe in a next world, not after what he had seen in this one.

The pathologist went down on one knee and leaned closer to the dead man. He reached and took his wrist. Punctilious to a fault, Rizzardi was checking his pulse. Brunetti looked away for a moment, and when he returned his attention, the pathologist had moved closer to the body and was lowering Franchini's shoulder to the floor, where it flopped to one side. He tried to straighten the bent knee but failed.

Rizzardi rose and, still crouching, stepped to the head of the body. He knelt again and examined the back of the head, tilting it to provide a better look. He got to his feet and approached Brunetti.

'What happened?' Brunetti asked.

'Someone kicked him. Someone wearing heavy shoes or boots.'

'In the head?' Brunetti asked.

'Yes: that's what killed him. But also in the face. His right cheek is cut almost all the way through, and at least four teeth are broken. But it's the ones in the back of his head that killed him.' He turned and gestured back to the scene. 'He tried to stand – God knows how – but he couldn't. Or the other one pulled him down.'

'But he was an old man,' Brunetti protested.

'Old people are better victims,' Rizzardi said, stripping off his gloves. He placed the gloves carefully face to face, then slipped them into the transparent package they came in before putting them into his pocket. 'They're weak and can't defend themselves.'

'You'd think people would respect them,' Brunetti said. 'That people would be . . . different.'

Rizzardi looked at Brunetti. 'You know, Guido, at times I find it difficult to believe you do the sort of work you do.'

Brunetti had observed for years the respect, almost reverence, with which Rizzardi treated the dead he was called to view, and so said nothing.

'It's hard to tell how many times he was kicked,' Rizzardi said. 'I'll be sure . . . later.'

'"The pleasure of those who injure you lies in your pain",' Brunetti found himself repeating.

'Excuse me?' Rizzardi asked.

'It's something Tertullian wrote,' he explained.

'Tertullian?'

'The theologian.'

Rizzardi gave a sigh he tried to make sound as patient as possible. 'I know who Tertullian is, Guido. I don't know why you're quoting him just now.'

'That's what he was called,' Brunetti said, nodding towards the dead man.

'You knew him?'

'I knew about him,' Brunetti said.

'Ah,' was Rizzardi's only response.

'He spent his time reading the Fathers of the Church at the Merula Library.'

'Why?'

'Maybe because they had them in Latin. And it was a place to go.'

'So are cinemas and restaurants,' Rizzardi observed.

'He used to be a priest,' Brunetti explained. 'So perhaps he felt more at home reading than going to see *Bambi*.'

'Do people still go to see *Bambi*?' Rizzardi asked.

'I didn't mean it literally, Ettore. It was the first film I thought of.'

'Oh.'

Brunetti thought that was the end of the conversation. The silence drew out, and just as he decided it was time to go back and talk to Franchini's brother, Rizzardi said, 'And now he's dead.' That said, the pathologist patted his pockets again, nodded to Brunetti, and left the room.

14

After telling Vianello to remain there until the boat came to take the body away, Brunetti went downstairs and started across the *campo*. As he approached the two men on the bench, he saw the back of Pucetti's head next to Franchini's. When he saw that they were turned towards one another, he stopped to observe them. Pucetti's shoulders moved minimally in synchrony with his hands as he gestured while saying something to the older man. Franchini nodded, then both of his shoulders moved as he folded his arms across his chest. Pucetti raised a hand and pointed at one of the buildings on the other side of the *campo*, and Franchini nodded again.

Brunetti grew nearer and heard Pucetti's voice: 'From the time I was seven until I was eleven.'

He could not make out Franchini's reply.

'To Santa Croce. Down by San Basilio. The apartment was bigger, and there were three of us kids by then.' Pucetti paused for a long time. 'I got my own room then, for the first time.'

Franchini then said something else Brunetti could not hear.

'I had two sisters, so they got to stay together. It would have been nice to have a brother.' Then, remembering, he said, 'I'm sorry, Signore. I . . .'

Brunetti watched Franchini turn as he gave Pucetti's knee a fleeting tap, but again couldn't hear what he said. He saw that Pucetti's neck had flushed red, and was relieved at this proof that the young man was still capable of embarrassment. He moved off to the left and came upon them from the side.

Pucetti got to his feet and saluted; Franchini looked at him with no sign of recognition.

Brunetti told Pucetti he could go back upstairs and took his place beside Franchini.

He let a minute pass, until finally Franchini asked, 'Did you see him?'

'Yes, I did, Signore. I'm sorry such a thing could happen to him. And to you.'

Franchini nodded, as if words would take too much effort.

'You said you were close, the two of you.'

Franchini leaned back and folded his arms, then

seemed to find that posture uncomfortable and leaned forward to resume his study of the pavement between his feet. 'Yes, I said that.'

'You said you studied the same things and were religious when you were young,' Brunetti reminded him. 'Were you still close enough to tell each other about your lives?'

After some time, Franchini said, 'There's not a lot to tell. I'm married, but we don't have children. My wife's a doctor. Paediatrician. I still teach, but I won't for much longer.'

'Because of your age?'

'No. Because students aren't interested in studying Greek or Latin any more. They want to learn about computers.' Before Brunetti could speak, Franchini went on. 'That's what they're interested in, in this world. What good are Greek and Latin?'

'They discipline the mind,' Brunetti said as if by rote.

'That's nonsense,' Franchini answered. 'They show an ordered structure, but that's not the same as disciplining the mind.'

Brunetti had to admit the truth of this; nor, for that fact, did he really see why a mind should be disciplined in the first place. 'Did your brother marry?' he asked.

Franchini shook his head. 'No, when he left, it was too late for that sort of thing.'

Brunetti decided not to inquire about that judgement and, instead, asked, 'Was his pension enough to let him live comfortably?'

'Yes,' Franchini replied. 'He had very few expenses. I told you: the house was ours, so he could live there. All he had to do was pay the gas and light.' He nodded at the ground a few times, trying perhaps to persuade the pavement that his brother's life had been comfortable.

'I see,' Brunetti said. 'Do you know if he had friends here, Signor Franchini?' When he saw the man's hands tighten, Brunetti said, 'I'm sorry to ask you these things, but we need to know as much as we can about him.'

'Will that bring him back?' Franchini asked, as had so many other people in the same circumstances.

'No. Nothing will, I'm afraid. We both know that. But things like this can't be allowed to happen . . .'

'It already has,' Franchini interrupted.

The Latin came to Brunetti unsummoned. '"*Nihil non ratione tractari intellegique voluit.*"'

The words washed over Franchini, who moved to the side and turned to take a better look at Brunetti. "There is nothing God does not wish to be understood and investigated by reason." He failed to hide his astonishment. 'How do you know that?'

'I learned it in school, years ago, and it seems to have remained with me.'

'Do you think it's true?'

Brunetti shook his head. 'Too many people already tell us what God wishes or wants. I don't have any idea.'

'But you quoted it. Did you think we still have to obey Tertullian?'

'I don't know why I said it, Signor Franchini. I'm sorry if it offended you.'

The man's face softened into a smile. 'No, it surprised me; it didn't offend me. It was the sort of thing Aldo was always doing. Not only from Tertullian, but from Cyprian and Ambrose. He had a quotation for everything,' he concluded and then had to wipe his eyes again.

'Signore,' Brunetti began, 'I think it's right to find out who killed your brother. Not because of God. Because things like this are wrong and should be punished.'

'Why?' he asked simply.

'Because.'

'That's not a reason,' Franchini said.

'For me, it is,' Brunetti answered.

Franchini studied Brunetti's face, then leaned back and spread his arms across the top of the back of the bench, looking as relaxed and casual as someone with nothing better to do but take the sun.

'Tell me what you know about your brother, please, Signore,' Brunetti said.

Franchini tilted his head back, face up to the sun. After a long time, he said, 'My brother was a thief and a blackmailer. He was also a liar and a fraud.'

Brunetti stared off at the police boat, where Foa stood on deck, bent over the pink pages of *La Gazzetta dello Sport*. He thought of something Paola often repeated, maintaining it was Hamlet's observation on his mother, that someone 'could smile and smile, and be a villain'.

'Tell me more, please,' he asked.

'There's little to tell, really. Aldo always claimed he changed when he lost his faith, but that was a lie, too. He never had any faith in anything but his own cleverness, never had a vocation: he saw becoming a priest as a way to succeed. But it didn't work for him, and he ended up teaching Latin to teenaged boys in a boarding school, not as a bishop with scores of people to obey him.'

'Is that what he wanted?'

Franchini lowered his face and turned to look at Brunetti. 'I never asked him. I don't think he knew, not really. He thought that being a priest would help him rise in the world: that's why he wanted to do it.'

Brunetti had no idea of what it meant to rise in the world and could not ask. Perhaps the thought of the answers he might get frightened him, especially after what Franchini had said about his brother. He realized his question had had no aim save to keep Franchini talking while he adjusted himself to this new vision of the dead man. Aldo Franchini was no longer a pious seeker of religious truth but a liar, thief, fraud, and blackmailer. No wonder he had not reported Nickerson to the staff of the library.

Brunetti thought back to the small figure crushed against the wall of the room upstairs and was relieved that he still felt a sense of loss and indignation that Tertullian had been made to suffer and die, regardless of what his brother had just said.

He had been a priest teaching at a boys' school,

and he was a blackmailer. 'Did these things you've told me about his character have anything to do with why he left the school where he was teaching?'

Franchini was incapable of disguising his surprise. Brunetti watched him as he followed the verbal path that might have led Brunetti to that question. 'Yes.' Then, after a moment, 'It's the obvious explanation, isn't it?'

'Did he tell you?'

'No, of course not. He never told me the truth, not about anything.'

'How did you learn it, then?'

'Oh, it's a small world we live in, people who teach what we do. I knew the man who replaced him – he wasn't a priest – and he told me what had happened.'

'What was that?'

'Aldo was blackmailing two of the priests.'

'Ah,' Brunetti sighed. 'What happened?'

'One of the boys finally told his parents about the priests, and they called the police.' Franchini paused, as if reliving his discovery of those events. Brunetti searched his memory for any such incident in the last few years in Vicenza and found nothing, but it was not uncommon for the arrest of a priest not to be made public.

'They were both arrested, the priests, and that's when they told their superior about the blackmail.'

'Did he tell the police?' Brunetti asked.

'I don't think so. Nothing happened to Aldo.' Franchini looked at the pavement again, flicked a cigarette butt away with one foot and said, 'You know, it's very strange. For a time, I used to console myself by saying he was only blackmailing them, and that meant he didn't do anything to the boys.' He looked up and gave Brunetti a grim smile, then looked back at the pavement. 'But that meant I was saying it was all right to be a blackmailer.' He let them both think about this for a moment, and then he said, 'I was so proud of him when I was a kid.'

'He lost his job,' Brunetti said when Franchini had not spoken for a while.

'Yes.'

'What happened to the two priests?'

'My friend told me they were sent on retreat for a month.'

'And then?'

'Sent to other schools, I imagine.'

'Did your brother do this to other people?'

Franchini shook his head. 'I don't know. But he always lived well and took nice vacations.'

'As a priest?'

'He had a great deal of autonomy. Especially while he was at the school. He was there for fifteen years. He said he gave private lessons.' He glanced at Brunetti and, seeing his confusion, said, 'To explain the money.'

'Ah,' Brunetti said.

As if losing patience with Brunetti's failure to ask the proper question, Franchini said, 'One of the priests was the Director of the school.'

This time, it was Brunetti who nodded.

'Do you know of any other things he did like this?'

'Blackmail, no. But he stole things.'

'For example?'

'Some of the things in our parents' house.'

'What things?'

'There were four good paintings that had been in the family for generations. They were there when my parents died, and when Aldo moved in. They aren't there now.'

Before Brunetti could ask, Franchini said, 'No, it wasn't today I noticed they were gone. I realized it years ago.'

'How long ago was that?'

'Two years. He'd been in the house a year. They were all gone.'

'Did you ask him about them?'

Franchini sighed and gave a shrug. 'What would be the sense? He'd only lie. Besides, I don't have anyone to leave them to. It's just more stuff to worry about.' Then, in a lighter voice, he added, 'If the money made him happy, then I'm glad of it.' Brunetti believed him.

'And the lying?' Brunetti asked.

'His whole life was a lie,' Franchini said tiredly. 'He pretended everything: pretended to want to be a priest, to be a good son, to be a good brother.' There followed a long silence which Brunetti had no desire to break.

'The only thing that was true about him was the Latin. He really loved it, and loved what was written in it.'

'Was he a good teacher?'

'Yes. It was the one thing he did with passion. He managed to inspire the boys in his class, to make them see the rigid clarity of the language, the profound sense of the way it put words, and ideas, together.'

'Did he tell you this?'

Franchini thought before he said, 'No, he taught me. He was already at university when I began *liceo*, and he helped me in the first years, helped me see how perfect both languages are.' He paused to think about this and then said, 'He showed me the passion.' Then, in a stronger voice, he added, 'I've met some of his former students, and they all said the classes with Aldo were fascinating and that they learned more from him than from any of their other teachers. He taught us to love the languages, and we loved him for that.'

Franchini's use of the word made Brunetti nervous. 'Was there any chance that your brother might have . . . with the boys, I mean?'

'Oh, no. Aldo loved women. He had lovers all over the Veneto. He told me once – he'd had a lot to drink – that he managed to make a lot of money from them. Asking them to give money to the Church.'

'They knew he was a priest?'

'Some of them, not all.'

'I see,' Brunetti said, then asked, 'You knew all of this?'

'I've had a long time to learn it. All my life,' Franchini said, and for the first time Brunetti heard betrayal in his voice.

'Yes,' Brunetti agreed. 'But how did you find out about him?'

'Friends we had in common,' Franchini said. 'Or I should say friends of mine who met him.' He sat back again and stretched out his legs. 'Or he would boast about it,' he added, his voice uneasy. 'I was the only person he could boast to: about the women and the money and being so much cleverer than anyone he met.'

'When did he do this?'

'It used to happen when we saw each other, but then I couldn't stand it any more – especially after the paintings disappeared – so I stopped coming here to visit him.' Franchini looked at the buildings on the other side of the canal. 'We grew up here. It was home.'

He opened his handkerchief and wiped his face with it, as if it were a towel, and put it back in the pocket of his trousers. 'For the last few years, all we had were the phone calls. For some reason, I couldn't stop calling him. Maybe I thought he would eventually listen to himself and hear how he sounded. But he never did. I think he had come to believe it, really, that he was so clever he could outsmart everyone.' He studied the houses on the opposite side of the canal and waved in their direction. 'That young policeman said he grew up here.' Then, in a sober voice, he added, 'It's still a good part of the city.'

He sat up straight and slapped his palms on his

thighs in a gesture meant to display activity or the desire for it. 'What do I have to do?'

'I'm afraid you'll have to identify him,' Brunetti said.

Franchini turned, his terror evident. 'I don't think I can see him again.' The tears came to his eyes, but he was unaware of them.

'Officially, Signor Franchini. I'm sorry, but that's the law. You have to make a formal identification.'

Franchini pushed himself back on the bench and shook his head. 'I don't think I can. Really.' The sight of the tears on his face led Brunetti to say, 'It will be enough if you go to see Doctor Rizzardi at the hospital and sign the papers there. I'll talk to the doctor: it won't be necessary for you to see him again.' Then it came to Brunetti to suggest, 'You won't have to do it until tomorrow or the next day. If you tell us the time your train from Padova arrives, Pucetti – the young man you were talking to – will meet you in a boat at the station.' He could not bring himself to say that Dottor Rizzardi would be in the morgue, so he added, 'He'll take you to the doctor's office.'

Franchini's face relaxed. 'Can I go now?' he asked, as if surprised he had not asked this before. He got to his feet.

'Yes,' Brunetti said, standing and taking the older man's arm, saying, 'The boat will take you to the station, Signore.'

Reluctant, Franchini made no attempt to walk towards the boat. 'It's a nice day. I could walk.'

'Yes, it is. But it's a long way to the station, and I think you'd be more comfortable in the boat.' Brunetti released his arm, turning the gesture into a wave in the direction of Foa.

'It's kind of you,' Franchini said.

Brunetti found nothing to say in response. 'I have a favour to ask you,' he finally said.

'Which is?'

'I'd like you to think over the conversations you had with your brother in the last few months.'

'I've been doing that for the last two hours, Signore,' Franchini said, then added, 'I'm sorry, I've forgotten your rank.'

'Commissario.'

'Commissario,' Franchini repeated formally.

'Was he any different?'

Franchini took a small step in the direction of the boat, and Brunetti, fearing he had pushed him too far, moved along at his side. Franchini stopped, took another step, then stopped again and looked up at the taller Brunetti. 'He was excited by something. I don't know what. I didn't ask, and Aldo didn't tell me. But he was excited. I know he wanted to tell me about it, but I couldn't listen.'

'Had this happened before?' Brunetti asked.

Franchini nodded. 'He was like a hunter at times. It thrilled him to find something – or someone – new. I'd watched and listened to it happen in the past, and I couldn't stand it any more. So I cut him off when he asked if I wanted to know what he was doing.

I just asked how he was and what he was reading. That's all I wanted to talk to him about.'

'I see,' Brunetti said, wondering how he could get him to reveal more: feelings, impressions, the unspoken sense of what his brother wanted to say.

'Once – about six months ago – he said he'd been sitting and waiting for years, and he'd finally found someone who would go hunting with him.' He paused and then added, surprised at his memory. '"In the chicken coop." That's exactly what he said.'

'What did he mean?' Brunetti asked, though he thought he knew.

'I don't know. I didn't ask. I didn't want to know.' With each short phrase, Franchini's voice grew louder.

He started to walk towards the boat again. 'Maybe I will accept your offer, Commissario,' he said.

15

When he returned to Franchini's apartment, Brunetti found the two crime-squad men just inside the door, busy snapping closed their equipment boxes. They still wore their protective suits, would keep them on until they returned to the Questura.

Pucetti and Vianello, both wearing booties and gloves, emerged from a door that led to the back of the apartment; Bocchese came along behind them, he too still fully suited up.

'Did you see the other room?' Vianello asked Brunetti.

'Yes.'

'What do you make of it?'

'He was reading. Someone rang the bell or knocked

on the door of the apartment, and he put his book face down on the table to go and answer it. Whoever it was killed him.' To Bocchese, he said, 'Did your men search the apartment?'

'You know we don't do that, Guido,' the technician said with exaggerated patience. 'We photograph traces that have been left and make a record of the scene and collect samples, but you gentlemen get to open things up and look around.'

Brunetti almost smiled but did not, unwilling to give Bocchese the satisfaction. 'Then let me rephrase the question: did any of you happen to see anything we might be interested in? Accidentally, as it were.'

'You're always a fine one for careful distinctions, aren't you?' Bocchese asked. 'It's Lorenzo who did the seeing, not one of mine.'

Brunetti turned his attention to Vianello. 'I was looking at the books in there,' the Inspector said, 'and some of them seemed different from the others.'

'Different' could mean many things, Brunetti knew. 'How?'

'They looked old,' Vianello said and smiled. Pucetti, standing behind him, nodded.

One of the technicians called over to Bocchese that they were ready to return to the Questura. 'I'll go with them,' Bocchese said, 'and leave the books to you.'

'Leave an evidence box, would you?' Brunetti asked the chief technician. 'Just in case.'

Bocchese nodded and walked away, his feet making a whooshing sound on the floor. Vianello led the way into the other room. Brunetti and Pucetti followed him to the walnut bookcase behind the chair where Franchini had been sitting. As they pulled on their plastic gloves, Brunetti began to study the books. The top shelves held the usual classics of Italian history and political thinking: Machiavelli, Guicciardini, Gramsci. Even Bobbio was there. Below them started the Latin writers: modern editions of Cicero, Pliny, Seneca, Propertius. He ran his eye across their predictable presence, but on the third shelf down he was surprised, for he found Valerius Flaccus, Arrian, and Quintilian. And Justinian's Codex, which he had never read – as, indeed, he had never read Valerius Flaccus. There was Sallust, *The Conspiracy of Catiline*, which he had read but forgotten entirely, and Varro's *On the Latin Language*, which Brunetti had always assumed no one had ever read.

On the shelf below were the playwrights, but between Seneca's *Phaedra* and Plautus' *Comedies* stood another book, far older than the modern editions. He pulled it from the shelf and took delight in the way the book nestled comfortably in his hand. Black morocco binding on what might be wooden boards, three raised horizontal bars on the spine. He looked at the cover and saw the double circle within a finely drawn rectangle of gold: CATVL TIBULLUS PROPER. Fumbling with his plastic-covered finger, he opened it to the title page and saw that it had been printed in Lyon by Gryphius in . . . he worked out the Roman numerals . . . 1534.

He stepped aside and set it on the cushion of the chair where Franchini had been sitting and returned his attention to the shelf. He took another book that was farther along the row and opened it. The title page identified it as Seneca's tragedies. He turned the page, again not without difficulty, and felt the comfortable jolt that beauty always gave him. The illuminator's hand had taken life from the elaborate N with which the page began and used it as the starting point for a chain of tiny flowers – red and gold and blue and looking as though they had been painted the day before – that enclosed the text. At the bottom, the flowers flowed across to meet and then slipped under a coat of arms with two lions rampant before dancing up the inside margin of the page and back to the originating N. He bent to read the text. '*NISI GRATIAS AGEREM tibi, vir optime*'. So the writer was giving thanks to a good man, Brunetti worked out. Perhaps Enrico Franchini was right, and being able to translate Latin did not discipline the mind.

He placed the book on top of the other and saw that there were three more such volumes on that shelf and even more on the ones below. On the bottom shelf, he saw a large volume lying horizontally and bent to retrieve it. Tacitus, the first five books. He set it on the back of the chair and opened it, flinching when he saw the inked notations in the margins. He paged through it, having once read it, though in Italian. He could translate phrases and whole sentences, but he could never read it in Latin, not after all these years and not after all the indiscipline of his mind. He tried to read the handwritten notes, but the calligraphy outwitted him and he gave it up.

He closed the Tacitus and placed it on the growing pile, then stepped back and studied the spines of the remaining books: the antique volumes were easily recognized: almost all of them showed signs of where their paper catalogue stickers had been removed.

He chose one at random and opened it without bothering to look at the title: the binding had told him its age and suggested its value. He cupped it in his hands and let it fall open where it willed. He saw the illuminated T, a man kneeling to the left of it, two sheep on the other side of the letter. The sight of the lines of poetry printed in italic script caused his heart, and then his hands, to tighten. He had first seen this same text more than twenty years before, during his initial, strained visit to Paola's parents – he an awkward university student from a humble family invited to dinner at Palazzo Falier – when the Conte had shown him some of the books in the library. He turned back to the title page, and memory was confirmed: the Manutius Virgil. He worked out the date: 1501. He turned to page 36 and looked on the bottom for the stamp with the Conte's seal, but it was not there.

Brunetti added the book to the pile. There was a fortune stacked on that chair, and not for an instant did he think that Franchini had come by the books honestly. 'A thief and a blackmailer, a liar and a fraud.'

Retrieving the Seneca from the pile, he opened it again, quickly finding the small oval stamp on the bottom left of the title page. 'Biblioteca Querini Stampaglia,' he read. He flipped ahead to pages 57 and then 157, where the same identification was repeated. And then, just to be sure – though there was no longer any need of that – he turned to the last page, where he saw the stamp again. It was the library's numbering pattern he had known since he was a student.

Vianello, who had been silently observing him all this time, said, 'I thought you'd understand what they are.' He picked one up: Catullus, Tibullus, and Propertius. 'I don't know anything about them,' he said. 'I can barely figure out the title and the date. I didn't have Latin at school.'

Pucetti broke in to say, 'For me it's old and that's all.'

'It's something you might enjoy,' Brunetti told the younger man.

'Perhaps,' Pucetti replied. Then, sounding so much like Raffi it made Brunetti's ears tingle, he asked, 'Are they interesting?'

'It depends on what you think is interesting, Roberto,' he stalled. 'I read them and I like them.'

'Why?'

Brunetti reached over and took the book from Vianello. 'I suppose it's because I like the past,' he said. 'Reading about it shows us that we really haven't changed much in all these centuries.'

'Why should we change?' Pucetti asked.

'It might be nice to get rid of some of the bad things,' Vianello interrupted to say.

'Put the likes of us all out of work,' Brunetti said and left them to go and ask the technicians if they had a box large enough to hold the books.

At the Questura, the three men went to Brunetti's office, he walking first, carrying the box of books. Inside, they put on their gloves again and, following his instructions, opened the books by latching their fingers under the front covers and turning each one to the title page to search for any indication of the rightful owner. The men were careful to touch the books as little as possible and to turn pages only by holding the corners.

Twelve had come from the Merula. In one that was not from the Merula, Brunetti found the familiar Manutius dolphin and anchor insignia and made out the Greek letters of Sophocles' name and the date, 1502. Below the insignia there was a modern nameplate with the initials 'P D' separated by a single upright dolphin. Two others came from a public library in Vicenza. The next he opened was a 1485 edition of Livy's *History*, printed in Treviso, also bearing the 'P D' insignia. Another – a 1470 edition of Cicero's *Rhetorica* – bore no identification whatsoever. For all Brunetti knew, Franchini could have bought it himself, though he doubted that.

Only when he had finished making a list of the books did he call Bocchese and ask him to send one of his men for them. Sooner or later, they might find a common fingerprint, other than Franchini's, on them.

When the books were gone and Vianello and Pucetti had said they'd return to Franchini's neighbourhood to speak to the people in the area, Brunetti called Dottoressa Fabbiani and told her about Franchini's death and then about the books they had found in the apartment.

'My God, poor Tertullian,' she said without giving a thought to the books. There followed a long pause Brunetti lacked the courage to interrupt. In an altered voice, she then thanked him for the information and told him that the rare book section would be closed until they had done a complete audit of the collection. He started to ask her something, but she cut him off and said she couldn't talk any more, and then she was gone.

After he hung up, Brunetti went to the window and told himself he was there to check on the advance of springtime. He looked at the trailing vines slipping over the top of the fence that enclosed the garden on the far side of the canal, but the buds and shoots could have lined up and danced the cancan for all he saw of them. Something at the back of his memory was irritating him, and he tried to work at it, as Dottoressa Fabbiani had at her nail. Push and pull and back and forth . . . what was the story he had been told that he couldn't now believe?

By Its Cover

And there it was, standing forthright in his memory. Viale Garibaldi, a woman sitting on the bench and talking to Franchini, sudden arrival of another man, the assault, Franchini's refusal to press charges. Look at it one way, and it might have been a random attack. Add in Franchini's fondness for women and blackmail, and the same events might tell a different story entirely.

He went back to his computer and punched in the assailant's surname and called up the file on him. On the second page he found his companion's name and address, the one who had a restraining order against him: Adele Marzi, Castello 999, the *sestiere* where Franchini had lived. He checked his address in Campo Ruga: 333. It was unlikely that the buildings could be close to one another, but still he pulled his *Calli, Campielli e Canali* out of the bottom drawer, found the coordinates and opened to map 45. He studied the incoherent numbers for a moment and then saw that 999 lay just at the bottom of Ponte S. Gioachin and thus – thanks to the chaos of the city – less than two minutes from Franchini's apartment.

He typed the woman's name into the system, but she was present there only for having requested the court order keeping Durà away from her. On her application for the request he found her *telefonino* number and dialled it.

'*Sì?*' a woman's voice answered on the fifth ring.

'Signora Marzi?' Brunetti asked.

'*Sì.*'

'This is Commissario Guido Brunetti,' he said and waited long enough for her to work out that he was a commissario of police. 'I'd like to speak to you.'

'What about?' she asked after a pause.

'That incident on Viale Garibaldi.'

She said nothing for a long time and then asked, 'What about it?'

'We've decided to take another look at it.'

'He's in jail,' she said.

'I know that, Signora. But it's still necessary that we discuss the incident.'

Her voice unsteady with the fear all citizens felt at any brush with the state, she said, 'I haven't heard from him.'

Brunetti wondered whether she meant her ex-companion or Franchini but did not ask. 'It's still necessary that we speak, Signora.'

'Why?'

'Because we need to know more about what happened.' It was a stupid answer, but he knew how fear could dull people's perceptions and make them uncritical.

'When?'

It sounded like negotiation, but he recognized it as surrender.

'Whenever is most convenient for you, Signora,' he said in a warm voice. He looked at his watch and saw that it was almost eight. 'Would tomorrow be convenient?'

'What time?'

'Whatever time you choose, Signora.'

'Where?' she asked.

'You could come here to the Questura, or . . .'

'No,' she said, cutting off his sentence.

The fear was back in her voice. He had been about to suggest a place close to where she lived, but that would only confirm that they knew where she lived; it would also put her, near her home, in the company of an unknown man, and she might not like that. 'We could meet at Florian's,' he suggested.

'All right,' she said grudgingly. 'What time?'

It might be better to let her have some time to worry about this, Brunetti found himself thinking. 'Three,' he said.

'All right,' she agreed after a silence during which he could almost hear her readjusting her day.

'Good. I'll see you there.' Before she could ask, he added, 'When you come in, ask for me, Brunetti: I'll leave my name with the waiters.'

'All right,' she said yet again and cut the line.

He opened his email and wrote to Signorina Elettra, surely gone home by now. 'Could you see what there is to know about Adele Marzi, Castello 999? I know that she was granted a restraining order against her ex-companion, Roberto Durà, but nothing else.' Then, with a not very subtle nudge, he added, 'I'm meeting her tomorrow afternoon.' He turned off his computer without bothering to see what mail was waiting for him and went home.

16

It was after nine before he got there, not having called to say he would be late. Paola was accustomed to his delays and lapses and usually left something for him in the oven or on the stove while she went back to her study to read or to grade student papers. Years ago, decades ago, he had felt guilty about being late, but his guilt had diminished in the face of her apparent lack of concern at his absences.

He had asked her about this once, and she had asked in return if he really thought she'd mind spending an hour with Trollope or Fielding instead of with two teenaged children and a husband preoccupied with some horrendous crime. There were times when it was difficult for Brunetti to reconcile the things

Paola said with his belief that she was a devoted wife and mother.

In the kitchen he found a large platter of artichokes, not the giant, vulgar Roman ones, but their own delicate *castraura*. There must have been a dozen of them. He picked up the fork that sat beside them and put five on a plate, then took a spoon from the drawer and covered them with olive oil from the bottom of the dish. Then a sixth. He opened the fridge and poured himself a glass of white wine without bothering to look at the label. He put two slices of bread on the side of the plate, noticing that it had dried out a bit. Brunetti could think of no fate more cruel than having to eat alone, so he went towards the back of the house and Paola's study.

The door was ajar and he went in without bothering to knock. She looked up from the sofa, where she had staked her territorial rights by lying across most of its length. He sat in the empty place at the end, and put his plate and glass on the low table.

'Guido,' she said as he picked up the wine and took a sip, 'someone's told me a very strange story.'

'About what?' he asked, piercing the first artichoke. They had been fried in olive oil and a bit of water, with a whole garlic clove left in and parsley added at the end. He cut it in half and shoved the pieces around in the olive oil, flipped them over and made sure the other sides got their fair share. He ate a piece, sipped the wine, and wiped up some olive oil with a fragment of bread. Taking his glass, he sat back in the sofa. 'Tell me.'

'I was talking to Bruno today.'

'The one who has the camping place?'

'Yes.'

'And he said he's going to run off to Rio with a German tourist and start a samba studio?' Bruno, whom Brunetti had known for years, was the uncle of a classmate of Paola's and ran a small hotel on the Lido. Because the Lido was removed from the city centre, the Guardia di Finanza was a less oppressive presence there, and so Brunetti had always assumed that Bruno was less than rigorous in his bookkeeping.

'Was it something about his clients?' Brunetti asked, convinced that the comments of tourists were often a window on the real world.

'No. It came out of the blue.'

'What?'

'Some time ago he had a phone call at home. A man, who knew his name, said they were making a survey of all the people who worked in the tourist industry.'

'They?' Brunetti asked and sipped at his wine.

'That's what he asked: who they were. The man said he was "La Finanza".' Paola saw his look and answered it. 'That's right, "La Finanza".'

'What's the Guardia di Finanza want from him?'

'The man said he thought he might be interested in subscribing to some magazines.'

'What sort of magazines?'

'He described five of them and said he was sure Bruno would want to subscribe to at least one of them.'

'What did he do?'

'What do you think he did? He agreed.'

'Why?'

'Because he's at risk, Guido. He's at risk like all of us. How many of us obey the law all the time? When we go to dinner in a restaurant, do you get a *ricevuta fiscale*?'

'Not if I know the people, no,' Brunetti answered indignantly, as if he'd been asked if he were a shoplifter.

'That's against the law, Guido. You're at risk too. In your case, they'd probably give you a break once you told them you were a policeman,' she said, then added, 'But they don't give breaks to people who aren't members of the club.'

'Like Bruno?' he asked.

'Like him and all the other people who are honest but who can't live honestly. His rent has been tripled in the last ten years, and fewer and fewer people want to stay on the Lido. So he's breaking the law to survive, earning money and not paying tax on it. Whoever called him knew that. And used it.'

'When did this happen?'

'About four months ago.'

Brunetti took another sip of his wine but left the artichokes where they were. 'Tell me more.'

'The magazines come by courier, and he has to

pay the courier every time. So he has no idea who they're coming from.'

'What magazines are they?'

'The history of the Guardia Costiera, the contribution of the Navy to our society. That sort of thing.'

He knew them well. Every police station in the country had them lying around, unread, unreadable histories of different branches of the state services.

'Did this person give any other information?' he asked. 'Other than to say he was calling for "La Finanza"?'

'No, nothing. And the phone he called from had the number blocked.'

Brunetti sat back. 'So there's only the courier, who gets the money. And he could come from anywhere.'

'Yes.'

'Why are you telling me this?' he asked.

'Because he paid them. Because the two possibilities are that it's a fraud – which I think it is – or that the Finanza is actually doing this. Bruno believed it was the Finanza. And paid what he believed was blackmail in order to be left alone.'

There was nothing he could say and nothing he could ask.

'That's how we live now, Guido. If some organ of the state calls and threatens us, or we believe it's an organ of the state, we pay them. That's what we're reduced to, paying blackmail money to the state to stay safe from it.'

Brunetti refused to rise to the bait. He wanted to

eat his artichokes in peace, finish his wine, and go back to the kitchen to see what was waiting for him in the oven. He did not want to get involved in this, did not even want to comment on it. How else did she expect Bruno to react to a threat like this?

He looked at the remaining artichokes, wondering what he should do. To eat them was to suggest lack of interest in what Paola had said; not to eat them was to have to talk. He picked up his plate and glass and went back to the kitchen. In the oven, he found an oval dish covered with aluminium foil. He touched the side with an exploratory finger, felt that he could safely pull it out. He did, then peeled back the foil.

Two tiny quails lay between a pile of fresh peas and an even larger pile of tiny roasted new pota- toes, the whole dish redolent of the cognac in which the quails had been baked. The woman might be a troublemaker, but she knew how to cook. Shoving his remaining artichokes to one side, he transferred everything in the dish to his plate, then set it on the table. He took the wine from the fridge. He'd stick with white. He retrieved *Il Gazzettino* from the living room, where he had left it that morning. Back in the kitchen, he placed the newspaper to the side of his plate and continued reading where he had left off. Like the food, that morning's news should not be leftovers for the following day: best to consume them while they were still warm.

When he had finished, he put his plate in the sink and ran hot water on it, then found a bottle of cognac and grabbed two glasses. He went down to Paola's study with what he thought of as a peace offering, though there was no need to establish peace.

She looked up and smiled as he came in, either at his return or at the bottle he brought with him. This time, she pulled back her feet to give him more room and set her book aside. 'I hope you liked them,' she said.

'Wonderful,' he said and held up the bottle. 'I thought I'd continue with the theme of cognac.'

She reached for the glass he offered her. 'That's very kind, Guido.' She took a sip and nodded her thanks.

'I came to tell you what's happened,' he said, sitting at her feet.

His second glass of cognac stood untouched in front of him when he finished telling Paola about Franchini's murder and the books they had found in his apartment.

'But why would anyone kill him?' she asked, and in response, he repeated the remark Franchini's brother had made.

That stopped her. She started to speak but, apparently finding no words, looked away and raised a hand into the air, only to let it drop.

'I believe him,' Brunetti said. 'I can't explain why I do, but I do. He kept crying, even after he told me.' Brunetti passed on the other things Franchini's brother had told him: the blackmailing, Aldo's fierce desire to rise in the world, talk of some new plan, and his happiness at having found someone to hunt with.

'And now he's dead,' Paola said.

'Yes.' In all these years, she had never asked him for details of the deaths he investigated. That someone was dead by the hand of another person was more than enough horror for Paola.

She set her glass on the table in the manner she had when she was finished drinking. Brunetti noticed that the glass was almost full. So, he was surprised to see when he looked at the cognac he no longer wanted, was his own.

'What do you do now?'

'Tomorrow afternoon I have an appointment to speak to a woman who knew him.'

'Knew him how?' Paola asked.

'That's one of the questions I'll ask her,' Brunetti said simply.

'And what else?'

'Why her ex-companion assaulted him.'

Her curiosity was evident in the look she gave him.

'It was about six months ago. They had some sort of run-in, and Franchini ended up in the hospital with a broken nose. He didn't press charges. The man who hit him's in jail now for something else. So he didn't do it.'

'At least that's something,' Paola said, then asked, 'Why talk to her?'

'To get her to tell me more about Franchini. All he is to me now is a former priest who sat in a library for years, reading the Fathers of the Church, but who, his brother said, was not an honest man. And whose house was filled with stolen books.' He paused for a moment and then added, 'I want to see if her story is the same as his brother's and which one is true.'

'But can't they both be?' Paola asked.

Brunetti considered this for some time and finally asked, 'Why not?'

17

Brunetti kept this in mind the following afternoon as he crossed the Piazza on his way to Florian's. He'd had lunch with Paola and the kids; by mutual agreement they had ignored last night's conversation in favour of trying to arrive at a general decision about where to go for a vacation that summer. 'Assuming your boss doesn't make you stay in the city to keep an eye out for pickpockets,' Chiara had observed, warning Brunetti that he was perhaps too open with his comments about his job.

'More likely it'll be boat licences and speeding on the Canal Grande,' Paola had suggested as he got to his feet. He leaned down to kiss the top of her head. 'I'll call if I'm going to be late,' he told her.

Though they had all talked about it, they had – as was ever the case – failed to agree where to spend their vacation. Paola didn't much care where they went, so long as she could loll around all day, reading, then go out to dinner in the evening. The children were content if they had a beach and could go swimming all day. Brunetti wanted the chance to walk long distances surrounded by mountains, come back in the afternoon and fall asleep over a book. Trouble lay ahead, he feared. Terrible thing, giving children the vote.

He came into the Piazza from the Merceria and cut across it in a diagonal that took him towards Florian's. He paused in the centre of the Piazza and turned to look at the façade of the Basilica. How absurd it was, how excessive, a building thrown together from bits and pieces of loot from Byzantium. What men in their right minds could have designed what he was looking at: the doors, the domes, the light glinting off golden tiles? Hoping to break the building's spell, he took his phone and dialled Signorina Elettra's number, struck by the oddness of making a phone call while looking at copies of the horses pillaged from Constantinople almost a thousand years before. Signorina Elettra, who had not appeared in the office that morning, did not answer, leaving him to meet Signora Marzi without the advantage to be had from information about her life and doings.

Inside the café he was struck, as he always was, by the elegant dilapidation of the place. The tablecloths were spotless; the waiters gleamed in white jackets and provided quick and friendly service. But the paint on the walls was faded and chipped, streaked with the marks from the backs of the chairs that had rubbed against them for decades. The velvet on the settees, smoothed by generations of tourists, reminded him of the bald patches on his children's long-abandoned teddy bears.

He told the waiter he was expecting a female guest and said she would ask for him by name. He went into the first room on the left and said he'd order when his companion arrived, then returned to the front door and selected that day's *Gazzettino* from the newspapers available for guests.

The story of Franchini's murder was at the bottom right of the front page of the second section and said only that he had been found dead 'in mysterious circumstances' and that the police were conducting an investigation. The victim's name and age were given correctly, and it was reported that he had formerly been a priest and had worked at a school in Vicenza. Brunetti wondered how they had learned all of this so quickly, which member of the police had spoken to them, and with what authority.

'Signor Brunetti?' a woman's voice asked.

He set the paper on the next table and got to his feet. 'Signora Marzi?' he asked, extending his hand.

She was tall, almost as tall as he, her hair a bit too blonde and her makeup more heavily applied than the hour warranted. Her eyes were so dark as almost to be black and were lined with mascara above and below. Her eyebrows had been plucked thin, then returned to their natural width by a black pencil that created the inverted 'V' so often seen in the eyebrows of cartoon characters.

Her nose was short and turned up at the end: two faint creases began under it and ran vertically to the top of her mouth. She could be anywhere in her forties; the years would increase or decrease depending on lighting and makeup, and probably on her mood. In either case, she was a woman most men would find attractive.

'Please,' he said, motioning her to the padded bench to his left and pulling out the table so she could slip behind it. She sat, rose for a moment to smooth out her skirt, and sat again. On a man, the double-breasted jacket of the dark grey suit she wore would have been traditional, almost boring: on a woman, especially one with hair as short as hers, it was faintly provocative. There was no disguising the quality of the fabric or the cut of the suit. Under it, she wore a round-necked black sweater and a single strand of pearls. This was not a woman who bought her clothing in Coin. She placed her handbag on the empty space to her right and looked out the window into the Piazza. Lowering her eyes, she studied the objects on the table as if she had never before seen a menu or an envelope containing sugar.

Brunetti caught the waiter's eye. When he came to the table, Brunetti said, '*Un macchiatone.*' The waiter turned his attention to the woman, who nodded. '*Due*,' Brunetti said.

When the waiter's footsteps had disappeared, she raised her eyes to Brunetti's and asked, 'What do you want to know?'

'I'd like you to tell me what happened that afternoon in Viale Garibaldi.'

'After half a year?' she asked. She gave him a steady look, licked at her lips, looked away.

Brunetti shrugged. 'Police work is like that. We settle something, and then something else happens and we have to go back and re-examine the original incident.'

'What's happened to make that necessary?'

She had paid no particular attention to the newspaper, so it was likely she had not read about Franchini's murder. He felt no obligation to mention it to her: let her talk as though the man were still alive.

'Nothing that affects you in any way, Signora,' he said, uncertain that this was true. 'I'd like you to tell me what happened.' He was careful not to ask about specific events or persons. He wanted her to believe he was interested only in the facts, as if he were simply double-checking the existing report.

She looked up and again met Brunetti's glance. 'I sometimes walk down the Viale to get the vaporetto. I like it because it's so wide and open, and there are trees.' Brunetti nodded, as would any Venetian. 'That morning, I saw someone I knew and stopped to talk to him. After I left, my ex-companion showed up and there was some sort of trouble between them. I wasn't there and didn't see what happened.' Then, a note of exasperation slipping into her voice, she said, 'I've already told the police all about this.' Before Brunetti could comment, the waiter returned and set their coffees and two small glasses of water in front of them. He moved the ceramic bowl with the sugar packets a centimetre closer to the woman, nodded to Brunetti, and left the room.

Brunetti poured sugar into his coffee and stirred it. He took a sip, replaced the cup. 'You said you knew the person?'

Instead of answering, she pulled the bowl closer. She took an envelope and tore it open slowly, poured it into her coffee and stirred it. Then she looked at Brunetti as if she had answered his question and were waiting for a different one.

'You said you knew the person?'

A trio of women, wearing hooded sweatshirts and running shoes, came in and moved chairs around until they all fitted at the table nearest the window. They spoke noisily in a language Brunetti did not recognize until one of them caught his glance and shushed the others to lower their voices.

He turned back to Signora Marzi, who said, 'He lived in the neighbourhood. People told me about him.' She folded her hands in her lap, her coffee apparently forgotten. Brunetti waited for her to say something else. Her right hand slid free of the other and began to finger the fabric of the tablecloth as though she were trying to decide if it were of a quality worth buying.

Brunetti finished his coffee, sat back and crossed his arms.

Looking up from the tablecloth, she said, 'I told you: I didn't see what happened.'

'How did you hear about it?' Brunetti asked.

She seemed genuinely surprised by the question. 'You called me.' Seeing his momentary confusion she explained: 'The police.' Making no attempt to disguise her exasperation, she went on, 'I'd already made a number of complaints about him, so they called me when they arrested him.' Then, truculently, 'Don't you people keep records?'

'The man was hurt,' he told her, ignoring her provocation.

'My ex-companion is a very strong man,' she said.

'You said you knew the man on the bench.'

'Why are you asking me all of this?'

'I don't understand why your companion would hit a man just because you spoke to him.'

Signora Marzi opened her purse and pulled out a cotton handkerchief covered with small pink roses. She used it to wipe at the corners of her mouth, even though she had yet to touch her coffee. The bright pink lip gloss she had been wearing when she came in had all but disappeared. She refolded the handkerchief and replaced it, opening the bag long enough for Brunetti to recognize the discreet Hermès logo on the inner lining.

'It's enough that I was talking to him,' she finally said. Again, she moistened her lips.

'Had you spoken to him before?'

'Someone told me he was a priest, so I thought I could trust him,' she offered by way of answer. She did not seem the type of woman who would trust a priest – or anyone, for that matter – but he nodded in understanding.

'Was it something you couldn't trust your friends with?' he asked.

She folded her hands in her lap again. 'I wanted to talk to someone about him.' Brunetti worked out the pronoun.

'I see. And did the priest help you?' he asked, failing to say that it seemed a strangely intimate subject to discuss with a man she barely knew. Standing in front of a park bench.

Her glance was quick and suspicious, as if she feared he knew far more than he was saying. She shook her head. 'No. He didn't help. He said he wasn't a priest any more and didn't have any advice to give me.'

She suddenly remembered her coffee and raised the cup to her lips but was surprised to find it cold. She set the cup back on the saucer.

'You'd spoken to him before, then?' Brunetti asked.

She greeted this question with a look of studied confusion but said nothing.

'The man on the bench,' Brunetti clarified. 'The one your ex-companion hit.' He waited a few beats before adding, 'He ended up in the hospital. Did you know that?'

She nodded. 'Yes.' Nothing more.

'Had you spoken to him before?'

She made a face to suggest irritation: lips pulled together in a straight line, eyes narrowed. Brunetti looked across at her calmly, like a man waiting for a cloud to pass so he could return to enjoying the sunshine.

'Maybe,' she conceded. Brunetti directed his gaze towards the window and the passing people in order to hide any involuntary sign of triumph. The waiter came in then and took the order of the three women, who were now speaking to one another in the sort of voices generally used in church. The waiter glanced at Brunetti, who shook his head. The waiter left.

'As a priest?' Brunetti inquired mildly, thinking how similar most interviews – although he always thought of them as interrogations – were. Once they started to talk and found that their interrogator believed them, people with things to hide felt safe enough to begin the minor lies that would end up trapping them. The only way to avoid this was to refuse to speak to the police about anything, without a lawyer, but few people had the sense to do this, believing themselves clever enough to talk their way out of most things.

Her voice grew more serious. 'When I met him, I didn't know he had been a priest.'

'Where did you meet him? How long ago?'

She should have been prepared for the question; perhaps she was. 'There. In the park. Some time last year. I used to go every now and then in the morning to sit in the sun. It's on the way to the boat, so if I leave early enough, I can stop there for half an hour on my way to work.' Brunetti said nothing, asked nothing.

'He used to sit there and read, and one day the only free seat was next to him, so I asked if I could sit there, and we started talking.'

'About his book?'

'No,' she said adamantly. 'I don't read.'

Brunetti nodded in understanding, as if this were the most normal thing in the world.

'We talked about things. Real things.' Take that, books, Brunetti thought. He was curious about how a woman of her age, apparently single, could have enough free time to spend her days sitting on a bench in Viale Garibaldi or, in fact, how she could be free at such short notice to come and talk to him.

She used the silence to drink her glass of water. All along, Brunetti had been attentive for any sign of her emotional response to the man on the bench – whose name they had not used – but there had been none. She had apparently been displeased when Brunetti asked about him, even more so when he persisted, but, for all the feeling she displayed at mention of the man, Brunetti might as well have been talking about the weather. In fact, the only emotion he could read, which filled the air around her as if with a low hum, was nervousness that her meeting with the man on the bench might be of interest to the police.

'You said you stopped there on your way to work, Signora. Could you tell me where you work?'

'Why do you want to know?' she asked, eyes sharp.

'Curiosity,' he said and smiled.

'I'm a secretary,' she said, then, seeing his response, added, 'though I'm really more what the English call an administrative assistant.' She gave it the pronunciation of someone who spoke the language with difficulty.

'Oh,' he said, sounding impressed by this career distinction: 'to a private person?'

'Yes, Marchese Piero Dolfin.'

The name conjured in Brunetti's memory the inside cover of the books in Franchini's apartment: 'P D' and the leaping dolphin on the two insignia.

As casually as he could make it sound, Brunetti said, 'He's a friend of my father-in-law.'

As if he had made a boast she had to better, Marzi said, 'Yes, it's a very old family, one of the oldest in the city.'

Indeed it was, Brunetti knew, although the branch of the family she was talking about had arrived from Genova at the time of Unification with an entirely different surname and had bought their title from the new King of Italy, deliberately choosing one of the oldest names in the city to attach it to.

As if unable to restrain his interest in so fascinating a job, Brunetti asked, 'What sorts of things do you do?'

While she answered, Brunetti considered the possibilities that might explain the presence of books from the Dolfin library in Franchini's bookshelf, though there could be only one. He turned back to what Signora Marzi was saying. '... founding members of the Rotary Club,' she concluded.

'That's certainly impressive,' Brunetti said, knowing that whatever she had said would surely have been intended to sound so. He smiled across at her, all the time asking himself, did she know or was she used?

Brunetti was suddenly aware that two other tables were now filled: at one sat a Japanese couple in late middle age, both of whom reminded him of the Contessa Morosini-Albani by sitting with at least ten centimetres between their backs and those of the chairs, and at another a pair of blonde teenaged girls, staring about with wide-eyed delight.

He retrieved the folded newspaper from the table beside him and passed it to Signora Marzi without comment. She was surprised but took it automatically, giving him a confused look.

Brunetti said nothing.

She lowered her head and glanced at the headlines. He waited. At a certain point, he saw her left hand contract, crumpling the paper and making a noise that could be heard at the tables near to them. When she finished, she set it on the table between them. She kept her eyes on the newspaper, refusing to look at him.

'What did you do for him?' Brunetti asked in a conversational voice.

'I don't know what you're talking about,' she said, a statement which had, by overuse, come to mean the opposite.

'Franchini,' Brunetti said, pointing at the newspaper. 'The man in the park, the man your companion sent to the hospital but who didn't press charges against him. What did you do for him?'

Brunetti was fishing. He'd linked different strands; although he didn't know how they were woven together, he knew they were joined. 'As you like,' he said and shrugged. But then he gave his best boyish smile and said, 'Il Marchese Dolfin will be delighted to have his Sophocles back, I'm sure.'

'His what?' she asked nervously.

'His copy of Sophocles. It's a Manutius. 1502. I'm sure he'll be relieved.' He gave that a moment to sink in, then asked, 'Has he noticed it's missing, do you know? Or the other one?'

Her voice was dull when she said, 'I don't know what you're talking about.' This time, he believed her.

'Books from his library. Rare books. That's why I think he'll be pleased to have them back.' Then, as if the thought had just come to him, he smiled again and said, 'And it's because of you he'll get them back, isn't it?' He stopped himself from leaning forward and patting her arm in congratulation, but he did nod his head in approval. 'Just think, if you hadn't told me you worked for Marchese Dolfin, I would never have realized that the books were his.'

He suspected he might be overplaying his hand, but she had irritated him with her dogged refusal to answer his questions, so he wanted at least to enjoy her discomfiture, base as he knew his desire to be. He met her glance, all smiles gone now.

'Are they valuable?'

'Very,' he answered.

'How much are they worth?'

'I have no idea. Ten thousand Euros, perhaps. Fifteen?' Her mouth fell open, and Brunetti added, 'Perhaps more.'

She astonished him by putting her elbows on the table and burying her face in her hands. He heard her moan. It struck him that he had, in the past, only read about this and had never actually heard anyone do it. It was ugly, a noise that would bring people to her aid, should they hear her and not know what was wrong. Even he, who had not warmed to her, felt an atavistic desire to help or comfort her.

Instead, he said, 'Of course, the Marchese will want to know how the books ended up in Franchini's possession, but that's perhaps explained by the fact that you know him, and have known him for some time. I hope he's not so narrow-minded, the Marchese, that he would hold it against you that your ex-companion knew the man in whose house the missing books were found. But you thought he was a priest, didn't you, not a thief?' He stopped himself then, not liking his tone, nor the fact that the noise she was making, though diminished, could still be heard. Nor did he like the fact that people at the two tables nearest them had turned to stare, as though they held him responsible for her moaning. Which, he admitted, he was.

She pulled her hands from her face, said, 'Outside,' got to her feet and pushed past him towards the front door of the café.

18

He left twenty Euros on the table to be sure. After all, Florian's was Florian's, and the last thing he wanted now was to be called back for not paying his bill. Outside, he stood on the steps and looked over the Piazza, hoping she had not been absorbed into the crowds.

And there she was, standing beside one of the tables at the edge of the serving space in front of the café, holding her handbag, which gaped open. Two men of about his age walked by, giving her appreciative glances. One of them stopped to speak to her, but she shook her head and moved away from them. The men continued on their way, though the one who had spoken to her turned to watch her as she walked away.

Brunetti followed her for a moment and then quickened his pace to reach her side. 'Signora Marzi,' he said, 'are you all right?'

She turned to face him, her glance level. She grasped her handbag and zipped it closed. 'He'll fire me if he finds out. You know that, don't you?' she demanded.

'It depends on what he finds out,' Brunetti answered.

'If you found the books, it means Franchini was in his apartment.' When Brunetti failed to confirm this, she demanded, 'How else could he take them?'

'With your help?' he asked.

'What?' she asked, missing a step; she came down heavily on her left foot and lurched into his side. She pulled away from him as though he'd put his hands upon her. 'Help him? Him? *Quello sporco ladro?*' she demanded, her face suffused with blood, saliva spitting as she said '*sporco*'. She had just read of the man's death, yet she called him a dirty thief.

'When did he steal them?' he asked.

She turned and started to walk away from him, heading for the far end of the Piazza. He followed her for some time, then stepped past a man and woman walking arm in arm to move up beside her. Matching his steps to hers, Brunetti said, 'Signora, I'm interested in his murder, not in stolen books.' This was not strictly true, but murder had trumped theft; he was interested in the more serious crime and would bargain away any interest in theft if it got him closer to understanding or solving the murder.

'I don't care about the books, Signora. If it will help you, I'll give you back the books Franchini took from the Marchese.'

That stopped her. She turned to him and demanded, 'In return for what?'

'Tell me what you know about Franchini and how he got the books, and you can have them.'

'But I must give them back to him?' she asked, voice high and tight, trying to provoke him into making that condition.

'The books are of no value to me, Signora. You're free to do whatever you want with them.'

Both her face and her voice softened. 'He's been good to me. He gave me this job and he trusts me. Of course I'll give them back.'

Suddenly Brunetti was conscious of how crowded the place was. There were people everywhere, hundreds of them – more than that: walking, standing, taking photos, making videos, posing with pigeons on their shoulders, tossing corn to the birds, looking into windows, pausing to talk to the person next to them. He looked around the Piazza and saw a multi-coloured sea of them, their noise like the disjointed slaps of choppy surf. He tried to think of somewhere to go to escape them, but he failed absolutely. Nowhere within a radius of two bridges, five minutes' walk, could he recall a quiet place. They would have to go into a bar or a shop or a church to wipe out the sight and sound of them.

'What's wrong?' she asked.

There was nothing he could tell her. She was Venetian: he knew that from having listened to her. 'Where are you going?' he asked.

'To work,' she said.

He had no idea where that might be, but still he asked, 'May I come along with you? We can talk.'

As if waking from a deep sleep, she looked around and saw the people, heard the low murmur. 'Yes,' she said. 'This way.' She turned towards XXII Marzo and walked quickly away from the Piazza. As they approached the bridge, the street widened and the crowds had room to spread out.

Just before the bridge, she said, 'I was involved with Aldo for a few months before that time in the park. He had been a friend of Roberto's for a long time.' Then, to be sure Brunetti understood, she said, 'My ex-companion.'

Brunetti nodded, and she started up the bridge. She stopped at the top and turned to look towards the Grand Canal. She folded her arms, one hand holding the bag. 'I think Roberto sold him things.'

'What sort of things?'

'Things he bought from people.'

'Stolen things?' Brunetti asked to save time.

'I think so.'

She knew so, or she wouldn't have mentioned it, but Brunetti said nothing. She went on. 'Some of them were books. I saw them a few times, when we were still living together and Aldo'd come to get the things Roberto sold to him.' And she didn't call the police,

Brunetti said to himself, but then he told that same self to shut up because most people wouldn't call them, either.

'Old books?' he asked, but only to make sure.

'Yes. He used to come to our apartment. He was always polite with me, even if he came when Roberto wasn't there. So it . . . so it just started. Roberto had to go to Cremona for a few days once, and . . . well, Aldo was always so nice to me.' Her eyes turned away from his and back to the canal and she said, 'In the beginning.'

'What happened?'

As if addressing her words to the water, she said, 'After Roberto came back and after it . . . happened, I suppose I was different with Aldo or when he was around, and Roberto saw it. That's when the trouble started.'

'Trouble?'

'Threats,' she said and looked at Brunetti again. 'But only to me. It was like Aldo had nothing to do with it. Once Roberto showed me a gun and said he'd use it if I ever talked to another man. That's when I went to the police. My sister was there when he said it, so there was a witness, thank God. I moved out. I left everything and moved out. The Marchese – I had just started to work for him – he had his lawyer help me, and that's how I got the order against Roberto.'

'And the books?' Brunetti asked. 'How did Franchini manage to steal them?'

She glanced down at the gondolieri sitting on

benches along the embankment, occasionally jumping up to welcome the tourists who came to talk to them or bargain for prices. As if anyone could out-bargain a gondoliere, Brunetti thought.

She cleared her throat a few times but then, he thought, forced herself to look at him as she said, 'The Marchese let me stay in a small guest apartment in the *palazzo* while I looked for something bigger.' He watched her fight against the temptation of silence, and then she said, 'Aldo sometimes came there with me.' Her voice was barely audible above the slap of footsteps on the bridge and the loud voices of the gondolieri. 'And once when we were there, he went into the other part of the *palazzo* when I was . . . asleep.' She backed away from the railing and stood up straight. 'That's when I knew what he wanted.'

'Had he done this before?' Brunetti asked.

Again, he watched her struggle. 'He must have,' she said at last.

'What did you do?'

'The next time he called me, I told him it was over.'

'And?'

She looked away before she answered this question. 'He laughed and said he was relieved.' Brunetti had always admired courage: hearing her say this in a steady voice, his estimation of her rose.

'Why did you talk to him in the park?'

'It was the first time I'd seen him since the phone call. I was surprised to see him there, so I stopped and asked him what he wanted, and he said he didn't want anything, that he was just sitting there, reading. That's what Roberto saw, the two of us talking, and when I left, he went and threatened him. And that's when it happened.'

'I see,' Brunetti said. 'Did you ever go to his home?'

'No. I didn't know he lived in Castello until I read it. Just now.' She waved back towards the Piazza, and Florian's, and the newspaper.

She began to walk down the bridge, Brunetti beside her, slipping eel-like through the streams. She turned right at the carpet shop, heading towards La Fenice, passed in front of the theatre, and continued on past the Ateneo Veneto. On the far side of the next bridge she stopped and opened her handbag. She pulled out a set of keys. 'It's down here,' she said, making it clear that he was to come no farther.

As if they had been talking all along and this was just another question in their conversation, he said, 'Did you ever get the sense that he was buying things from other people, not only from Roberto?'

Franchini had sat in the same room as Nickerson for weeks, had certainly had the opportunity to observe his behaviour. 'My brother was a thief and a blackmailer, a liar and a fraud.' Like a favourite bar of music, the words sounded in his mind.

She ran the keys through her fingers as if they were a metal rosary. Finally she said, 'His only interest in other people was finding their weak spot and using it to get what he wanted from them.' She let the keys jangle in her hand, then added, 'But I think he'd buy from other people; yes.'

Brunetti studied the houses on the other side of the canal. Her voice was replaced by the continued click of the keys against one another and then by the footsteps of people coming down the *calle* and crossing the bridge.

'I remember,' she said, 'one time, when Roberto showed him a book, he said he already had a copy but he'd take it anyway.'

'Do you remember what the book was?'

'No. They all looked the same to me: old, with leather covers. I don't know why anyone would want them.'

Even before Brunetti could decide not to try to explain, she added, 'But if he could sell them for a lot of money, then they're worth something, aren't they?'

He nodded, gave her his card and asked her to call him on his *telefonino* if she remembered anything else.

He was surprised that she offered him her hand and even more surprised that he was not unpleased to shake it.

19

He backtracked and took the Number One from Santa Maria del Giglio to save time as well as to avoid the crowds, though the vaporetto, at this hour, was perhaps not the better choice. The disembarking and embarking at the few stops he had to pass seemed to take for ever, with crowds blocking the exit, both from the boat and from the landing. After a six-minute delay – he timed it – at Vallaresso, he was ready to commandeer the boat or dial Foa's number and tell him to come and rescue him. He calmed himself for the rest of the ride with the scene of Foa's pulling up beside the moving vaporetto – much in the way he had picked them up at the Punta della Dogana – and himself leaping from one to the other while the remaining passengers viewed the event with a mixture of astonishment and envy.

He pushed this scenario from his mind and concentrated on what Signora Marzi had told him: a man apparently without a conscience, who would not only buy stolen books but, if the opportunity arose, also steal them himself. Yet they had found only seventeen volumes in his apartment, hardly the hoard of a major fence and thief. They had found no diary, nor an address book – not even a computer – only the simplest uncharged *telefonino* that had not a single number programmed into it and had not made or received a call in more than three months.

When he reached the Questura, he stopped in the officers' squad room, but neither Vianello nor Pucetti was there. He went to Signorina Elettra's office, where he found her in conversation with Commissario Claudia Griffoni, Signorina Elettra at her desk and Griffoni leaning against the windowsill, the place Brunetti had come to consider, over the years, as his. They stopped when he came in, and he said, before thinking, 'I don't want to interrupt,' realizing, as soon as the words were out, how much he sounded like a jealous husband.

Claudia laughed and said, 'All you've interrupted is a discussion of a way to access the files of the Department of Foreign Affairs.' The memory of her saying this, and so lightly, and the amusement her remark caused Signorina Elettra, would no doubt pull him out of a sound sleep, at some future time, when the whole lot of them were under investigation by the Security Services for the unauthorized pillaging – he thought he should use the proper word – these two women, their friendship so long in forming, were now capable of committing. Pucetti and Vianello, he feared, had also been corrupted by them, sucked into a cyber-gyre that could lead – or so he feared in his darkest moments – to ineluctable ruin.

'For what purpose?' he asked, calmly.

'There's a rumour going around,' Signorina Elettra said, not supplying either the source or scope of that rumour, 'that someone in the Department has managed to make a copy of the Mafia–Stato conversations. We thought it would be interesting to listen to them.'

The Romans, he knew, honoured the goddess Fama, she of the thousand-windowed house of reverberating bronze, she who heard and repeated everything, first in whispers, then in a booming voice. Surely she would be interested in repeating the telephone conversations of politicians, recorded decades ago, in which they discussed seriously the possibility of making a non-aggression pact with the Mafia. True or not? Fact or fiction? The highest court had ruled that the tapes of those purported conversations be destroyed, but Rumour declared they had been copied before that could be done.

Brunetti remembered a time when he had cared about things like this, felt indignation and rage that such things could happen, even that people could believe that they could happen. And now he listened and nodded, neither believing nor disbelieving, wanting only to get on with his work and then go home and be with his family and read the literary record left by the people to whom Rumour was indeed a goddess.

'May I help you, Commissario?' Signorina Elettra asked.

Griffoni moved away from the windowsill, but Brunetti held up a hand to stop her from leaving. He turned to Signorina Elettra. 'It's about Signora Marzi,' he said.

He saw from her look that she had found nothing and so was prepared when she said, 'I have birth certificate, school reports, health records, certificate of residence, job history, bank statements, tax returns, but there's nothing in any way unusual. She's never been arrested, was once questioned as a possible witness – when Franchini was assaulted – but there was nothing she could say because she wasn't present when it happened. She also had an injunction served against her former companion, who had threatened her in the presence of a witness.'

Brunetti was not surprised. She had spent time living with a petty criminal, but that did not make her one, and she had certainly shown loyalty and gratitude to her employer. Even though he recognized these things, Brunetti could not erase her bland indifference to her own ignorance.

Changing the subject, he asked, 'Anything from Rizzardi?'

Signorina Elettra shook her head. 'It's still early,' she said, reminding him that only a day had passed since Franchini had been discovered.

'And Contessa Morosini-Albani's donation to the library?'

Signorina Elettra nodded. 'The gift was made in honour of her late husband and at the time was said to be worth several hundred thousand Euros,' she said, and then added, with a note of disappointment, 'I haven't had time to verify the value of the individual volumes, so that's the only amount I can provide.'

After a pause, she added, 'I've spoken to people at some of the other libraries, and they all insist that they have systems in place that will prevent theft.' Brunetti glanced at Griffoni, who raised her eyebrows but said nothing.

'I sent them copies of Nickerson's passport photo and letter of recommendation and suggested they see if he had done research in their libraries.'

'Had he?' Brunetti asked.

'No one seemed to know. But all of them said they'd check their records for his name.'

'And if he used a different name?' Griffoni broke in to ask. 'What records would they check?'

'Is one of their systems a central record of people who have stolen from other libraries?' Brunetti asked.

Signorina Elettra's only answer was an angry snort.

He turned to Griffoni and said, 'You want to come

down to Castello and help take another look at his apartment?'

She smiled. 'Let me go and get my jacket.'

On the way, she made it clear that she was familiar with the facts of the case; she even knew about Signora Marzi and Roberto Durà. Brunetti told her about his meeting with Marzi and his certainty that Franchini had been in the business of stealing books as well as buying stolen copies.

Griffoni seemed aware of the fascination rare books exercised over many people. When he asked about this, she explained that she had once had a *fidanzato* who was doing research on musical manuscripts in the Girolamini. 'He was sure the lost manuscript of Monteverdi's *Arianna* is there,' she said.

Seeing his confusion, she went on, 'It was performed in his lifetime, and there are copies of the libretto, but the music's lost, except for her Lament.' Seeing that she had captured his interest, she went on, 'From what I understood when he talked about it, it's the Loch Ness Monster of musicology: the manuscript was sighted ages ago, and people believe it's still around.'

'Were you ever in the Girolamini?'

She stopped, as if unable to walk and talk about this at the same time. 'Yes, and it was paradise. There are more than a hundred thousand volumes, hundreds of incunabula. My friend was there for the musical manuscripts, but I spent two days looking at the books on the history of Naples: incredible things.'

'It's closed now, isn't it?' Brunetti asked.

'The Carabinieri put seals on everything when they went in.' She started walking again. 'It would make a stone weep. They looted the place.'

'It makes what happened at the Merula seem like petty theft,' Brunetti said.

Her voice grew savage, and she said, 'I'd cut their hands off.'

'Excuse me?'

'People who steal books or deface paintings or vandalize things. I'd cut their hands off.'

'You're speaking metaphorically, I hope,' he said, wondering what they taught children in schools in Naples these days.

'Of course I'm speaking metaphorically. I'd seize everything they own until they've paid for what they've destroyed or stolen, or I'd keep them in jail until they've paid enough.'

'And if they couldn't pay?' he asked.

She stopped abruptly to face him and said, 'Oh, stop being so literal, Guido: you know I don't mean it. But it makes me wild, something like this. We gave the world so much beauty, and then to see it stolen or destroyed . . . and lost.' She let her voice trail away, and they resumed walking; then they were crossing the bridge into the *campo*, and Franchini's house came into view.

Brunetti let them in with the keys he had kept. As they climbed the steps, Griffoni asked, 'Do we know what we're looking for?'

Brunetti stopped in front of the door to the apartment and put the key in the lock. 'If I tell you that we're looking for anything that might be suspicious, will you promise not to laugh?'

'I can't count the places I've searched for "anything that might be suspicious".'

'Ever find anything?'

'I once found twenty kilos of cocaine.'

'Where?'

'In a private kindergarten outside of Naples. The woman who ran it was the cousin of the local boss. There was a fire in the kitchen, and the firemen found it there, hidden in a cupboard. They called us.'

'What happened?'

'Same as always. Nothing.'

'What?'

'We seized the drugs, but they disappeared the same night from the basement of the Questura. So there was no evidence to produce against her, and everyone in the kitchen swore it was flour.'

He opened the door and held it for her. 'Are you making this up?'

'No. I wish I were.'

He followed her inside and switched on the lights. 'All right,' he said. 'Anything that might be suspicious.'

An hour later, they had failed to find anything that might be suspicious. Before they entered, Brunetti had warned her about the blood on the walls and floor, and Griffoni told him she'd seen her first Mafia victim when she was six, his body lying in the street across from her school.

Franchini possessed an expensive wardrobe: hand-made shirts, five cashmere jackets, and countless pairs of very expensive shoes. There was nothing hidden under the bed or the mattress, and the top shelves of the wardrobe held only bed linen and towels. The toilet cistern contained only water, and the medicine cabinet aspirin and toothpaste. In a desk in the study, Brunetti found bank statements which showed that Franchini received a pension of 659 Euros a month.

Disgruntled at having been deprived of a quick reward for his intuition, he looked inattentively at the other papers in Franchini's desk, receipts for his water, electric, gas and garbage bills. Brunetti's mind wandered, as it sometimes did, to books he had read, and he found himself remembering a short story about a detective sent to search a suspect's home for an important letter. Though he hunted everywhere, he found no trace of the letter, not, that is, until he noticed the file of letters in open view in the room. And there it was, a letter hidden among other papers.

He set the folder with Franchini's pension records on the desk and went over to the bookcase. He knelt down – a burglar having once told him that people always try to hide things from thieves in places near the floor – and pulled out a modern hardback edition of Machiavelli's *Mandragola*. He fanned through the pages, then opened it to the middle and read a few lines, closed it and set it on the floor. Next to it were his *Discourses on Livy*, a book Brunetti had always preferred to *The Prince*. As he opened it to read a few paragraphs, he felt something slip through his fingers. His right hand caught it halfway and helped to free it, like a knife from a sheath. He saw the age-dulled brown morocco binding, and he understood.

'Claudia,' he called, getting to his feet. After a moment she emerged from the kitchen, where she had been going through the cabinets. In her right hand she held a potato peeler: when she saw him staring at it, she said, 'It can be a screwdriver. I'm trying to remove the baseboard.'

'I think that can wait,' he said, holding up the cover and the book he had discovered inside it. 'Look what I've found.'

Griffoni was wearing plastic gloves, but Brunetti had forgotten to put his back on. He placed the book on the floor and took his gloves from his pocket. He picked it up again and studied the binding. 'It's in Hebrew,' he said, holding the book out to her. She opened it and together they studied the double-columned page, the five illuminated letters at the top of the page on the right. She closed it, but they knew nothing more about the text than they had when she opened it. 'Where was it?' she asked.

'Hidden in a book,' he said, retrieving the empty cover and fitting the Hebrew text inside it.

'Oh, the clever devil,' she said, unable to disguise her admiration.

She looked at the backs of the books still on the shelves. 'All of them?' she asked, assessing the job in front of them.

'It's finally something that might be suspicious,' Brunetti said, 'so it's the least we can do.' He reached for another book.

An hour later, they had examined all of the books in the case and found thirty-seven more ancient texts hidden within modern volumes, so many that Brunetti had to call Foa and ask him to come and get them. Along the wall to their left they had discarded stacks of books, cascades of books, mounds of books, some intact and some the gutted volumes that Franchini had used as camouflage.

Along with the books he had found – hidden inside a first edition of Marx's *Das Kapital* – records from a private bank in Lugano and one in Luxembourg containing a joint total of 1.3 million Euros on deposit. The Lugano account was more than twelve years old, the one in Luxembourg only three. Most deposits had been in cash, though there were a number of bank transfers; all withdrawals had been in cash. Since this was now an investigation of murder, and not just theft, the banks could be forced to divulge the source of those transfers. It also occurred to Brunetti that the Art Theft people might be interested in the numbers of the accounts from which the money had been sent.

Brunetti had thought to tell Foa to bring along two cardboard boxes, and when he rang the bell from downstairs, Brunetti buzzed him in. By that time Brunetti and Griffoni had carried all of the books into the hallway and piled them on a table near the door. When Foa arrived, Brunetti asked the gloveless pilot to hold the boxes, one after the other, while he and Griffoni packed the books.

In the hallway, Brunetti locked the door, then took one of the boxes from Foa and started down the stairs.

'What about the books we left?' Griffoni asked.

Brunetti shrugged. Someone would have to re-shelve them, probably Franchini's brother if he decided to keep the house. His attention was devoted to the bank records and trying to think of someone he could ask about the value of the books they had just found. The bank deposits, in easily expressed numbers, would create no confusion of interpretation.

When they emerged from Franchini's house, Brunetti was surprised to find that darkness had fallen on the *campo*. He looked at his watch and saw that it was after nine: they'd been inside for more than three hours, and he was both exhausted and, now that he thought about it, very hungry. But things were moving, finally, and he dismissed tiredness and hunger.

As they turned on to the canal that led to the Questura, Brunetti considered the people who might be of help to him. The man who came to mind lived in Rome now, and Brunetti had not spoken to him for years, but Sella had been engaged to a cousin of Brunetti's a decade ago, and the two men had remained in occasional contact since then. 'Why not?' he said out loud.

'Excuse me?' Griffoni called above the noise of the motor.

'Someone I know,' Brunetti answered, stepping closer to her. 'He can tell us what the books are worth.' They had already cost, he reflected, Franchini's life, but he saw no reason to say that. Even before they pulled up to the Questura, he had dialled Sella's number.

Disregarding the usual formalities, Brunetti asked if there were any way Sella could give him an idea of the market value of a number of books.

'Guido,' Sella said into the sudden silence left when Foa cut the engine, 'I have no idea what you're calling me for at this hour, and I also don't know what century you think you're living in.'

'What?' Brunetti asked, fearing that the sound of the motor had blocked out something Sella had said.

'Ever hear of the internet?'

'What do you mean?'

'You can find almost everything there.' Brunetti's silence must have reminded Sella of the man he was speaking to because, after some time, he said, 'If you'll send me the publication information, Guido, I'll find out for you.' Before Brunetti could thank him, Sella asked, referring to his wife, 'You know Regina's a psychologist?'

Brunetti had forgotten, but he said, 'Yes, I know. Why do you ask?'

'In her language, this is referred to as learned help-lessness,' Sella said, then asked, 'Have you seen these books you're talking about?'

Ignoring the first remark, Brunetti answered, 'Some of them.' The thud of the boat against the dock made him dance around a bit, but he kept his hand on the phone and his mind on the conversation.

'What sort of shape do they seem to be in?' Sella asked.

'The ones I looked at seemed fine, but I'm not an expert.'

'Well,' Sella said with a laugh, 'I am. So send me a list of everything that's written on the title pages and tell me if something looks in bad condition to you.' He paused for a long time before saying, 'Am I correct in assuming these are stolen books?'

'Yes.'

'Then they'll be in good shape.'

'Why are you so sure of that?'

'No one would go to the trouble of stealing a book that wasn't.'

It took them more than an hour to add the thirty-eight titles and publication information to the list that already contained the other books. Griffoni sat at the computer and Brunetti opened the books one by one and read out the information on the title pages about author, date, and place of publication. As Sella had foretold, all the books were in very good condition as far as Brunetti could judge. The work went even more slowly because, when a book had the stamp of a library or collection, Griffoni copied that information to a second list, one that was not meant for Sella.

Twenty-one of the books were from libraries, and three had indications that they were from private collections; two of these had the dolphin insignia and the letters P D. Brunetti suspected that the remaining fourteen had been taken from other collections, either by Franchini or by the persons who had sold him the books. The same was true of those with the library seals. As to a client list, Franchini probably kept that in his head, though his bank statements might provide names.

If Sella was half as good as he had always told Brunetti he was, he should be able to discover their value quickly.

When the lists were done and the first one sent to Sella, Griffoni swivelled away from the screen to face Brunetti. 'What now?' she asked.

'We see what's come in and then we both go home,' Brunetti said, nodding in the direction of the computer. They exchanged places. The first email was from Rizzardi, who confirmed that three blows from a thick and heavy object, most likely a shoe or boot, had shattered the victim's skull and broken his jaw. The blow to the jaw, which would not have been fatal, was the source of the heavy bleeding. The blows to the back of the head had fractured the man's skull and pounded his brain to such a degree that death was inevitable. There were other signs of violence: bruises on his upper arms and another on his right shoulder, where he had hit the wall or floor. A splinter from the parquet was lodged in the palm of his right hand.

He might have survived minutes, though very few, Rizzardi wrote, after the kicks to the back of his head, although his motor skills might still have got him to his feet and let him take a few steps in an instinctive attempt to escape. But the blows had initiated a process that could lead only to death as the brain shut down the various systems necessary to maintain life. Then, in the last sentences, and as if in response to a question from Brunetti, the pathologist added, 'It is unlikely that he suffered anything other than the immediate pain of the blows. His brain had received sufficient damage to render him unaware of what was happening to him.'

So he would have been spared the knowledge that he was injured or dying. But how could Rizzardi be so sure of this? And why did he think it important that Brunetti be told?

There was an email from Bocchese stating that the three right-side footprints found in the room had been made by a size forty-three boot with a thick waffle sole. He did not speculate on the reason for the prints' disappearance, though he did add that it had rained heavily the night after the murder, thus eliminating any chance of finding traces of blood in the *campo* in front of the house.

The technician also reported on the fingerprints, stating that his laboratory had had time only to check those pages facing the pages that had been sliced from the books from the Biblioteca Merula. The finger-prints of the dead man had not been present on any of those books, though all of them did bear prints from the same unknown person, as well as many other unidentifiable prints. Dottoressa Fabbiani's prints and those of the guard, whom Bocchese referred to as Pietro Sartorio, appeared on the binding of the Cortés as well as on some of the facing pages.

In a third paragraph, he wrote that the only blood found in the apartment was the victim's. They had found traces of other DNA material on his clothing, but that information was useless until a suspect was arrested and the samples could be matched. Or not.

Brunetti stepped aside to let Griffoni read both emails. 'What do you make of it?' he asked.

'So much violence,' she said, and then, in a heavy voice, 'Kicking. Whoever did it lost control.' Then she added, 'No one *plans* to do something like this.'

Brunetti agreed with her. This was rage or madness.

He looked at his watch and saw that it was after midnight. 'I think we should go home,' he said, needing to be away from the thought of violence and madness. 'There'll be a pilot on night duty. We can go together. My place is on the way,' he added, though he had only a vague idea that she lived in Canareggio, over near the Misericordia. She nodded and they left the Questura together.

20

Brunetti went in early the next morning and was sitting on a chair outside Bocchese's laboratory, reading *Il Gazzettino*, when the technician came in at eight. The two boxes of books were on the floor beside his chair. 'Can you check the bindings, just the bindings?' Brunetti said in greeting.

'For fingerprints?' Bocchese asked, opening the door with his key.

Brunetti bent down and picked up one of the boxes, followed the technician into the lab. 'Yes,' he said and went outside to bring in the other.

'You get any sleep last night?' the technician asked, flipping on the lights.

'Very little,' Brunetti answered as he set down the second box. 'Can you do it? This morning?'

'Will I have any peace if I don't?' Bocchese asked, removing his jacket and slipping on his white lab coat. He walked to his desk and tapped his computer into life.

'No,' Brunetti admitted.

'Don't bother me before noon,' Bocchese said, picking up the first box and carrying it to a table at the back of the room. 'Now go and get yourself another coffee and leave me alone.'

Nervous with lack of sleep and too much coffee, Brunetti could not wait to be summoned, but went down to Patta's office at eleven, by which time he thought his superior might have arrived, as indeed he had. Brunetti found him in the corridor that led to his office, talking to his assistant, Lieutenant Scarpa.

'Ah, Commissario,' Patta said. 'We were just talking about you.'

Brunetti nodded a greeting to them as he approached, choosing to ignore the Vice-Questore's remark. 'I've come to tell you what we've learned about the death of Aldo Franchini, Dottore,' he said with rigorous formality.

As he waited for Patta's response, Brunetti calculated the situation in terms of rank: Patta could say just about anything he chose to either one of them; Brunetti could be passively aggressive to Patta, actively so to Scarpa; while Scarpa was limited to deference and respect in his dealings with Patta and dared not exceed ironic disrespect with Brunetti. All three of them, however, treated Signorina Elettra with the maximum respect: Patta from what he probably didn't realize was fear, Brunetti from open admiration, and Scarpa from a mixture of active dislike and unacknowledged fear.

'What is that?' Patta asked in his brisk leader-of-men voice.

Scarpa, taller than Patta and the same height as Brunetti, glanced in his direction as though he were owed part of the explanation. He would occasionally display curiosity, the way a snake might every so often take an interest in the temperature.

'It would seem that he knew his killer. He left a book face down in his living room when he went to answer the door and returned to the room with the person who killed him.'

'How was he killed?' Patta asked, adding, 'I haven't had time to read the pathologist's report.' Just as he had not, Brunetti added to himself, had time to learn the pathologist's name in all these years.

'Dottor Rizzardi believes he was knocked or thrown to the floor and kicked in the head but that he still had sufficient strength to pull himself to his feet. He died of the blows to his head, probably within a short time of the attack.'

'And his killer?' Scarpa interrupted to ask, then turned to Patta and said, 'If you don't mind my asking, Vice-Questore.' If he had been wearing a hat with a plume, he would have removed it and bowed, sweeping it in a graceful arc.

Brunetti spoke directly to Patta. 'We have no information suggesting who he might be, Dottore. We have found evidence, however, that Franchini was involved in the theft of books from libraries and private homes, and that might help lead us to his killer.'

'He?' Scarpa asked. If voices had eyebrows, his would have been raised.

'He,' Brunetti said. 'Or a woman wearing size forty-three boots.'

'I beg your pardon.' This from Patta.

'There were three footprints from a size forty-three boot.'

'Three?' Scarpa asked, as though Brunetti had tried to tell a joke the Lieutenant had failed to understand or appreciate. Brunetti turned and looked at him until he looked away.

'Anything else?' Patta asked.

'No, Dottore.'

'What are you doing about all of this?' Patta asked in a cooler voice.

'I'm waiting for word from banks in Lugano and Luxembourg, to find out who transferred money to Franchini's account, probably in payment for stolen books. And I'm still waiting to see if Interpol has an identification for the man called Nickerson.'

'Who?' Patta asked.

'It's the name used by the man who stole the pages from the books in the Merula,' Brunetti said evenly, quite as if he believed this was the first time his superior would have had reason to hear this name. 'We've contacted the Art Theft police and Interpol, but we haven't had any response.'

Patta put on a long-suffering expression and sighed as though he, too, were familiar with the long delays of Interpol. 'I see, I see,' he said and turned away. 'Let me know when you learn anything.'

'Certainly, Vice-Questore,' Brunetti answered and, ignoring the Lieutenant, left them there.

He stopped in the officers' squad room on the way to his office and heard from Vianello that their hours of questioning in the neighbourhood had contributed nothing that might be of use. If the neighbours remembered Franchini, it was as a boy and then as a young priest: none of them had had contact with him since he had returned to live in the family apartment after his parents' death. No one Vianello and Pucetti had spoken to seemed to find his isolation strange in any way: they seemed to assume that his decision to leave the priesthood had somehow removed him from the purlieus of human contact.

No one could, or would, say anything about him, or had any memory of ever having seen him in the company of another person; everyone they talked to expressed astonishment at his murder.

Back in his office, Brunetti sat at his desk, thinking of Tertullian – not the one Saint Jerome said lived to extreme old age, but the one kicked to death in Castello.

He seemed to have had no close dealings with another person. A weekly phone call from his brother, even after he'd stolen part of his inheritance, and a woman he seduced so that he could steal books hardly counted. He wanted to rise in the world, and he did this by theft, seduction, and blackmail.

Brunetti's thoughts wandered to the other Tertullian and, prompted by curiosity, he turned on his computer and started to search for him there. Having found him, he looked for what he had said, or, at least, what was attributed to him. 'The entire fruit is already present in the seed.' 'Out of the frying pan into the fire.' So that's where that one came from. And then this: 'He who lives to benefit only himself confers on the world a benefit when he dies.' Oh, they were a savage bunch, those early Christians. And another: 'If you say you are a Christian when you are a dice player, you say what you are not, for you are a partner with the world.'

Under his breath, as he always did when a book said something that antagonized him, Brunetti responded, but the only thing he could think of to ask was, 'What's wrong with playing dice?'

Then it came back to him: Sartor had distanced himself from gambling by referring to it as *'roba da donne'*. Women's things. Why would Sartor be calculating odds on the sex of a woman's child if he had no interest in gambling? And why would his pocket be full of lottery slips? Would he lie about such a trivial thing and, if so, why? To save face with the police? With the *police*?

He looked at his watch and saw it was three minutes after noon. He took the phone and dialled Bocchese's number.

'You're turning into a nagging old woman, Guido,' the technician greeted him by saying.

'Those books – have you had a chance to check them?'

'Nagging, *impatient* old woman,' Bocchese amended.

'How many?'

'Wait a minute.' The sound grew muffled as Bocchese covered the mouthpiece with his hand and shouted to someone in the laboratory with him. He came back. 'Thirteen.'

'Are there prints from Sartor – not Sartorio – the guard?'

Again, the sound grew muffled and all he heard was the hum and thud of Bocchese's voice. He was back. 'Six.'

'Where?'

'On the covers.'

'Book people call them bindings,' Brunetti said, hoping he sounded like a nagging, impatient, fussy old woman. Then, in order to leave no doubt about that, he asked, 'Were they from the Merula?'

'Oh, for God's sake,' Bocchese said and set the phone down loudly. Brunetti could hear his footsteps as he stomped away from his desk. After a moment, they stomped back and Bocchese said, 'Yes. His prints were on the binding' – which word he pronounced with heavy emphasis – 'of all six books from the Merula.'

'Thanks,' Brunetti said, then asked, 'When will you be finished with them?'

Bocchese's sigh was theatrical. 'If you're interested only in *his* prints, I can tell you tomorrow morning.' Then, perhaps to save Brunetti the trouble of further nagging, he offered, 'If you promise not to call me again and ask about it, maybe by the end of the afternoon.'

'If I want to know about all of the prints?'

'Minimum two days.'

'I'll wait for your call,' Brunetti said and hung up.

The inconsistency between Sartor's dismissal of gambling as *'roba da donne'* and his apparent interest in it was so insignificant as to be nothing. Perhaps the lottery slips did belong to his wife, and perhaps his interest in his colleague's child was only innocent concern. But his fingerprints were on those books. Brunetti pulled out the phone book and opened to the Cs, hunting for the number of the *casinò*, a place that had been the subject of frequent investigations, although not for the last year or so. He dialled the main number, gave his name, and asked to be connected with the Director.

The call went through immediately and without question: Brunetti wondered if that was what Franchini meant by rising in the world.

'Ah, Dottor Brunetti,' he heard the Director say in his friendliest tones, 'how may I be of service?'

'Dottor Alvino,' Brunetti responded, honey in his voice, 'I hope things are fine there.'

'Ah,' came the drawn-out sigh, 'as well as can be.'

'Still losing money?' Brunetti asked, using his best bedside manner.

'Unfortunately, yes. No one can explain it.'

Brunetti could, but this was a friendly call, and so he said only, 'I'm sure things will change.'

'We can but trust in good fortune,' Dottor Alvino said, echoing the faith of his clients, and then, 'What can I do for you, Dottore?'

'I'd like to ask a favour.'

'A favour?'

'Yes, I'd like you to give me some information.'

'About what, if I might ask?'

'About a . . .' What was he to call those poor deluded saps? 'About a client of yours, or a possible client.'

'What sort of information?'

'I'd like to know how often he visits and whether he wins or loses, and how much.'

'You know we're required to register all guests,' Dottor Alvino said, pretending that Brunetti had not, over the years, become an expert in the laws governing the conduct of the *casinò*, as well as its less formal organizational practices. 'So of course we have the names of the people who come and the dates when they do. I'd be happy to give those to you.' Allowing a significant pause, the Director added, 'Is this in response to a request from a magistrate, by any chance?'

'Dottore, how astute of you to ask. There's need for

haste, you see, so I thought I'd come to you directly. Personally.'

'For a favour?'

'Yes. A favour.' It was so like what they did at the *casinò*: Brunetti was placing his chip on the table, offering it to the Director for him to pick it up and use at some future time.

'As to the second part of your question: you know we have no official record of that.' The Director, his tone made it clear, was a person familiar with poker and with upping the ante.

'Yes, I know there's no formal record of that information, Dottore, but I thought you might have a sort of informal list of special guests, perhaps those who come most frequently or who play for stakes higher than the average. Something like that.' How many of the croupiers he had questioned over the years had told him that?

'So this is the favour you mentioned, Dottore?'

'Yes, it is. I'd be more than grateful.'

'I hope so,' Alvino said in a normal voice, and then, 'What's his name?'

'Sartor, Piero.'

'One moment,' he said, and the phone clicked against a hard surface.

Minutes passed. Brunetti gazed from his window. Four swallows flew by from right to left. The Romans would have seen an omen there.

'Dottore?' he heard and harkened to the voice of the Oracle.

'Yes.'

'He's been here twenty-three times in the last year.' Brunetti waited: this was not the part of the question his favour would pay for. 'And he's lost something between thirty and fifty thousand Euros in that time.'

'I see,' Brunetti said. Then, as if he had no idea how it happened, he asked, 'How is it you know this amount, Dottore?'

'Our croupiers keep an eye on certain guests and let us know what it is they win or lose. In an approximate sense, you realize.'

'Of course, of course,' Brunetti agreed, stopping himself from saying how pleasant it must be for the Director to hear of a guest who lost so heavily. Though they all did in the end, didn't they, or why have a *casinò*? Opening the honey Jar again, he said, 'I can't tell you how grateful I am for your information, Dottore.'

'I'm always happy to be of service to any agency of the state, Dottore. I hope I've given proof of that.'

'You have, indeed. Amply,' Brunetti said, wondering if Alvino was going to say he hoped Brunetti would keep that in mind, should they ever meet again.

But he did not, and Brunetti liked him for that. All the Director said was, 'If I can ever be of service again, please don't hesitate to call, Dottor Brunetti.'

There followed the usual pleasantries, and then Brunetti set down his phone.

21

Brunetti thought of Griffoni: which would she think worse – that Sartor might be a killer or that he had stolen and sold as much as fifty thousand Euros' worth of rare books from the Merula and perhaps from other libraries and then gambled away this small part of the patrimony of Italy? He thought the first would be her final choice, but not before she overcame the temptation of the second.

His own response was more measured. He realized he had proof neither that Sartor had stolen the books nor that he had killed Franchini. You couldn't hang a man for prevarication, nor for fingerprints on a book. He thought of how blithely he had listened to Sartor's talk of his interest in the books Nickerson and the other researchers read. Brunetti ran his memory back to their first conversation and the charming sincerity of the unschooled man who affirmed his admiration for books. He had displayed the just and fitting modesty of the man of low station who could still aspire to things beyond him. He was not a guard: he was a reader.

Like a ripe pear, Brunetti had fallen into believing in the man Sartor presented himself to be.

His phone rang. 'Commissario,' Signorina Elettra said when he answered. 'Interpol has got back to me. Doctor Nickerson, the American scholar, is not a doctor, nor is he Nickerson, nor is he American, nor is he a scholar.'

'Italian?' Brunetti asked.

'One of Napoli's own: Filippo D'Alessio,' she said. 'Do you want me to send you their file?'

'Please.'

'It's on the way,' she said and was gone. He liked it that she had called him first to tell him what she had, like a child on the beach who wants to be praised for finding the lovely seashell before passing it proudly to you.

By the time he turned on his computer, the mail had arrived. Filippo D'Alessio had a long history of impersonation and theft, the first at the service of the second. He was fluent in German, Italian, English, French, and Greek and was now sought by the police of the countries where those languages were spoken.

He had been arrested in Italy twice for credit card theft and three times for postal fraud. He was also wanted in three countries for the theft of books and pages from books. The pattern was the same: he assumed an identity as a scholar and started his research, sometimes in a museum, but most often in a library. Josef Nicolai had served for Austria and Germany, and José Nicandro had worked in Spain. Joseph Nickerson was wanted by the police in New York and Urbana, and his cognates in Berlin and Madrid. No one knew what the Greek police wanted.

Interpol had sent his photo to some libraries; the librarians had sent it on to colleagues, many of whom had already registered the desolation left in the wake of the affable young scholar. Brunetti suspected that many libraries had still to discover the results of the research conducted by, say, Joseph Nicollet at the Bibliothèque Nationale or Jozef Something Else at the library of the University of Kraków.

To the Art Theft police, he was a professional who could be hired to steal specific volumes or pages to order. His family claimed to have lost touch with him, but recently his father, a retired shoemaker, had bought a six-room apartment in the centre of Naples: the money for it was sent to his bank from an 'aunt in the Cayman Islands'.

Brunetti finished reading the file and found himself, after the intense activity of the last few days, with nothing to do save wait for Bocchese's call. He pulled a piece of paper towards him and began to sketch out a possible scenario, putting 'Books' in a circle at the centre of the page and drawing a straight line to another circle, in which he wrote, 'Nickerson/D'Alessio', then going back to the first circle and connecting it to 'Franchini' and to 'Sartor'. Then, as possibility offered itself to him, he connected 'Nickerson/D'Alessio' and 'Franchini' and drew a question mark above the line.

What had occupied the ex-priest's mind over the years as he sat reading Saints Ambrose, Cyprian, and Jerome? He was already trafficking in books with the help of Durà and adding to the store of books he had probably acquired from libraries in Vicenza during the time he worked there as a priest. After all these years, he would have a client list, Brunetti was certain.

Three years of reading in the Merula would have given Franchini time to enlist Sartor, and so he could connect them with a double-headed arrow. But then Dottor Nickerson had arrived to start mining what Franchini had staked out as his claim. And then what? And then what?

Brunetti got up and went to stand at the window and contemplated the newly opened door of the church of San Lorenzo at the far end of the *campo* on the other side of the canal. The archaeological excavations had recently been resumed from one day to the next: one day the door to the church was closed, as it had been for decades; the next it was open. He watched people enter and emerge from the church, some of them wearing white overalls and yellow hard hats, others suits and ties.

He returned to his desk, his thoughts on the dead man. With Franchini lying unconscious or dead on the floor of his apartment, the killer had free access to the books, yet the books, their antiquity glaring at even the most ignorant glance, had not been touched. The killer had stopped only to remove his shoe.

How to dispose of a shoe? Would he be foolish enough to keep it? In the garbage, in the water?

He dialled Bocchese's number.

The technician picked up on the eighth ring and said, 'What is it now, Guido?'

'The blood that was on the floor, that the killer stepped in – could it be removed from his shoe?' He wondered if anyone ever called Bocchese to ask him when it was time to plant dahlias or whether he thought Juve was going to be league champion.

The answer was almost a minute in coming. 'There were traces of Franchini's blood in the sink in the kitchen,' the technician said.

'Fingerprints?'

'I would have told you that, wouldn't I, Guido?'

'Yes. Of course. Sorry. Could he get rid of the blood?'

'No. He could wash it off. But he couldn't get rid of it. They were waffle-soled boots: worst thing a killer could wear.' Bocchese paused, then added, 'If he watches television, he'd know that, so he'd try to get rid of them.'

'Thanks,' Brunetti said, 'for all your help.'

Bocchese made a noise, then said, 'You're keeping me from those books, Guido.' But then he laughed and was gone.

Brunetti decided that this conversation and these thoughts were not what he wanted on a fine spring day. He called home and asked Paola if she thought they could meet over on the Zattere and go for a walk and have lunch outside, on the *riva*.

'And the children?' she asked in that pro forma maternal voice he knew so well.

'Leave them lunch and a note and meet me at Nico's for a drink; then we can walk down to the end and eat.'

'What a wonderful idea,' she said. 'Though you're missing gnocchi with ragù.'

A man less versed in the ways of married life would have said they could order the same at the restaurant, but such a remark would lead only to trouble. 'Oh, I'm sorry to miss them.'

'I can cook half of them for the kids, and then you and I can have the rest for dinner,' she said.

'If we stuff ourselves with *moecche*, we won't be very hungry tonight,' he suggested, eager for the first soft-shelled crabs of the season.

'You?' she asked in her best false-innocent voice. 'Stuff?'

'Very funny,' he said, added that he'd leave immediately, and hung up.

*

Because he kept himself from mentioning his specu-
lations about the men who had met at the Biblioteca
Merula, lunch was a pleasant meal, during which
they agreed they would go to the seaside – though
not which seaside – that summer. They walked back
together as far as the Accademia *imbarcadero*, where
they got on their separate boats going in different
directions, Brunetti conscious of how unwilling he
was, ever and always, to see Paola move away from
him. Much as he chided himself for his unmanly
behaviour, he could never overcome the continual
fear that – in this most peaceful of cities – Paola
was somehow in peril the instant she was out of
his sight. It passed off as quickly as it came, but the
impulse never disappeared, just as he could never
bring himself to confess it to her.

They had lingered over coffee and idle chat, so it
was after four when he got back to his office. When
he entered, he saw a blue plastic folder on his desk.
Inside, as years of working with the technician had
told him it would be, was a copy of Bocchese's report,
left there with no explanation. It contained two lists:
the first contained all of the books examined, followed
by the names of the persons whose prints had been
detected on the bindings of those books.

Franchini's prints were present on all of them.
Sartor's were on all of the books taken from the
Merula; Dottoressa Fabbiani's were on three of them.

It might not persuade a judge, but it was more

than sufficient to send Brunetti back to his desk and to his original diagram. He darkened the circles around 'Franchini' and 'Sartor'. It was enough for him. He dialled Griffoni's number to ask her to come up. He wanted to see if it was enough for her.

22

It was. 'The Trojan Horse,' Griffoni said and smiled. 'He's inside, trusted. For God's sake, his job is to see that the books are safe. Who's going to be curious if they see him coming from the stacks with a book? Who's going to take a look in his bag when he goes home at night?'

'And Franchini?' Brunetti asked.

She said nothing for so long that he thought she had nothing to add, but then she said, 'We can't talk to him, but we can talk to Sartor.'

'Now?'

'It's still early enough to go and have a word with him.'

Brunetti thought he should call to see if the guard

was at the library and was glad he had when he learned that Sartor's wife had called two days before to say he was very sick and would not be in until he felt better.

So as not to call special attention to their interest in Sartor, Brunetti told the person he thought was the young man who had been at the front desk that they wanted to ask Piero – Brunetti was careful to use Sartor's first name and say it in a friendly manner – if he could remember any other conversations he might have had with Nickerson but that it could easily wait until the following week.

When the young man asked if there had been any progress or if they thought there was any hope of getting the books back, Brunetti said, making himself sound sad, that he thought it unlikely. If for any reason the young man were to talk to Sartor, it was best the guard be told the police were pessimistic about finding the books.

When he hung up, Brunetti explained the missing half of the conversation to Griffoni, who had figured it out in any case.

Her voice could not have been more dispassionate when she said, 'His wife called the day after you talked to him. The day after Franchini died.'

Brunetti called Signorina Elettra and asked her if Sartor's address was on file. After a moment, she told him the guard lived two *calli* behind the Accademia, gave him the *numero civico*, and told him where to turn left, and then right.

Calle larga Nani. He hadn't been there for years,

perhaps decades. He remembered that there had been a tobacco shop on the corner, but beyond that, he had no memory of the place. They took the Number Two, got off at Accademia, and found the house with no difficulty, four doors down from the *tabaccaio*, who was still there.

Before Brunetti rang the bell, he looked at Griffoni, wondering if they should decide on a strategy for questioning Sartor. 'We just *do* it,' she said, and he realized she was right: there was no way to prepare for it. He rang the bell.

Minutes passed and no one answered. He rang again and asked himself why he had not thought of requesting a warrant from a magistrate to search for other books. He feared the cause was his refusal to abandon his belief in readers.

The door opened. A woman who might have been in her fifties stood there: tall, too thin, haggard, confused to see people at her door. 'Are you the doctor?' she asked, staring first at one and then the other. 'You said you couldn't come, and now there's two of you.' She was puzzled, not angry. The dark circles under her eyes spoke of worry and lack of sleep, as did the way she glanced from one to the other, as if hoping to force one of them to speak.

'We've come to see Signor Sartor,' Brunetti said.

'Then you *are* the doctor?' she asked, in exasperation.

'No, not a doctor.' When she seemed to have registered that, he said, 'I'm sorry to hear that he's sick. What is it?'

She shook her head and looked more pained, more confused. 'I don't know. He came home two nights ago and said he was sick. He hasn't said much since then.'

'Where is he?'

'In bed.' Then, as if she thought they might be able to help, she said, 'The Ospedale told me to call Sanitrans to take him there, but I told them we can't afford that, and besides, he won't go. That was . . .' she looked at her watch and continued, 'two hours ago. I had to go out to call: I can't find Piero's *telefonino*, and we don't have a phone in the house any more. So I thought maybe they changed their minds and finally sent a doctor.' She gave a short smile, little more than a grimace, and said, 'He really won't go.'

'If you'd like us to try, Signora,' Griffoni said in a soft voice. 'We could call the Guardia Medica.'

A young couple appeared at the far end of the *calle*, and the woman said, 'Come inside, please.' She put her hand on Griffoni's arm and all but pulled her into the house. Brunetti followed, and the woman closed the door behind them and stood with her back against it, looking relieved.

He was surprised to see that they were not standing in an entrance hall but in what must be the living room of the apartment itself. It was on the ground floor, with windows to the *calle* on either side of the door, both of them protected by heavy curtains and, visible in the narrow opening that let in a bit of light, bars. A light fixture hung from the centre of the ceiling and tried to illuminate the room. An enormous old-fashioned television with a rabbit-eared antenna stared at a spavined green sofa. There was nothing else in the room: no chairs, nothing on the walls, no carpets. Nothing. It looked as though human locusts had passed through but had scorned the television and the sofa and had decided to leave the single light bulb to its futile attempt to relieve the gloom. The tile floor glistened with humidity as if to show its eternal resistance to sun or warmth or the arrival of springtime.

The woman stood with one arm across her chest, hand gripping the opposite shoulder, her lips pulled tight, still not certain who they were or why they were there. She blinked a few times to try to get them into clearer focus. She took a step to one side and braced herself on the back of the sofa.

'Signora?' Griffoni asked. 'Have you had anything to eat today?'

The woman's head swivelled to look at her. 'What?'

'Have you had anything to eat today?'

'No, no, of course not. I'm too busy,' she said with an agitation of hands.

'Could I trouble you for a glass of water, do you think?' Griffoni asked.

Her request seemed to reignite the sense of social obligation that required the neighbours not to know anything about what was going on. 'Yes, yes,' she said. 'Come with me. I can offer you a coffee. We still have some.' She turned away from the sofa and, now that their eyes had adjusted to the diminished light, Brunetti and Griffoni saw a curtained doorway leading off to the left. The woman started towards it, Griffoni a step behind her. As she reached to pull the curtain aside, she looked back at Brunetti and pointed to a door behind the sofa. 'My husband's in there. Maybe he'll . . .' she began, but abandoned the sentence as if she were no longer able to think of what her husband might do.

Brunetti waited until he heard the sound of water running, followed by the clash of metal on metal. He had seen that look of parched desolation on the faces of victims of crime or people who had been involved in accidents. Get sugar and water into them; something to eat if you could. Keep them warm. It was then he realized how cold the room was, the humidity complicit in making it worse.

He walked to the door and opened it without bothering to knock. The smell hit him, the fetid, dank stink of an animal's cage or the home of an old person who had given up on life and ceased to bathe or eat with any regularity. The fact that the room was warm made it worse. He searched for the source and saw an electric heater in the corner, five red bars glowing in defiance of the cold. Light filtered in through a single curtained window, illuminating little but giving shape to the few objects in the room: a double bed, a small table, and an empty glass. The locusts had passed through here, as well. They had overlooked the man in the bed, lying on his back, eyes closed. A grubby white sheet was folded back over the top of a dark blue blanket.

Sartor's face was rough with beard; the light from the window hollowed and darkened the cheek it illuminated. The collar of his T-shirt exposed his stubble-covered neck. His breathing was audible.

The room was so small that two steps brought Brunetti close to the side of the bed. A chair stood beside it; he sat. Nestled in the hair on Sartor's neck, Brunetti saw, was a small coral bull's horn on a silver chain, worn by many men – though usually in the South – as a totem to ward off bad luck and call down good.

He had left the door of the room open in automatic response to the smell: he decided to leave it: cold was better than this. He heard a ping that might have been a cup or, he hoped, a plate. When he turned his attention back to Sartor, he realized the man's breathing had quickened. Sudden footsteps approached, and Brunetti got to his feet, reluctant to permit either of the women into the room.

When the footsteps passed away, moving down the *calle* and away from the house, Brunetti was struck by the strangeness of living in a place where you had no idea if people were in the house with you or out on the street. He sat down again and said, careful to speak in a normal voice, 'Signor Sartor, it's Brunetti. We met at the library.'

Sartor opened his eyes and looked at him. Brunetti saw recognition in them; Sartor nodded and said, 'Yes, I remember.'

'I came because of the books.'

This time Sartor did no more than nod.

Changing the subject, Brunetti said, 'You've been in bed for two days, is that right?'

'I don't know.'

'Are you sick?'

'No,' he answered. 'Not really.'

'Then why are you in bed?' Brunetti asked, posing it as a normal question.

'There's nowhere else I can go.'

'You could go to work. You could go for a walk. You could go to a bar for a coffee.'

Sartor moved his head from side to side on the pillow. 'No. That's over.'

'What is?' Brunetti asked.

'My life.'

Brunetti let his surprise show. 'But you're talking to me, and your wife is in the kitchen, so your life isn't over.'

'Yes it is,' he said with childlike insistence.

'Why do you think that?'

Sartor closed his eyes for a moment, opened them and looked at Brunetti. 'Because I'll lose my job.'

'Why is that?' Brunetti asked innocently.

Sartor stared at him and then closed his eyes. Brunetti sat and waited. After more than a minute, Sartor opened his eyes and said, 'I stole books.'

'From the library?'

Sartor nodded.

'Why did you steal them?'

'To pay him.'

'Pay who?' Brunetti asked, doing his best to sound confused.

'Tertullian. Franchini.'

'Pay him what? Why?' Brunetti asked. He thought there could be only one reason a gambler would have to pay someone.

'He gave me money. Lent me.'

'I don't understand,' Brunetti said. 'Why would you borrow money from him?'

'To pay other debts,' Sartor said. He closed his eyes and pulled his mouth tight at the thought of those debts.

'What happened?' Brunetti asked.

'I needed money. Two years ago. So I went to someone who lends it.'

'Not to a bank?'

Sartor dismissed the idea with a heavy snort. 'Someone in the city.'

'Ah, I understand,' Brunetti said. There were more than a few usurers in Venice: sign your house over as collateral and you can have what you want. Your mother's gold? Your father's life insurance? Your furniture? Nothing easier. Sign here and you can have whatever money you need. Only 10 per cent interest. Per month. Everything they did was indecent; nothing could be done to stop them.

'We had to pay interest every month. We gave him that, but then he wanted the money back.'

Brunetti found it interesting that Sartor borrowed the money, but 'we' had to pay it back.

'When did this start?'

'I told you: two years ago. We managed for a year, paying the interest, but then it got to be too much.' One of Sartor's hands contracted under the covers, bunching and pulling at the sheet and blanket. 'When he told me he wanted the money back, I said we couldn't pay it.' His hand emerged to finger the coral horn for a moment, then slipped back to safety. 'He came here with a friend and talked to my wife.' He left it to Brunetti to imagine the tenor of that conversation.

'So you asked Franchini to lend it to you?' Brunetti asked.

The question shocked Sartor. 'No. Of course not. He was one of our readers.'

Brunetti was no less shocked by the answer than by the vehemence with which Sartor gave it.

The rhythm of these conversations changed constantly, Brunetti knew: it was time for even more softness. 'I see,' he said. 'How did it happen, then?'

He watched as Sartor tried to formulate an answer, saw the way he pulled his lips inside his teeth, as if by closing his mouth like that, he could remain silent for a longer time; perhaps until Brunetti forgot about the question.

Brunetti sat and waited. He imagined that he was a plant, perhaps a lilac bush, and he had just dug his roots into this chair. If he sat here long enough he would become a permanent part of the chair, of the room, of Sartor's life: the man would never rid himself of the sight of Brunetti, rooted into his life.

'One day,' Sartor finally said, 'when he was leaving the library – we always exchanged a few words when he came in and when he left – he said he thought I looked worried and asked if there was anything he could do to help me.'

'You knew he had been a priest?'

'Yes.'

'And?'

'And we went and had a coffee, and I told him – like you say, he was a priest once – that I was worried about money.' Brunetti did not see the connection, believing that priests were meant for other things, but he said nothing. 'He offered to lend it to me. I said I couldn't take it, and he said if I wanted, we could make it official.'

'Official?'

'With a paper that I'd sign.' A hand emerged from the covers to make a signing gesture in the air.

'So there was interest?'

'No,' Sartor said, sounding almost offended. 'Just that he had lent me the money.'

'How much was it?'

He watched Sartor get ready to lie, and then he did. 'A thousand Euros.'

Brunetti nodded in apparent belief.

There was a long pause, as if Sartor could, by wishing, make all of this be over.

Brunetti was tiring of it, of the lies and delays, and so he asked, to hurry things, 'And then what happened?'

The look Sartor flashed at him suggested Brunetti had nudged him too hard or insulted him. He turned his head away and stared at the wall. Brunetti waited.

'After a few months, Franchini told me he needed the money back,' Sartor muttered, to the wall. 'But I didn't have it. When I told him that, he said I could help him, instead.'

'How?'

Sartor turned suddenly and shot Brunetti a sharp glance. 'By giving him books, of course,' he said in a tight voice. Brunetti realized that either Sartor's patience or his powers of invention were nearly exhausted.

'Did he tell you what books?' Brunetti asked.

'Yes. He found them in the catalogue and told me their titles.'

'Did you give them to him?' Brunetti asked, conscious of the verb and its suggestion that the books were Sartor's to give.

'I had no choice.' Sartor sounded indignant.

'And Nickerson?' Brunetti asked, hoping to surprise him with the question.

Sartor's response was immediate, his voice tight. 'What about him?'

'Did he know Franchini?'

Sartor looked across at him quickly, unable to disguise his surprise, and Brunetti wondered if he had asked the wrong question, or asked it too soon. Sartor's glance sharpened, but then he closed his eyes and remained silent for so long that Brunetti feared they had reached the point he had known was coming when Sartor would refuse to say anything more. He waited, making evident his retreat from the conversation, but Sartor remained motionless, eyes closed. From the other room, he heard a noise and hoped that the women would not choose this moment to return.

Sartor opened his eyes. His face looked different, more alert; even his beard, which had seemed scraggly and unkempt, now appeared to be the result of an exercise in studied negligence.

'Yes,' he said, finally answering Brunetti's question. 'He was very clever. Franchini.'

Not clever enough, Brunetti wanted to say but, instead, asked, 'What do you mean?'

'He told me he recognized him, Nickerson. From before,' Sartor began. Slowly, he continued, considering every word, as if it were necessary to make what he was saying clear. 'He didn't tell me where. Or when. Just that he knew him.'

'Were they working together?' Brunetti asked.

It took so long for Sartor to answer that Brunetti again feared he had decided to stop speaking, but then he said, 'Yes.'

'And you helped?'

'Very little. Franchini told me to leave Nickerson alone.'

'At the exit?' Brunetti asked.

Sartor lowered his head to indicate embarrassment. 'Yes,' he muttered, as if he didn't want even Brunetti to hear this confession. His eyes were rich with appeal when he asked, 'What else could I do?' When Brunetti didn't answer, he said, 'I just didn't bother to look in his briefcase.'

Sartor moved his left hand to the side of the bed and took hold of the hem of the sheet. He started to roll the edge between his thumb and middle finger, turning it into a thin cylinder. Back and forth, back and forth, like someone stroking a cat.

'Then what happened?' Brunetti asked, hoping this was the question Sartor wanted to hear.

'Nickerson wanted the Doppelmayr.'

'The what?' Brunetti asked, though he knew the book of maps.

'It's an atlas of the heavens,' Sartor said with the condescension of the expert. 'There's one in the library, and Nickerson said he wanted it.'

'Why that one?'

'For a client. That's what Franchini told me.'

'What happened?'

'Franchini was a cautious man, and he said it was too important to take. And too big. He told Nickerson he'd have nothing to do with it, no matter what he said or what he offered.'

Brunetti made his face as blank as possible and asked, 'What happened?'

Brunetti watched Sartor think of how to answer.

'He told me, the day before Nickerson left, to go into the reading room and the next day say I had to take one of the books he was using back to the desk because it had to be sent to another library. He told me that would frighten him away. And it did.'

'Why did he tell you to do that?' Brunetti asked.

'Franchini said they'd had an argument about the Doppelmayr; then they argued about money.' Sartor saw what looked like raw curiosity on Brunetti's face, and said, 'He told me – Franchini did – that he wanted to get rid of him because he was afraid of him.'

Ah, there it was, Brunetti thought, finally, the thing he was meant to believe. He had no doubt that an argument about money was the cause of Franchini's death, but perhaps not a fight between those two men.

Brunetti had long been of the opinion that one of the handicaps of stupidity was its inability to imagine intelligence. Though stupid people might know the word 'intelligent' and have seen that some people understood things more quickly, their own mono-chrome intelligence could never truly fathom the difference. So Sartor would never see how transpar-ent his story was. Brunetti didn't know whether to hit him or pity him.

He was distracted from the need to make that decision by the sound of footsteps, this time not from the *calle* but from the next room. 'Commissario,' he heard Griffoni call.

He got to his feet and went to the door. Claudia was in the middle of the room, Sartor's wife in the opening that led to the kitchen. 'We've been talking, the Signora and I,' Claudia said, turning to the woman and smiling at her. The soft voice she used filled him with fear.

Brunetti closed the door to the bedroom and walked closer to Claudia.

'We've been talking,' she said, 'about how hard it is to make ends meet with only one salary.' In the background, the woman nodded in agreement with these truths only women seemed to understand. She looked calmer; perhaps Claudia had managed to get some sugar into her, even some food.

Turning to her, Claudia asked, 'That's right, isn't it, Gina?'

'Yes. And with the crisis, salaries stay the same and everything becomes more expensive.' She was a more composed person than the shattered woman who had pulled them into the apartment.

'So we all have to be careful,' Claudia said with heavy emphasis. 'No waste: make do with what we have.' She turned to Brunetti and said, with shrieking falsity that the other woman could not sense, 'The Signora's told me that her husband's frightened he might lose his job.' A cloud crossed the woman's face, and her hands came together to console one another.

Brunetti wondered if Claudia was perhaps in need of some sugar herself, but her voice had warned him that all of this was leading somewhere. Then, as if suddenly reminded of that fact, she turned to the woman and said, 'That's why it's so wise of you not to have let your husband throw those boots away.'

The woman smiled, proud of her housekeeping skills. 'They've got a good few years left in them,' she said. 'He paid a hundred and forty-three Euros for them, only four years ago.' A pause, and then she said, 'We couldn't afford to buy them, not now: things are so bad.'

'Can't be too careful, Signora,' Brunetti said with an approving smile, while thinking that it was going to destroy her to have done this. Then, his voice caught between two emotions, he said, 'Signora, do you think I could have a glass of water, too?'

'Oh, let me make you a coffee, Dottore,' she said and turned back towards the kitchen.

As he followed her, he turned to Griffoni and said, 'Call them and tell them we need a warrant to search this place for the boots.'

Instead of the easy compliance he had come to expect from her, Griffoni said, 'I've been Judas once; I don't want to do it again.'

Brunetti pulled out his phone and dialled the number of the Questura and requested the warrant, then he went into Signora Sartor's kitchen to accept her hospitality.

ALSO BY DONNA LEON

THE GOLDEN EGG

The twenty-second instalment in the bestselling Brunetti series.

A local deaf-mute man has been found dead and an empty bottle of pills points to suicide. Fearing the case may be more sinister than at first it seems, Brunetti investigates further.

It is a surprise to Brunetti just how little was known about this man-child. His mother is angry and contradictory when questioned about his death, and Brunetti can find no official records to prove he even existed. With the help of Inspector Vianello and the ever-resourceful Signorina Elettra, the Commissario sets out to discover the truth in what rapidly becomes a dark and troubling case.

'The doyenne of Italian crime fiction'
Herald

'The familiar characters and Venetian location are described with remarkable freshness . . . both amusing and thought-provoking'
Sunday Telegraph

BEASTLY THINGS

The twenty-first instalment in the bestselling Brunetti series

When a body is found floating in a canal, strangely disfigured and with multiple stab wounds, Commissario Brunetti is called to investigate and is convinced he recognises the man from somewhere. With the help of Signorina Elettra, Brunetti soon realises he remembers the dead man from a farmers' protest. But what does this have to do with his murder?

Brunetti and Inspector Vianello's investigation eventually takes them to a slaughterhouse on the mainland, where they discover a whole world of blackmail and corruption.

'*Beastly Things* is a perfect accompaniment to a hot day and a cool glass of white wine. Superb.'
Crimesquad

'Written with that depth of thought about crime and humanity that characterises the best of Leon's work.'
Independent

*For all of you who find
a crime story irresistible.*

Discover the very best crime and thriller books on our dedicated website – hand-picked by our editorial team so you have tailored recommendations to help you choose what to read next.

We'll introduce you to our favourite authors and the brightest new talent. Read exclusive interviews and specially commissioned features on everything from the best classic crime to our top ten TV detectives, join live webchats and speak to authors directly.

Plus our monthly book competition offers you the chance to win the latest crime fiction, and there are DVD box sets and digital devices to be won too.

**Sign up for our newsletter at
www.deadgoodbooks.co.uk/signup**

Join the conversation on: